CW00521095

EX LI

VINTAGE CLASSICS

THE CHRONICLES OF CAPTAIN BLOOD

Rafael Sabatini was born in Jesi, Italy in 1875 to an English mother and Italian father, both renowned opera singers. At a young age, Rafael travelled frequently, and could speak six languages fluently by the age of seventeen. After a brief stint in the business world, he turned to writing. He worked prolifically, writing short stories in the 1890s, with his first novel published in 1902. *Scaramouche* was published in 1921 to widespread acclaim, and was soon followed by the equally successful *Captain Blood*. He died on 13 February 1950 in Switzerland.

OTHER WORKS BY RAFAEL SABATINI

The Lovers of Yvonne
The Tavern Knight
Bardelys the Magnificent
The Trampling of the Lilies
Love-at-Arms
The Shame of Motley
St. Martin's Summer
Mistress Wilding
The Lion's Skin
The Strolling Saint
The Gates of Doom
The Fortunes of Captain Blood
The Snare
Captain Blood
The Sea Hawk
Fortune's Fool
The Carolinian

Bellarion the Fortunate
The Hounds of God
The Romantic Prince
The King's Minion
Scaramouche the Kingmaker
The Black Swan
The Stalking Horse
Venetian Masque
Chivalry
The Lost King
The Sword of Islam
The Marquis of Carabas
Columbus
King in Prussia
The Gamester
Scaramouche

RAFAEL SABATINI

The Chronicles of Captain Blood

VINTAGE BOOKS
London

Published by Vintage 2011

2 4 6 8 10 9 7 5 3 1

The Chronicles of Captain Blood was first published by Hutchinson
and Co in 1929.

Vintage
Random House, 20 Vauxhall Bridge Road,
London SW1V 2SA

www.vintage-classics.info

Addresses for companies within The Random House Group Limited
can be found at: www.randomhouse.co.uk/offices.htm

The Random House Group Limited Reg. No. 954009

A CIP catalogue record for this book
is available from the British Library

ISBN 9780099528463

The Random House Group Limited supports The Forest
Stewardship Council (FSC), the leading international forest
certification organisation. All our titles that are printed on
Greenpeace approved FSC certified paper carry the FSC logo.
Our paper procurement policy can be found at:
www.randomhouse.co.uk/environment

Printed and bound in Great Britain by
CPI Antony Rowe, Chippenham and Eastbourne

FSC
Mixed Sources
Product group from well-managed
forests and other controlled sources
Cert no. SGS-COC-2953
www.fsc.org
© 1996 Forest Stewardship Council

INTRODUCTION

THE ODYSSEY of Captain Blood, given to the world some years ago, was derived from various sources, disclosed in the course of its compilation. Of these the most important is the log of the *Arabella*, kept by the young Somersetshire ship-master Jeremy Pitt. This log amounts to just such a chronicle of Blood's activities upon the Caribbean as that which Esque-meling, in similar case, has left of the exploits of that other great buccaneer, Sir Henry Morgan.

The compilation of the Odyssey, whilst it exhausted all other available collateral sources of information, was very far from exhausting the material left by Pitt. From that log of his were taken only those episodes which bore more or less directly upon the main outline of Blood's story, which it was then proposed to relate and elucidate. The selection presented obvious diffi-culties; and omissions, reluctantly made, were compelled by the necessity of presenting a straightforward and consecutive narrative.

It has since been felt, however, that some of the episodes then omitted might well be assembled in a supplementary volume which may shed additional light upon the methods and habits of the buccaneering fraternity in general and of Captain Blood in particular.

It will be remembered by those who have read the volume entitled *Captain Blood: His Odyssey,* and it may briefly be repeated here for the information of those who have not, that Peter Blood was the son of an Irish medicus, who had desired that his son should follow in his own honourable and humane profession. Complying with this parental wish, Peter Blood had received, at the early age of twenty, the degree of baccalaureus medicinae at Trinity College, Dublin. He showed, however, little disposition to practise the peaceful art for which he had brilliantly qualified. Perhaps a roving strain derived from his

Somersetshire mother, in whose veins ran the blood of the Frobishers, was responsible for his restiveness. Losing his father some three months after taking his degree, he set out to see the world, preferring to open himself a career with the sword of the adventurer rather than with the scalpel of the surgeon.

After some vague wanderings on the continent of Europe we find him in the service of the Dutch, then at war with France. Again it may have been the Frobisher blood and a consequent predilection for the sea which made him elect to serve upon that element. He enjoyed the advantage of holding a commission under the great de Ruyter, and he fought in the Mediterranean engagement in which that famous Dutch Admiral lost his life. What he learnt under him Pitt's chronicle shows him applying in his later days when he had become the most formidable buccaneer leader on the Caribbean.

After the Peace of Nimeguen and until the beginning of 1685, when he reappears in England, little is known of his fortunes, beyond the fact that he spent two years in a Spanish prison – where we must suppose that he acquired the fluent and impeccable Castilian which afterwards served him so often and so well – and that later he was for a while in the service of France, which similarly accounts for his knowledge of the French language.

In January of 1685 we find him at last, at the age of thirty-two, settling down in Bridgwater to practise the profession for which he had been trained. But for the Monmouth Rebellion, in whose vortex he was quite innocently caught up some six months later, this might have been the end of his career as an adventurer. And but for the fact that what came to him, utterly uninvited by him, was not in its ultimate manifestation unacceptable, we should have to regard him as one of the victims of the ironical malignity of Fortune aided and abetted, as it ever is, by the stupidity and injustice of man.

In his quality as a surgeon he was summoned on the morning after the battle of Sedgmoor to the bedside of a wounded gentleman who had been out with Monmouth. The dignity of his calling did not permit him to weigh legal quibbles or consider the position in which he might place himself in the eyes of a rigid and relentless law. All that counted with him was that a human being required his medical assistance, and he went to give it.

Surprised in the performance of that humanitarian duty by a party of dragoons who were hunting fugitives from the battle, he was arrested together with his patient. His patient being convicted of high-treason, for having been in arms against his king, Peter Blood suffered with him the same conviction under the statute which ordains that who succours or comforts a traitor is himself a traitor.

He was tried at Taunton before Judge Jeffreys in the course of the Bloody Assize, and sentenced to death.

Afterwards the sentence was commuted to transportation, not out of any spirit of mercy, but because it was discovered that to put to death the thousands that were implicated in the Monmouth Rebellion was to destroy valuable human merchandise which could be converted into money in the colonies. Slaves were required for work in the plantations, and the wealthy planters overseas who were willing to pay handsomely for the Negroes rounded up in Africa by slavers would be no less ready to purchase white men. Accordingly, these unfortunate rebels under sentence of death were awarded in batches to this lady or that gentleman of the Court to be turned by them to profitable account.

Peter Blood was in one of these batches, which included also Jeremy Pitt and some others who were later to be associated with him in an even closer bond than that of their present common misfortune.

This batch was shipped to Barbados, and sold there. And then, at last, Fate eased by a little her cruel grip of Peter Blood. When it was discovered that he was a man of medicine, and because in Barbados medical men of ability were urgently required, his purchaser perceived how he could turn this slave to better account than by merely sending him to the sugar plantations. He was allowed to practise as a doctor. And since the pursuit of this demanded a certain liberty of action, this liberty, within definite limits, was accorded him. He employed it to plan an escape in association with a number of his fellow slaves.

The attempt was practically frustrated, when the arrival of a Spanish ship of war at Bridgetown and the circumstances attending it suddenly disclosed to the ready wits and resolute will of Peter Blood a better way of putting it into execution.

The Spaniards, having subjected Bridgetown to bombardment, had effected a landing there and had taken possession of the place, holding it to ransom. To accomplish this, and having nothing to fear from a town which had been completely subdued, they had left their fine ship, the *Cinco Llagas* out of Cadiz, at anchor in the bay with no more than a half score of men aboard to guard her. Nor did these keep careful watch. Persuaded, like their brethren ashore, that there was nothing to be apprehended from the defeated English colonists, they had abandoned themselves that night, again like their brethren ashore, to a jovial carousal.

This was Blood's opportunity. With a score of plantation slaves to whom none gave a thought at such a time, he quietly boarded the *Cinco Llagas*, overpowered the watch and took possession of her.

In the morning, when the glutted Spaniards were returning in boats laden with the plunder of Bridgetown, Peter Blood turned their own guns upon them, smashed their boats with roundshot, and sailed away with his crew of rebels-convict to turn their reconquered liberty to such account as Fate might indicate.

1

THE BLANK SHOT

CAPTAIN EASTERLING, whose long duel with Peter Blood finds an important place in the chronicles which Jeremy Pitt has left us, must be regarded as the instrument chosen by Fate to shape the destiny of those rebels-convict who fled from Barbados in the captured *Cinco Llagas*.

The lives of men are at the mercy of the slenderest chances. A whole destiny may be influenced by no more than the set of the wind at a given moment. And Peter Blood's, at a time when it was still fluid, was certainly fashioned by the October hurricane which blew Captain Easterling's ten-gun sloop into Cayona Bay, where the *Cinco Llagas* had been riding idly at anchor for close upon a month.

Blood and his associates had run to this buccaneer stronghold of Tortuga, assured of finding shelter there whilst they deliberated upon their future courses. They had chosen it because it was the one haven in the Caribbean where they could count upon being unmolested and where no questions would be asked of them. No English settlement would harbour them because of their antecedents. The hand of Spain would naturally be against them not only because they were English, but, further, because they were in possession of a Spanish ship. They could trust themselves to no ordinary French colony because of the recent agreement between the Governments of France and England for the apprehension and interchange of any persons escaping from penal settlements. There remained the Dutch, who were neutral. But Blood regarded neutrality as the most incalculable of all conditions, since it implies liberty of action in any direction. Therefore he steered clear of the Dutch as of the others and made for Tortuga, which, belonging to the French West India Company, was nominally

9

French, but nominally only. Actually it was of no nationality, unless the Brethren of the Coast, as the buccaneering fraternity was called, could be deemed to constitute a nation. At least it can be said that no law ran in Tortuga that was at issue with the laws governing that great brotherhood. It suited the French Government to give the protection of its flag to these lawless men, so that in return they might serve French interests by acting as a curb upon Spanish greed and aggressiveness in the West Indies.

At Tortuga, therefore, the escaped rebels-convict dwelt in peace aboard the *Cinco Llagas* until Easterling came to disturb that peace and force them into action and into plans for their future, which, without him, they might have continued to postpone.

This Easterling – as nasty a scoundrel as ever sailed the Caribbean – carried under hatches some tons of cacao of which he had lightened a Dutch merchantman homing from the Antilles. The exploit, he realized, had not covered him with glory, for glory in that pirate's eyes was measurable by profit; and the meagre profit in this instance was not likely to increase him in the poor esteem in which he knew himself to be held by the Brethren of the Coast. Had he suspected the Dutchman of being no more richly laden he would have let her pass unchallenged. But having engaged and boarded her, he had thought it incumbent upon him and his duty to his crew of rascals to relieve her of what she carried. That she should have carried nothing of more value than cacao was a contingency for which he blamed the evil fortune which of late had dogged him – an evil fortune which was making it increasingly difficult for him to find men to sail with him.

Considering these things, and dreaming of great enterprises, he brought his sloop *Bonaventure* into the shelter of the rock-bound harbour of Tortuga, a port designed by very Nature for a stronghold. Walls of rock, rising sheer, and towering like mountains, protect it upon either side and shape it into a miniature gulf. It is only to be approached by two channels demanding skilful pilotage. These were commanded by the Mountain Fort, a massive fortress with which man had supplemented the work of Nature. Within the shelter of this harbour, the French and English buccaneers who made it their lair might deride the might of the King of Spain, whom they regarded as their natural enemy, since it was his persecution of them when they had been peaceful boucan-hunters which had driven them to the grim trade of sea rovers.

Within that harbour Easterling dismissed his dreams to gaze upon a curious reality. It took the shape of a great red-hulled ship riding proudly at anchor among the lesser craft, like a swan amid a gaggle of geese. When he had come near enough to read the name *Cinco Llagas* boldly painted in letters of gold above her counter, and under this the port of origin, Cadiz, he rubbed his eyes so that he might read again. Thereafter he sought in conjecture an explanation of the presence of that magnificent ship of Spain in this pirates' nest of Tortuga. A thing of beauty she was, from gilded beak-head, above which the brass cannons glinted in the morning sun, to towering sterncastle, and a thing of power as announced by the forty guns which Easterling's practised eye computed her to carry behind her closed ports.

The *Bonaventure* cast anchor within a cable's length of the great ship, in ten fathoms, close under the shadow of the Mountain Fort on the harbour's western side, and Easterling went ashore to seek the explanation of this mystery.

In the market-place beyond the mole he mingled with the heterogeneous crowd that converted the quays of Cayona into an image of Babel. There were bustling traders of many nations, chiefly English, French and Dutch; planters and seamen of various degrees; buccaneers who were still genuine boucan-hunters and buccaneers who were frankly pirates; lumbermen, beachcombers, Indians, fruit-selling half-castes, Negro slaves, and all the other types of the human family that daily loafed or trafficked there. He found presently a couple of well-informed rogues very ready with the singular tale of how that noble vessel out of Cadiz came to ride so peacefully at anchor in Cayona Bay, manned by a parcel of escaped plantation slaves.

To such a man as Easterling it was an amusing and even an impressive tale. He desired more particular knowledge of the men who had engaged in such an enterprise. He learned that they numbered not above a score and that they were all political offenders – rebels who in England had been out with Monmouth, preserved from the gallows because of the need of slaves in the West Indian plantations. He learned all that was known of their leader, Peter Blood; that he was by trade a man of medicine, and the rest.

It was understood that, because of this, and with a view to resuming his profession, Blood desired to take ship for Europe at the first occasion and that most of his followers would accompany him. But one or two wilder spirits, men who had been trained to the sea, were likely to remain behind and join the Brotherhood of the Coast.

All this Easterling learned in the market-place behind the mole, whence his fine, bold eyes continued to con the great red ship.

With such a vessel as that under his feet there was no limit to the things he might achieve. He began to see visions. The fame of Henry Morgan, with whom once he had sailed and under whom he had served his apprenticeship to piracy, should become a pale thing beside his own. These poor escaped convicts must be ready enough to sell a ship which had served its purpose by them, and they should not be exorbitant in their notions of her value. The cacao aboard the *Bonaventure* should more than suffice to pay for her.

Captain Easterling smiled as he stroked his crisp black beard. It had required his own keen wits to perceive at once an opportunity to which all others had been blind during that long month in which the vessel had been anchored there. It was for him to profit by his perceptions.

He made his way through the rudely built little town by the road white with coral dust – so white under the blazing sun that a man's eyes ached to behold it and sought instinctively the dark patches made by the shadows of the limp exiguous palms by which it was bordered.

He went so purposefully that he disregarded the hails greeting him from the doorway of the tavern of The King of France, nor paused to crush a cup with the gaudy buccaneers who filled the place with their noisy mirth. The Captain's business that morning was with Monsieur d'Ogeron, the courtly, middle-aged Governor of Tortuga, who in representing the French West India Company seemed to represent France herself, and who, with the airs of a minister of state, conducted affairs of questionable probity but of unquestionable profit to his company.

In the fair, white, green-shuttered house, pleasantly set amid fragrant pimento trees and other aromatic shrubs, Captain Easterling was received with dignified friendliness by the slight, elegant Frenchman who brought to the wilds of Tortuga a faint perfume of the elegancies of Versailles. Coming from the white glare outside into the cool spacious room, to which was admitted only such light as filtered between the slats of the closed shutters, the Captain found himself almost in darkness until his eyes had adjusted themselves.

The Governor offered him a chair and gave him his attention.

In the matter of the cacao there was no difficulty. Monsieur d'Ogeron cared not whence it came. That he had no illusions on the subject was shown by the price per quintal at which he announced himself prepared to purchase. It was a price representing rather less than half the value of the merchandise. Monsieur d'Ogeron was a diligent servant of the French West India Company.

Easterling haggled vainly, grumbled, accepted, and passed to the major matter. He desired to acquire the Spanish ship in the bay. Would Monsieur d'Ogeron undertake the purchase for him from the fugitive convicts who, he understood, were in possession of her.

Monsieur d'Ogeron took time to reply. "It is possible," he said at last, "that they may not wish to sell."

"Not sell? A God's name what use is the ship to those poor ragamuffins?"

"I mention only a possibility," said Monsieur d'Ogeron.

13

"Come to me again this evening, and you shall have your answer."

When Easterling returned as bidden, Monsieur d'Ogeron was not alone. As the Governor rose to receive his visitor, there rose with him a tall, spare man in the early thirties from whose shaven face, swarthy as a gipsy's, a pair of eyes looked out that were startlingly blue, level, and penetrating. If Monsieur d'Ogeron in dress and air suggested Versailles, his companion as markedly suggested the Alameda. He was very richly dressed in black in the Spanish fashion, with an abundance of silver lace and a foam of fine point at throat and wrists, and he wore a heavy black periwig whose curls descended to his shoulders.

Monsieur d'Ogeron presented him: "Here, Captain, is Mr Peter Blood to answer you in person."

Easterling was almost disconcerted, so different was the man's appearance from anything that he could have imagined. And now this singular escaped convict was bowing with the grace of a courtier, and the buccaneer was reflecting that these fine Spanish clothes would have been filched from the locker of the commander of the *Cinco Llagas*. He remembered something else.

"Ah yes. To be sure. The physician," he said, and laughed for no apparent reason.

Mr Blood began to speak. He had a pleasant voice whose metallic quality was softened by a drawling Irish accent. But what he said made Captain Easterling impatient. It was not his intention to sell the *Cinco Llagas*.

Aggressively before the elegant Mr Blood stood now the buccaneer, a huge, hairy, dangerous-looking man, in coarse shirt and leather breeches, his cropped head swathed in a red-and-yellow kerchief. Aggressively he demanded Blood's reasons for retaining a ship that could be of no use to him and his fellow convicts.

Blood's voice was softly courteous in reply, which but increased Easterling's contempt of him. Captain Easterling heard himself assured that he was mistaken in his assumptions. It was probable that the fugitives from Barbadoes would employ the vessel to return to Europe, so as to make their way to France or Holland.

"Maybe we're not quite as ye're supposing us, Captain. One of my companions is a shipmaster, and three others have served, in various ways, in the King's Navy."

"Bah!" Easterling's contempt exploded loudly. "The notion's crazy. What of the perils of the sea, man? Perils of capture? How will ye face those with your paltry crew? Have ye considered that?"

Still Captain Blood preserved his pleasant temper. "What we lack in men we make up in weight of metal. Whilst I may not be able to navigate a ship across the ocean, I certainly know how to fight a ship at need. I learnt it under de Ruyter."

The famous name gave pause to Easterling's scorn. "Under de Ruyter?"

"I held a commission with him some years ago."

Easterling was plainly dumbfounded. "I thought it's a doctor ye was."

"I am that, too," said the Irishman simply.

The buccaneer expressed disgusted amazement in a speech liberally festooned with oaths. And then Monsieur d'Ogeron made an end of the interview. "So that you see, Captain Easterling, there is no more to be said in the matter."

Since, apparently, there was not, Captain Easterling sourly took his leave. But on his disgruntled way back to the mole he thought that although there was no more to be said there was a good deal to be done. Having already looked upon the majestic *Cinco Llagas* as his own, he was by no means disposed to forgo the prospect of possession.

Monsieur d'Ogeron also appeared to think that there was still at least a word to be added, and he added it after Easterling's departure. "That," he said quietly, "is a nasty and a dangerous man. You will do well to bear it in mind, Monsieur Blood."

Blood treated the matter lightly. "The warning was hardly necessary. The fellow's person would have announced the blackguard to me even if I had not known him for a pirate."

A shadow that was almost suggestive of annoyance flitted across the delicate features of the Governor of Tortuga.

"Oh, but a filibuster is not of necessity a blackguard, nor is the career of a filibuster one for your contempt, Monsieur Blood. There are those among the buccaneers who do good service to your country and to mine by setting a restraint upon the rapacity of Spain, a rapacity which is responsible for their existence. But for the buccaneers, in these waters, where neither France nor England can maintain a fleet, the Spanish dominion would be as absolute as it is inhuman. You will remember that your country honoured Henry Morgan with a knighthood and the deputy-governorship of Jamaica. And he was an even worse pirate, if it is possible, than your Sir Francis Drake, or Hawkins, or Frobisher or several others I could name, whose memory your country also honours."

Followed upon this from Monsieur d'Ogeron, who derived considerable revenues from the percentages he levied by way of harbour dues on all prizes brought into Tortuga, solemn counsels that Mr Blood should follow in the footsteps of those heroes. Being outlawed as he was, in possession of a fine ship and the nucleus of an able following, and being, as he had proved, a man of unusual resource, Monsieur d'Ogeron did not doubt that he would prosper finely as a filibuster.

Mr Blood didn't doubt it himself. He never doubted himself. But he did not on that account incline to the notion. Nor, probably, but for that which ensued, would he ever have so inclined, however much the majority of his followers might have sought to persuade him.

Among these, Hagthorpe, Pitt, and the giant Wolverstone, who had lost an eye at Sedgmoor, were perhaps the most persistent. It was all very well for Blood, they told him, to plan a return to Europe. He was master of a peaceful art in the pursuit of which he might earn a livelihood in France or Flanders. But they were men of the sea, and knew no other trade. Dyke, who had been a petty officer in the Navy before he embarked on politics and rebellion, held similar views, and Ogle, the gunner, demanded to know of heaven and hell and

Mr Blood what guns they thought the British Admiralty would entrust to a man who had been out with Monmouth.

Things were reaching a stage in which Peter Blood could see no alternative to that of parting from these men whom a common misfortune had endeared to him. It was in this pass that Fate employed the tool she had forged in Captain Easterling.

One morning, three days after his interview with Mr Blood at the Governor's house, the Captain came alongside the *Cinco Llagas* in the cockboat from his sloop. As he heaved his massive bulk into the waist of the ship, his bold, dark eyes were everywhere at once. The *Cinco Llagas* was not only well-found, but irreproachably kept. Her decks were scoured, her cordage stowed, and everything in place. The muskets were ranged in the rack about the mainmast, and the brasswork on the scuttlebutts shone like gold in the bright sunshine. Not such lubberly fellows, after all, these escaped rebels-convict who composed Mr Blood's crew.

And there was Mr Blood himself in his black and silver, looking like a Grandee of Spain, doffing a black hat with a sweep of claret ostrich plume about it, and bowing until the wings of his periwig met across his face like the pendulous ears of a spaniel. With him stood Nathaniel Hagthorpe, a pleasant gentleman of Mr Blood's own age, whose steady eye and clear-cut face announced the man of breeding; Jeremy Pitt, the flaxen-haired young Somerset shipmaster; the short, sturdy Nicholas Dyke, who had been a petty officer and had served under King James when he was Duke of York. There was nothing of the ragamuffin about these, as Easterling had so readily imagined. Even the burly, rough-voiced Wolverstone had crowded his muscular bulk into Spanish fripperies for the occasion.

Having presented them, Mr Blood invited the captain of the *Bonaventure* to the great cabin in the stern, which for spaciousness and richness of furniture surpassed any cabin Captain Easterling had ever entered.

A Negro servant in a white jacket – a lad hired here in

Tortuga – brought, besides the usual rum and sugar and fresh limes, a bottle of golden Canary which had been in the ship's original equipment and which Mr Blood recommended with solicitude to his unbidden guest.

Remembering Monsieur d'Ogeron's warning that Captain Easterling was dangerous, Mr Blood deemed it wise to use him with all civility, if only so that being at his ease he should disclose in what he might be dangerous now.

They occupied the elegantly cushioned seats about the table of black oak, and Captain Easterling praised the Canary liberally so as to justify the liberality with which he consumed it. Thereafter he came to business by asking if Mr Blood, upon reflection, had not perhaps changed his mind about selling the ship.

"If so be that you have," he added, with a glance at Blood's four companions, "considering among how many the purchase money will be divided, you'll find me generous."

If by this he had hoped to make an impression upon those four, their stolid countenances disappointed him.

Mr Blood shook his head. "It's wasting your time, ye are, Captain. Whatever else we decide, we keep the *Cinco Llagas*."

"Whatever you decide?" The great black brows went up on that shallow brow. "Ye're none so decided than as ye was about this voyage to Europe? Why, then, I'll come at once to the business I'ld propose if ye wouldn't sell. It is that with this ship ye join the *Bonaventure* in a venture – a bonaventure," and he laughed noisily at his own jest with a flash of white teeth behind the great black beard.

"You honour us. But we haven't a mind to piracy."

Easterling gave no sign of offence. He waved a great ham of a hand as if to dismiss the notion.

"It ain't piracy I'm proposing."

"What then?"

"I can trust you?" Easterling asked, and his eyes included the four of them.

"Ye're not obliged to. And it's odds ye'll waste your time in any case."

It was not encouraging. Nevertheless, Easterling proceeded. It might be known to them that he had sailed with Morgan. He had been with Morgan in the great march across the Isthmus of Panama. Now it was notorious that when the spoil came to be divided after the sack of that Spanish city it was found to be far below the reasonable expectations of the buccaneers. There were murmurs that Morgan had not dealt fairly with his men; that he had abstracted before the division a substantial portion of the treasure taken. Those murmurs, Easterling could tell them, were well founded. There were pearls and jewels from San Felipe of fabulous value, which Morgan had secretly appropriated for himself. But as the rumours grew and reached his ears, he became afraid of a search that should convict him. And so, midway on the journey across the Isthmus, he one night buried the treasure he had filched.

"Only one man knew this," said Captain Easterling to his attentive listeners – for the tale was of a quality that at all times commands attention. "The man who helped him in a labour he couldn't ha' done alone. I be that man."

He paused a moment to let the impressive fact sink home, and then resumed.

The business he proposed was that the fugitives on the *Cinco Llagas* should join him in an expedition to Darien to recover the treasure, sharing equally in it with his own men and on the scale usual among the Brethren of the Coast.

"If I put the value of what Morgan buried at five hundred thousand pieces of eight, I am being modest."

It was a sum to set his audience staring. Even Blood stared, but not quite with the expression of the others.

"Sure, now, it's very odd," said he thoughtfully.

"What is odd, Mr Blood?"

Mr Blood's answer took the form of another question. "How many do you number aboard the *Bonaventure*?"

"Something less than two hundred men."

"And the twenty men who are with me make such a difference that you deem it worth while to bring us this proposal?"

Easterling laughed outright, a deep, guttural laugh. "I see that ye don't understand at all." His voice bore a familiar echo of Mr Blood's Irish intonation. "It's not the men I lack so much as a stout ship in which to guard the treasure when we have it. In a bottom such as this we'ld be as snug as in a fort, and I'ld snap my fingers at any Spanish galleon that attempted to molest me."

"Faith, now I understand," said Wolverstone, and Pitt and Dyke and Hagthorpe nodded with him. But the glittering blue eye of Peter Blood continued to stare unwinkingly upon the bulky pirate.

"As Wolverstone says, it's understandable. But a tenth of the prize, which, by heads, is all that would come to the *Cinco Llagas*, is far from adequate in the circumstances."

Easterling blew out his cheeks and waved his great hand in a gesture of bonhomie. "What share would you propose?"

"That's to be considered. But it would not be less than one-fifth."

The buccaneer's face remained impassive. He bowed his gaudily swathed head. "Bring these friends of yours to dine tomorrow aboard the *Bonaventure*, and we'll draw up the articles."

For a moment Blood seemed to hesitate. Then in courteous terms he accepted the invitation.

But when the buccaneer had departed he checked the satisfaction of his followers.

"I was warned that Captain Easterling is a dangerous man. That's to flatter him. For to be dangerous a man must be clever, and Captain Easterling is not clever."

"What maggot's burrowing under your periwig, Peter?" wondered Wolverstone.

"I'm thinking of the reason he gave for desiring our association. It was the best he could do when bluntly asked the question."

"It could not have been more reasonable," said Hagthorpe, emphatically. He was finding Blood unnecessarily difficult.

"Reasonable!" Blood laughed. "Specious, if you will.

Specious until you come to examine it. Faith now, it glitters, to be sure. But it isn't gold. A ship as strong as a fort in which to stow a half million pieces of eight, and this fortress ship in the hands of ourselves. A trusting fellow this Easterling for a scoundrel!"

They thought it out, and their eyes grew round. Pitt, however, was not yet persuaded. "In his need he'll trust our honour."

Blood looked at him with scorn. "I never knew a man with eyes like Easterling's to trust to anything but possession. If he means to stow that treasure aboard this ship, and I could well believe that part of it, it is because he means to be in possession of this ship by the time he does so. Honour! Bah! Could such a man believe that honour would prevent us from giving him the slip one night once we had the treasure aboard, or even of bringing our weight of metal to bear upon his sloop and sinking her? It's fatuous you are, Jeremy, with your talk of honour."

Still the thing was not quite clear to Hagthorpe. "What, then, do you suppose to be his reason for inviting us to join him?"

"The reason that he gave. He wants our ship, be it for the conveyance of his treasure, if it exists, be it for other reasons. Didn't he first seek to buy the *Cinco Llagas*? Oh, he wants her, naturally enough; but he wants not us, nor would he keep us long, be sure of that."

And yet, perhaps because the prospect of a share in Morgan's treasure was, as Blood said, a glittering one, his associates were reluctant to abandon it. To gain alluring objects men are always ready to take chances, ready to believe what they hope. So now Hagthorpe, Pitt and Dyke. They came to the opinion that Blood was leaping to conclusions from a prejudice sown in him by Monsieur d'Ogeron, who may have had reasons of his own to serve. Let them at least dine tomorrow with Easterling, and hear what articles he proposed.

"Can you be sure that we shall not be poisoned?" wondered Blood.

But this was pushing prejudice too far. They mocked him freely. How could they be poisoned by meat and drink that Easterling must share with them? And what end would thus be served? How would that give Easterling possession of the *Cinco Llagas*?

"By swarming aboard her with a couple of score of his ruffians and taking the men here unawares at a time when there would be none to lead them."

"What?" cried Hagthorpe. "Here in Tortuga? In this haven of the buccaneers? Come, come, Peter! I must suppose there is some honour among thieves."

"You may suppose it. I prefer to suppose nothing of the kind. I hope no man will call me timorous; and yet I'ld as soon be called that as rash."

The weight of opinion, however, was against him. Every man of the rebels-convict crew was as eager for the enterprise when it came to be disclosed as were the three leaders.

And so, despite himself, at eight bells on the morrow, Captain Blood went over with Hagthorpe, Pitt, and Dyke, to dine aboard the *Bonaventure*. Wolverstone was left behind in charge of the *Cinco Llagas*.

Easterling welcomed them boisterously, supported by his entire crew of ruffians. Some eight score of them swarmed in the waist, on the forecastle, and even on the poop, and all were armed. It was not necessary that Mr Blood should point out to his companions how odd it was that all these fellows should have been summoned for the occasion from the taverns ashore which they usually frequented. Their presence and the leering mockery stamped upon their villainous countenances made Blood's three followers ask themselves at last if Blood had not been justified of his misgivings, and made them suspect with him that they had walked into a trap.

It was too late to retreat. By the break of the poop, at the entrance of the gangway leading to the cabin, stood Captain Easterling waiting to conduct them.

Blood paused there a moment to look up into the pellucid sky above the rigging about which the gulls were circling. He glanced round and up at the grey fort perched on its rocky eminence, all bathed in ardent sunshine. He looked towards the mole, forsaken now in the noontide heat, and then across the crystalline sparkling waters towards the great red *Cinco Llagas* where she rode in majesty and strength. To his uneasy companions it seemed as if he were wondering from what quarter help might come if it were needed. Then, responding to Easterling's inviting gesture, he passed into the gloom of the gangway, followed by the others.

Like the rest of the ship, which the first glance had revealed for dishevelled and unclean, the cabin was in no way comparable with that of the stately *Cinco Llagas*. It was so low that there was barely headroom for tall men like Blood and Hagthorpe. It was ill-furnished, containing a little more than the cushioned lockers set about a deal table that was stained and hacked. Also, for all that, the horn windows astern were open, the atmosphere of the place was heavy with an acrid blend of vile smells in which spunyarn and bilge predominated.

The dinner proved to be much as the surroundings promised. The fresh pork and fresh vegetables had been befouled in cooking, so that, in forcing himself to eat, the fastidious stomach of Mr Blood was almost turned.

The company provided by Easterling matched the rest. A half dozen of his fellows served him as a guard of honour. They had been elected, he announced, by the men, so that they might agree the articles on behalf of all. To these had been added a young Frenchman named Joinville, who was secretary to Monsieur d'Ogeron and stood there to represent the Governor and to lend, as it were, a legal sanction to what was to be done. If the presence of this rather vacuous, pale-eyed gentleman served to reassure Mr Blood a little, it served to intrigue him more.

Amongst them they crowded the narrow confines of the cabin, and Easterling's fellows were so placed along the two sides of the table that no two of the men from the *Cinco Llagas* sat together. Blood and the captain of the *Bonaventure* immediately faced each other across the board.

Business was left until dinner was over and the negro who waited on them had withdrawn. Until then the men of the *Bonaventure* kept things gay with the heavily salted talk that passed for wit amongst them. At last, the table cleared of all save bottles, and pens and ink being furnished together with a sheet of paper each to Easterling and Blood, the captain of the *Bonaventure* opened the matter of the terms, and Peter Blood heard himself for the first time addressed as Captain. Easterling's first words were to inform him shortly that the one-fifth share he had demanded was by the men of the *Bonaventure* accounted excessive.

Momentarily Peter Blood's hopes rose.

"Shall we deal in plain terms now, Captain? Do you mean that they'll not be consenting to them?"

"What else should I mean?"

"In that case, Captain, it only remains for us to take our leave, in your debt for this liberal entertainment and the richer for the improvement in our acquaintance."

The elaborate courtesy of those grossly inaccurate terms did not seem to touch the ponderous Easterling. His bold, craftily-set eyes stared blankly from his great red face. He mopped the sweat from his brow before replying.

"You'll take your leave?" There was a sneering undertone to his guttural voice. "I'll trouble you in turn to be plain with me. I likes plain men and plain words. D'ye mean that ye'll quit from the business?"

Two or three of his followers made a rumbling challenging echo to his question.

Captain Blood – to give him now the title Easterling had bestowed upon him – had the air of being intimidated. He hesitated, looking as if for guidance to his companions, who returned him only uneasy glances.

"If," he said at length, "you find our terms unreasonable, I must assume ye'll not be wishing to go further, and it only remains for us to withdraw."

He spoke with a diffidence which amazed his own followers, who had never known him other than bold in the face of any odds. It provoked a sneer from Easterling, who found no more than he had been expecting from a leech turned adventurer by circumstances.

"Faith, Doctor," said he, "ye were best to get back to your cupping and bleeding, and leave ships to men as can handle them."

There was a lightning flash from those blue eyes, as vivid as it was transient. But the swarthy countenance never lost its faint air of diffidence. Meanwhile Easterling had swung to the Governor's representative, who sat on his immediate right.

"What d'ye think of that, Mossoo Joinville?"

The fair, flabby young Frenchman smiled amiably upon Blood's diffidence. "Would it not be wise and proper, sir, to hear what terms Captain Easterling now proposes?"

"I'll hear them. But—"

"Leave the buts till after, Doctor," Easterling cut in. "The terms we'll grant are the terms I told ye. Your men share equally with mine."

"But that means no more than a tenth for the *Cinco Llagas*." And Blood, too, now appealed to M. Joinville. "Do you, sir, account that fair? I have explained to Captain Easterling that for what we lack in men we more than make up in weight of metal, and our guns are handled by a gunner such as I dare swear has no compeer in the Caribbean. A fellow named Ogle – Ned Ogle. A remarkable gunner is Ned Ogle. The very devil of a gunner, as you'ld believe if you'ld seen him pick those Spanish boats off the water in Bridgetown Harbour."

He would have continued upon the subject of Ned Ogle had not Easterling interrupted him. "Hell, man! What's a gunner more or less?"

"Oh, an ordinary gunner, maybe. But this is no ordinary gunner. An eye he has. Gunners like Ogle are like poets; they are born, so they are. He'll put you a shot between wind and water, will Ogle, as neatly as you might pick your teeth."

Easterling banged the table. "What's all this to the point?"

"It may be something. And meanwhile it shows you the valuable ally ye're acquiring." And he was off again on the

25

subject of his gunner. "He was trained in the King's Navy, was Ned Ogle, and a bad day for the King's Navy it was when Ogle took to politics and followed the Protestant Champion to Sedgmoor."

"Leave that," growled one of the officers of the *Bonaventure*, a ruffian who answered to the name of Chard. "Leave it, I say, or we'll waste the day in talk."

Easterling confirmed this with a coarse oath. Captain Blood observed that they did not mean to spare offensiveness, and his speculations on their aims starting from this took a fresh turn.

Joinville intervened. "Could you not compromise with Captain Blood? After all, there is some reason on his side. He might reasonably claim to put a hundred men aboard his ship, and in that case he would naturally take a heavier share."

"In that case he might be worth it," was the truculent answer.

"I am worth it as it is," Blood insisted.

"Ah, bah!" he was answered, with a flick of finger and thumb under his very nose.

He began to suspect that Easterling sought to entice him into an act of rashness, in reply to which he and his followers would probably be butchered where they sat, and M. Joinville would afterwards be constrained to bear witness to the Governor that the provocation had proceeded from the guests. He perceived at last the probable reason for the Frenchman's presence.

But at the moment Joinville was remonstrating. "Come, come, Captain Easterling! Thus you will never reach agreement. Captain Blood's ship is of advantage to you, and we have to pay for what is advantageous. Could you not offer him an eighth or even a seventh share?"

Easterling silenced the growl of disagreement from Chard, and became almost suave. "What would Captain Blood say to that?"

Captain Blood considered for a long moment. Then he shrugged. "I say what you know I must say: that I can say nothing until I have taken the wishes of my followers. We'll resume the discussion when I have done so – another day."

"Oh, s'death!" roared Easterling. "Do you play with us? Haven't you brought your officers with you, and ain't they empowered to speak for your men same as mine? Whatever we settles here, my men abides by. That's the custom of the Brethren of the Coast. And I expect the same from you. And I've the right to expect it, as you can tell him, Mossoo Joinville."

The Frenchman nodded gloomily, and Easterling roared on.

"We are not children, by God! And we're not here to play, but to agree terms. And, by God, we'll agree them before you leave."

"Or not, as the case may be," said Blood quietly. It was to be remarked that he had lost his diffidence by now.

"Or not? What the devil do you mean with your 'or not'?" Easterling came to his feet in a vehemence that Peter Blood believed assumed, as the proper note at this stage of the comedy he was playing.

"I mean or not, quite simply." He accounted that the time had come to compel the buccaneers to show their hand. "If we fail to agree terms, why, that's the end of the matter."

"Oho! The end of the matter, eh? Stab me, but it may prove the beginning of it."

Blood smiled up into his face, and cool as ice he commented: "That's what I was supposing. But the beginning of what, if you please, Captain Easterling?"

"Indeed, indeed, Captain!" cried Joinville. "What can you mean?"

"Mean?" Captain Easterling glared at the Frenchman. He appeared to be extremely angry. "Mean?" he repeated. "Look you, Mossoo, this fellow here, this Blood, this doctor, this escaped convict, made believe that he would enter into articles with us so as to get from me the secret of Morgan's treasure. Now that he's got it, he makes difficulties about the articles. He no longer wants to join us, it seems. He proposes to withdraw. It'll be plain to you why he proposes to withdraw, Mossoo Joinville; just as it'll be plain to you why I can't permit it."

27

"Why, here's paltry invention!" sneered Blood. "What do I know of his secret beyond his tale of a treasure buried somewhere?"

"Not somewhere. You know where. For I've been fool enough to tell you."

Blood actually laughed, and by his laughter scared his companions, to whom the danger of their situation was now clear enough.

"Somewhere on the Isthmus of Darien! There's precision, on my soul! With that information I can go straight to the spot and set my hand on it! As for the rest, Monsieur Joinville, I invite you to observe it's not myself is making difficulties about the articles. On the one-fifth share which I asked from the outset, I might have been prepared to join Captain Easterling. But now that I'm confirmed in all that I suspected of him, and more, why, I wouldn't join him for a half share in this treasure, supposing it to exist at all, which I do not."

That brought every man of the *Bonaventure* to his feet as if it had been a signal, and they were clamorous too, until Easterling waved them into silence. Upon that silence cut the tenor voice of M. Joinville.

"You are a singularly rash man, Captain Blood."

"Maybe, maybe," said Blood, light and airily. "Time will show. The last word's not yet been said."

"Then here's to say it," quoth Easterling, quietly sinister on a sudden. "I was about to warn you that ye'll not be allowed to leave this ship with the information ye possess until the articles is signed. But since ye so clearly show your intentions, why, things have gone beyond warnings."

From his seat at the table, which he retained, Captain Blood looked up at the sinister bulk of the captain of the *Bonaventure*, and the three men from the *Cinco Llagas* observed with mingled amazement and dismay that he was smiling. At first so unusually diffident and timid; now so deliberately and recklessly provoking. He was beyond understanding. It was Hagthorpe who spoke for them.

"What do you mean, Captain? What do you intend by us?"

"Why, to clap you into irons, and stow you under hatches, where you can do no harm."

"My God, sir—" Hagthorpe was beginning, when Captain Blood's crisp pleasant voice cut across his speech.

"And you, Monsieur Joinville, will permit this without protest?"

Joinville spread his hands, thrust out a nether lip, and shrugged. "You have brought it on yourself, Captain Blood."

"So that is what you are here to report to Monsieur d'Ogeron! Well, well!" He laughed with a touch of bitterness.

And then, abruptly, on the noontide stillness outside came the thunder of a gun to shake them all. Followed the screaming of startled gulls, a pause in which men eyed one another, and then, a shade uneasily, came the question from Easterling, addressed to no one in particular:

"What the devil's that?"

It was Blood who answered him pleasantly. "Now don't let it alarm ye, Captain darling. It's just a salute fired in your honour by Ogle, the gunner – the highly skilful gunner – of the *Cinco Llagas*. Have I told you about him yet?" His eyes embraced the company in the question.

"A salute?" quoth Easterling. "By hell, what do you mean? A salute?"

"Why, just a courtesy, as a reminder to us and a warning to you. It's a reminder to us that we've taken up an hour of your time, and that we must put no further strain upon your hospitality." He got to his feet, and stood, easy and elegant in his Spanish suit of black and silver. "It's a very good day we'll be wishing you, Captain."

Inflamed of countenance, Easterling plucked a pistol from his belt. "You play-acting buffoon! Ye don't leave this ship!"

But Captain Blood continued to smile. "Faith, that will be very bad for the ship, and for all aboard her, including this ingenuous Monsieur Joinville, who really believes you'll pay him the promised share of your phantom treasure for bearing false witness against me, so as to justify you in the eyes of the Governor for seizing the *Cinco Llagas*. Ye see, I am under no delusions concerning you, my dear Captain. For a rogue ye're a thought too transparent."

Easterling loosed a volley of minatory obscenity, waving his pistol. He was restrained from using it only by an indefinable uneasiness aroused by his guest's bantering manner.

"We are wasting time," Blood interrupted him, "and the moments, believe me, are growing singularly precious. You'd best know where you stand. My orders to Ogle were that if within ten minutes of his firing that salute I and my friends here were not over the side of the *Bonaventure*, he was to put a round shot into your forecastle along the waterline, and as many more after that as may be necessary to sink you by the head. I do not think that many will be necessary. Ogle is a singularly skilful marksman. He served with distinction as a gunner in the King's Navy. I think I've told you about him."

It was Joinville who broke the moment's silence that followed. "God of my life!" he bleated, bounding to his feet. "Let me out of this!"

"Oh, stow your squealing, you French rat!" snarled the infuriated Easterling. Then he turned his fury upon Blood, balancing the pistol ominously. "You sneaking leech! You college offal! You'd ha' done better to ha' stuck to your cuppings and bleedings, as I told you."

His murderous intention was plain. But Blood was too swift for him. Before any could so much as guess his purpose, he had snatched up by its neck the flagon of Canary that stood before him and crashed it across Captain Easterling's left temple.

As the captain of the *Bonaventure* reeled back against the cabin bulkhead, Peter Blood bowed slightly to him.

"I regret," said he, "that I have no cup; but, as you see, I can practise phlebotomy with a bottle."

Easterling sagged down in a limp unconscious mass at the foot of the bulkhead. The spectacle stirred his officers. There was a movement towards Captain Blood, and a din of raucous voices, and someone laid hands upon him. But above the uproar rang his vibrant voice.

"Be warned! The moments are speeding. The ten minutes

30

have all but fled, and either I and my friends depart, or we all sink together in this bottom."

"In God's name, bethink you of it!" cried Joinville, and started for the door.

A buccaneer who did bethink him of it and who was of a practical turn of mind, seized him about the body and flung him back.

"You there!" he shouted to Captain Blood. "You and your men go first. And bestir yourselves! We've no mind to drown like rats."

They went as they were bidden, curses pursuing them and threats of a reckoning to follow.

Either the ruffians aswarm on the deck above were not in the secret of Easterling's intentions, or else a voice of authority forbade them to hinder the departure of Captain Blood and his companions.

In the cock-boat, midway between the two vessels, Hagthorpe found his voice at last.

"On my soul's salvation, Peter, there was a moment when I thought our sands were run."

"Ay, ay," said Pitt with fervour. "And even as it was they might have been." He swung to Peter Blood, where he sat in the stern-sheets. "Suppose that for one reason or another we had not got out in those ten minutes, and Ogle had opened fire in earnest? What then?"

"Ah!" said Blood. "Our real danger lay in that he wasn't like to do it."

"But if you so ordered him?"

"Nay, that's just what I forgot to do. All I told him was to loose a blank shot when we had been gone an hour. I thought that however things went it might prove useful. And on my soul, I believe it did. Lord!" He took off his hat and mopped his brow under the staring eyes of his companions.

"I wonder now if it's the heat that's making me sweat like this."

2

THE TREASURE SHIP

IT WAS a saying of Captain Blood's that the worth of a man
manifests itself not so much in the ability to plan great
undertakings as in the vision which perceives opportunity and
the address which knows how to seize it.

He had certainly displayed these qualities in possessing
himself of that fine Spanish ship the *Cinco Llagas*, and he had
displayed them again in foiling the designs of that rascally
buccaneer Captain Easterling to rob him of that noble vessel.

Meanwhile his own and his ship's near escape made it clear
to all who followed him that there was little safety for them in
Tortuga waters, and little trust to be placed in buccaneers. At
a general council held that same afternoon in the ship's waist
Blood propounded the simple philosophy that when a man is
attacked he must either fight or run.

"And since we are in no case to fight when attacked, as no
doubt we shall be, it but remains to play the coward's part if
only so that we may survive to prove ourselves brave men some
other day."

They agreed with him. But whilst the decision to run was
taken, it was left to be determined later whither they should
repair. At the moment all that mattered was to get away from
Tortuga and the further probable attentions of Captain Easterling.

Thus it fell out that in the dead of the following night, which,
if clear, was moonless, the great frigate which once had been
the pride of the Cadiz shipyards weighed anchor as quietly as
such an operation might be performed. With canvas spread to
the faint favouring breeze from the shore, and with the ebb tide
to help the manoeuvre, the *Cinco Llagas* stood out to sea. If
groan of windlass, rattle of chain, and creak of blocks had

betrayed the action to Easterling aboard the *Bonaventure*, a cable's length away, it was not in Easterling's power to thwart Blood's intention.

At least three-quarters of his rascally crew were in the taverns ashore, and Easterling was not disposed to attempt boarding operations with the remnant of his men, even though that remnant outnumbered by two to one the hands of the *Cinco Llagas*. Moreover, even had his full complement of two hundred been aboard, Easterling would still have offered no opposition to that departure. Whilst in Tortuga waters he might have attempted to get possession of the *Cinco Llagas* quietly and by strategy, not even his recklessness could consider seizing her violently by force in such a sanctuary, especially as the French Governor, Monsieur d'Ogeron, appeared to be friendly disposed towards Blood and his fellow fugitives.

Out on the open sea it would be another matter; and the tale he would afterwards tell of the manner in which the *Cinco Llagas* should have come into his possession would be such as no one in Cayona would be in a position to contradict.

So Captain Easterling suffered Peter Blood to depart unhindered, and was well content to let him go. Nor did he display any undue and betraying haste to follow. He made his preparations with leisureliness, and did not weigh anchor until the afternoon of the morrow. He trusted his wits to give him the direction Blood must take and depended upon the greater speed of the *Bonaventure* to overhaul him before he should have gone far enough for safety. His reasoning was shrewd enough. Since he knew that the *Cinco Llagas* was not victualled for a long voyage, there could be no question yet of any direct attempt to sail for Europe.

First she must be equipped, and since to equip her Blood dared approach no English or Spanish settlement, it followed that he would steer for one of the neutral Dutch colonies, and there take his only remaining chance. Nor was Blood likely without experienced pilotage to venture among the dangerous reefs of the Bahamas. It was therefore an easy inference that his destination would be the Leeward Islands with intent to put in at San Martin, Saba, or Santa Eustacia. Confident, then, of overtaking him before he could make the nearest of those Dutch settlements, two hundred leagues away, the pursuing *Bonaventure* steered an easterly course along the northern shores of Hispaniola.

Things, however, were not destined to be so simple as Easterling conjectured. The wind, at first favourable, veered towards evening to the east, and increased throughout the night in vehemence; so that by dawn – an angry dawn with skies ominously flushed – the *Bonaventure* had not merely made no progress, but had actually drifted some miles out of her course. Then the wind shifted to the south towards noon, and it came on to blow harder than ever. It blew up a storm from the Caribbean, and for twenty-four hours the *Bonaventure* rode it out with bare yards and hatches battened against the pounding seas that broke athwart her and tossed her like a cork from trough to crest.

It was fortunate that the burly Easterling was not only a stout fighter but also an able seaman. Under his skilled handling the *Bonaventure* came through the ordeal unscathed, to resume the chase when at last the storm had passed and the wind had settled to a steady breeze from the south-west. With crowded canvas the sloop now went scudding through the heaving seas which the storm had left.

Easterling heartened his followers with the reminder that the hurricane which had delayed them must no less have delayed the *Cinco Llagas*; that, indeed, considering the lubbers who handled the erstwhile Spanish frigate, it was likely that the storm had made things easier for the *Bonaventure*.

What exactly the storm had done for them they were to discover on the following morning, when off Cape Engaño they sighted a galleon which at first, in the distance, they supposed to be their quarry, but which very soon they perceived to be some other vessel. That she was Spanish was advertised not only by the towering build, but by the banner of Castile which she flew beneath the Crucifix at the head of her mainmast. On the yards of this mainmast all canvas was close-reefed, and under the spread of only foresail mizzen and sprit she was labouring clumsily towards the Mona Passage with the wind on her larboard quarter.

The sight of her in her partially maimed condition stirred Easterling like a hound at sight of a deer. For the moment the quest of the *Cinco Llagas* was forgotten. Here was more immediate prey, and of a kind to be easily reduced.

At the poop rail he bawled his orders rapidly. In obedience the decks were cleared with feverish speed and the nettings spread from stem to stern to catch any spars that might be shot down in the approaching action. Chard, Easterling's lieutenant, a short, powerful man, who was a dullard in all things save the handling of a ship and the wielding of a cutlass, took the helm. The gunners at their stations cleared the leaden aprons from the touch-holes and swung their glowing matches, ready for the word of command. For however disorderly and unruly Easterling's crew might be at ordinary times, it knew the need for discipline when battle was to be joined.

Watchful on the poop, the buccaneer captain surveyed the Spaniard upon which he was rapidly bearing down, and observed with scorn the scurry of preparation on her decks. His practised eye read her immediate past history at a glance, and his harsh guttural voice announced what he read to Chard, who stood below him at the whipstaff.

"She would be homing for Spain when the hurricane caught her. She's sprung her mainmast and likely suffered other damage besides, and she's beating back to San Domingo for repairs." Easterling laughed in his throat and stroked his dense black beard. The dark, bold eyes in his great red face glinted wickedly. "Give me a homing Spaniard, Chard. There'll be treasure aboard that hulk. By God, we're in luck at last."

He was indeed. It had long been his grievance, and the true reason of his coveting the *Cinco Llagas*, that his sloop the *Bonaventure* was unequal to tackling the real prizes of the Caribbean. And he would never have dared to attack this heavily armed galleon but that in her crippled condition she

35

was unable to manoeuvre so as to bring her guns to bear upon his flanks.

She gave him now a broadside from her starboard quarter, and by doing so sealed her own doom. The *Bonaventure*, coming head on, presented little target, and save for a round shot in her forecastle took no damage. Easterling answered the fire with the chasers on his prow, aiming high, and sweeping the Spaniard's decks. Then, nimbly avoiding her clumsy attempt to go about and change their relative positions, the *Bonaventure* was alongside on the quarter of her empty guns. There was a rattling, thudding jar, a creak of entangled rigging, a crack and clatter of broken spars and the thud of grapnels rending into the Spaniard's timbers to bind her fast, and then, tight-locked, the two vessels went drifting down wind, whilst the buccaneers, led by the colossal Easterling, and after discharging a volley of musketry, swarmed like ants over the Spaniard's bulwarks. Two hundred of them there were, fierce fellows in loose leathern breeches, some with shirts as well, but the majority naked to the waist, and by that brown muscular nakedness the more terrific of aspect.

To receive them stood a bare fifty Spaniards in corselet and morion, drawn up in the galleon's waist as if upon parade, with muskets calmly levelled and a hawk-faced officer in a plumed hat commanding them.

The officer spoke an order, and a volley from the muskets momentarily checked the assault. Then, like an engulfing wave, the buccaneer mob went over the Spanish soldiers, and the ship, the *Santa Barbara*, was taken.

There was not perhaps upon the seas at the time a more cruel, ruthless man than Easterling; and those who sailed with him adopted, as men will, their captain's standard of ferocity. Brutally they exterminated the Spanish soldiery, heaving the bodies overboard, and as brutally they dealt with those manning the guns on the main deck below, although these unfortunates readily surrendered in the vain hope of being allowed to keep their lives.

Within ten minutes of the invasion of the *Santa Barbara*

36

there remained alive upon her of her original crew only the captain, Don Ildefonso de Paiva, whom Easterling had stunned with the butt of a pistol, the navigating officer, and four deck-hands, who had been aloft at the moment of boarding. These six Easterling spared for the present because he accounted that they might prove useful.

Whilst his men were busy in the shrouds about the urgent business of disentangling and where necessary repairing, the buccaneer captain began upon the person of Don Ildefonso the investigation of his capture.

The Spaniard, sickly and pallid and with a lump on his brow where the pistol-butt had smitten him, sat on a locker in the handsome roomy cabin, with pinioned wrists, but striving nevertheless to preserve the haughty demeanour proper to a gentleman of Castile in the presence of an impudent sea robber. Thus until Easterling, towering over him, savagely threatened to loosen his tongue by the artless persuasions of torture. Then Don Ildefonso, realizing the futility of resistance, curtly answered the pirate's questions. From these answers and his subsequent investigations Easterling discovered his capture to exceed every hope he could have formed.

There had fallen into his hands – which of late had known so little luck – one of those prizes which had been the dream of every sea rover since the days of Francis Drake. The *Santa Barbara* was a treasure ship from Porto Bello, laden with gold and silver which had been conveyed across the Isthmus from Panama. She had put forth under the escort of three strong ships of war, with intent to call at San Domingo to revictual before crossing to Spain. But in the recent storm which had swept the Caribbean she had been separated from her consorts, and with damaged mainmast had been driven through the Mona Passage by the gale. She had been beating back for San Domingo in the hope of rejoining there her escort or else awaiting there another fleet for Spain.

The treasure in her hold was computed by Easterling when his gleaming eyes came to consider those ingots at between two and three hundred thousand pieces of eight. It was a prize such as does not come the way of a pirate twice in his career, and it meant fortune for himself and those who sailed with him.

Now the possession of fortune is inevitably attended by anxiety, and Easterling's besetting anxiety at the moment was to convey his prize with all possible speed to the security of Tortuga.

From his own sloop he took twoscore men to form a prize crew for the Spaniard, and himself remained aboard her because he could not suffer himself to be parted from the treasure. Then, with damage hurriedly repaired, the two ships went about, and started upon their voyage. Progress was slow, the wind being none too favourable and the *Santa Barbara* none too manageable, and it was past noon before they had Cape Raphael once more abeam. Easterling was uneasy in this near proximity to Hispaniola, and was for taking a wide sweep that would carry them well out to sea, when from the crow's-nest of the *Santa Barbara* came a hail, and a moment later the object first espied by the lookout was visible to them all.

There, rounding Cape Raphael, not two miles away, and steering almost to meet them, came a great red ship under full sail. Easterling's telescope confirmed at once what the naked eye had led him incredulously to suspect. This vessel was the *Cinco Llagas*, the original object of his pursuit, which in his haste he must have outsailed.

The truth was that, overtaken by the storm as they approached Samana, Jeremy Pitt, who navigated the *Cinco Llagas*, had run for the shelter of Samana Bay, and under the lee of a headland had remained snug and unperceived, to come forth again when the gale had spent itself.

Easterling, caring little how the thing had happened, perceived in this sudden and unexpected appearance of the *Cinco Llagas* a sign that Fortune, hitherto so niggardly, was disposed now to overwhelm him with her favours. Let him convey himself and the *Santa Barbara*'s treasure aboard that stout red ship, and in strength he could make good speed home.

Against a vessel so heavily armed and so undermanned as the *Cinco Llagas* there could be no question of any but boarding tactics, and it did not seem to Captain Easterling that this should offer much difficulty to the swifter and more easily handled *Bonaventure*, commanded by a man experienced in seamanship and opposed by a lubberly follower who was by trade a surgeon.

So Easterling signalled Chard to be about the easy business, and Chard, eager enough to square accounts with the man who once already had done them the injury of slipping like water through their fingers, put the helm over and ordered his men to their stations.

Captain Blood, summoned from the cabin by Pitt, mounted the poop and, telescope in hand, surveyed the activities aboard his old friend the *Bonaventure*. He remained in no doubt of their significance. He might be a surgeon, but hardly a lubberly one, as Chard so rashly judged him. His service under de Ruyter in those earlier adventurous days when medicine was neglected by him had taught him more of fighting tactics than Easterling had ever known. He was not perturbed. He would show these pirates how he had profited by the lessons learnt under that great admiral.

Just as for the *Bonaventure* it was essential to employ boarding tactics, so for the *Cinco Llagas* it was vital to depend on gunfire. For with no more than twenty men in all, she could not face the odds of almost ten to one, as Blood computed them, of a hand-to-hand engagement. So now he ordered Pitt to put down the helm, and, keeping as close to the wind as possible, to steer a course that would bring them on to the *Bonaventure*'s quarter. To the main deck below he ordered Ogle, that sometime gunner of the King's Navy, taking for his gun crew all but six of the hands who would be required for work above.

Chard perceived at once the aim of the manoeuvre and swore through his teeth, for Blood had the weather gauge of him. He was further handicapped by the fact that since the *Cinco Llagas* was to be captured for their own purposes, it must be no part of his work to cripple her by gunfire before attempting to board. Moreover, he perceived the risk to himself of the

39

attempt, resulting from the longer range and heavier calibre of the guns of the *Cinco Llagas*, if she were resolutely handled. And there appeared to be no lack of resolution about her present master.

Meanwhile the distance between the ships was rapidly lessening, and Chard realized that unless he acted quickly he would be within range with his flank exposed. Unable to bring his ship any closer to the wind, he went about on a southeasterly course with intent to circle widely and so get to windward of the *Cinco Llagas*.

Easterling, watching the manoeuvre from the deck of the *Santa Barbara*, and not quite understanding its purpose, cursed Chard for a fool. He cursed him the more virulently when he saw the *Cinco Llagas* veer suddenly to larboard and follow as if giving chase. Chard, however, welcomed this, and taking in sail allowed the other to draw closer. Then with all canvas spread once more, the *Bonaventure* was off with the wind on her quarter to attempt her circling movement.

Blood understood, and took in sail in his turn, standing so that as the *Bonaventure* turned north she must offer him her flank within range of his heavy guns. Hence, Chard, to avoid this, must put up his helm and run south once more.

Easterling watched the two ships sailing away from him in a succession of such manoeuvres for position, and, purple with rage, demanded of heaven and hell whether he could believe his eyes, which told him only that Chard was running away from the lubberly leech. Chard, however, was far from any such intention. With masterly patience and self-control he awaited his chance to run in and grapple. And with equal patience and doggedness Blood saw to it that he should be given no such chance.

In the end it became a question of who should commit the first blunder, and it was Chard who committed it. In his almost excessive anxiety to avoid coming broadside on with the *Cinco Llagas*, he forgot the chasers on her beakhead, and at last in playing for position allowed her to come too near. He realized his blunder when those two guns roared suddenly behind him and the shot went tearing through his shrouds. It angered him, and in his anger he replied with his stern chasers; but their inferior calibre left their fire ineffective. Then, utterly enraged, he swung the *Bonaventure* about, so as to put a broadside athwart the hawse of the other, and by crippling her sailing powers lay her at the mercy of his boarders.

The heavy ground swell, however, combined with the length of the range utterly to defeat his object, and his broadside thundered forth in impotence to leave a cloud of smoke between himself and the *Cinco Llagas*. Instantly Blood swung broadside on, emptied his twenty larboard guns into that smoke cloud, hoping to attain the *Bonaventure*'s exposed flank beyond. The attempt was equally unsuccessful, but it served to show Chard the mettle of the man he was engaging – a man with whom it was not safe to take such chances. Nevertheless, one more chance he took, and went briskly about, so as to charge through the billowing smoke, and so bear down upon the other ship before she could suspect the design. The manoeuvre, however, was too protracted for success. By the time the *Bonaventure* was upon her fresh course the smoke had dispersed sufficiently to betray her tactics to Blood, and the *Cinco Llagas*, lying well over to larboard, was ripping through the water at twice the speed of the *Bonaventure*, now ill-served by the wind.

Again Chard put the helm over and raced to intercept the other and to get to windward of her. But Blood, now a mile away, and with a safety margin of time, went about and returned so as to bring his starboard guns to bear at the proper moment. To elude this Chard once more headed south and presented no more than his counter as a target.

In this manner the two vessels worked gradually away until the *Santa Barbara*, with the raging, blaspheming Easterling aboard, was no more than a speck on the northern horizon; and still they were as far as ever from joining battle.

Chard cursed the wind, which favoured Captain Blood, and cursed Captain Blood, who knew so well how to take and maintain the advantage of his position. The lubberly surgeon appeared possessed of perfect understanding of the situation and uncannily ready to meet each move of his opponent. Occasional shots continued to be exchanged by the chasers of each vessel, each aiming high so as to damage the other's sailing powers, yet, at the long range separating them, without success.

Peter Blood at the poop rail, in a fine back-and-breast and cap of black damascened steel, which had been the property of the original Spanish commander of the *Cinco Llagas*, was growing weary and anxious. To Hagthorpe similarly armed beside him, to Wolverstone, whom no armour aboard would fit, and to Pitt at the whipstaff, immediately below, he confessed it in the tone of his question:

"How long can this ducking and dodging continue? And however long it continues, what end can it have but one? Sooner or later the wind will drop or veer, or else it's ourselves will drop from sheer weariness. When that happens we'll be at that scoundrel's mercy."

"There's always the unexpected," said young Pitt.

"Why, so there is, and I thank you for reminding me of it, Jerry. Let's put our hopes in it, for all that I can't see whence it's to come."

It was coming at that moment, and coming quickly, although Blood was the only one of them who recognized it when he saw it. They were standing in towards the land at the end of a long westerly run, when round the point of Espada, less than a mile away, a towering heavily-armed ship came sailing as close to the wind as she dared, her ports open and the mouths of a score of guns gaping along her larboard flank, the banner of Castile flapping aloft in the breeze.

At the sight of this fresh enemy of another sort Wolverstone loosed an oath that sounded like a groan.

"And that's the end of us!" he cried.

"I'm by no means sure, now, that it may not be the beginning," Blood answered him, with something that sounded like laughter in his voice, which when last heard had been jaded and dispirited. And his orders, flowing fast, showed clearly what was in his mind. "Run me the flag of Spain aloft, and bid Ogle empty his chasers at the *Bonaventure* as we go about."

As Pitt put the helm over, and with straining cordage and creaking blocks the *Cinco Llagas* swung slowly round, the gold and scarlet banner of Castile broke bravely from her main-truck. An instant later the two guns on her forecastle thundered forth, ineffectually in one way but very effectually in another. Their fire conveyed very plainly to the Spanish newcomer that here he beheld a compatriot ship in pursuit of an English rover.

Explanations no doubt must follow, especially if upon the discovery of the identity of the *Cinco Llagas* the Spaniards should happen to be already acquainted with her recent history. But that could not come until they had disposed of the *Bonaventure*, and Blood was more than content to let the future take care of itself.

Meanwhile the Spanish ship, a guarda-costa from San Domingo, which whilst on patrol had been attracted beyond the Point of Espada by the sound of gunfire out at sea, behaved precisely as was to be expected. Even without the flag now floating at her masthead, the Spanish origin of the *Cinco Llagas* was plain to read in the lines of her; that she was engaged with this equally obvious English sloop was no less plain. The guarda-costa went into the fight without a moment's hesi-tation, and loosed a broadside at the *Bonaventure* as she was in the act of going about to escape this sudden and unforeseen peril.

Chard raged like a madman as the sloop shuddered under blows at stem and stern and her shattered bowsprit hung in a tangle of cordage athwart her bows. In his frenzy he ordered the fire to be returned, and did some damage to the guarda-costa, but not of a kind to impair her mobility. The Spaniard, warming to the battle, went about so as to pound the sloop with her starboard guns, and Chard, having lost his head by now, swung round also so as to return or even anticipate that fire.

Not until he had done so did it occur to him that with empty guns he was helplessly vulnerable to an onslaught from the

Cinco Llagas. For Blood, too, espying the opportunity whilst yet it was shaping, had gone about, drawn level, and hurled at him the contents of his heavy artillery. That broadside at comparatively short range swept his deck, shattered the windows of the coach, and one well-placed shot opened a wound in the bows of the *Bonaventure* almost on the waterline, through which the sea rushed into the hold at every roll of the crippled vessel.

Chard realized that he was doomed, and his bitterness was deepened by perception of the misapprehension at the root of his destruction. He saw the Spanish flag at the masthead of the *Cinco Llagas,* and grinned in livid malice.

On a last inspiration, he struck his colours in token of surrender. It was his forlorn hope that the guarda-costa, accepting this, and ignorant of his strength in men, would rush in to grapple him, in which case he would turn the tables on the Spaniards and, possessing himself of the guarda-costa, might yet come out of the adventure with safety and credit.

But the vigilant Captain Blood guessed, if not the intention, at least the possibility, as well as the alternative possibility of explanations dangerous to himself from the captured Chard to the Spanish commander. To provide against either danger, he sent for Ogle, and under his instructions that skilful gunner crashed a thirty-two-pound shot into the *Bonaventure*'s waterline amidships, so as to supplement the leakage already occurring forward.

The captain of the guarda-costa may have wondered why his compatriot should continue to fire upon a ship that had struck her colours, but the circumstance would hardly seem to him suspicious, although it might be vexatious, for its consequence appeared to be the inevitable destruction of a vessel that might yet have been turned to account.

As for Chard, he had no time for speculations of any kind. The *Bonaventure* was now making water so fast that his only hope of saving the lives of himself and his men lay in attempting to run her aground before she sank. So he headed her for the shoals at the foot of the Point of Espada, thanking God that she might now run before the wind, although at an ominously diminishing speed, despite the fact that the buccaneers heaved their cannon overboard to lighten her as they went. She grounded at last in the shallows, with the seas breaking over her stern and forecastles, which alone remained above water. These and the shrouds were now black with the men who had climbed to safety. The guarda-costa stood off with idly flapping sails, waiting, her captain wondering to behold the *Cinco Llagas* half a mile away already heading northwards.

Aboard her presently Captain Blood was inquiring of Pitt if a knowledge of Spanish signals was included in his lore of the sea, and if so would he read the signals that the guarda-costa was flying. The young shipmaster confessed that it was not, and expressed the opinion that as a consequence they had but escaped the frying-pan to fall into the fire.

"Now here's a lack of faith in Madame Fortune," said Blood. "We'll just be dipping our flag in salute to them, to imply that we've business elsewhere, and be off to attend to it. We look like honest Spaniards. Even through a telescope, in this Spanish armour Hagthorpe and I must look like a pair of dons. Let's go and see how it's faring with the ingenious Easterling. I'm thinking the time has come to improve our acquaintance with him."

The guarda-costa, if surprised at the unceremonious departure of the vessel she had assisted in the destruction of that pirate sloop, cannot have suspected her bona fides. Either taking it for granted that she had business elsewhere, or else because, too intent upon making prisoners of the crew of the *Bonaventure*, she made no attempt to follow.

And so it fell out that some two hours later Captain Easterling, waiting off the coast between Cape Raphael and Cape Engaño, beheld to his stupefaction and horror the swift approach of Peter Blood's red ship. He had listened attentively and in some uneasiness to the distant cannonade, but he had assumed its cessation to mean that the *Cinco Llagas* was taken. The sight now of that frigate, sailing briskly, jauntily, and undamaged, defied belief. What had happened to Chard? There was no sign of him upon the sea. Could he have blundered so badly as to have allowed Captain Blood to sink him?

Speculation on this point was presently quenched by speculation of an infinitely graver character? What might be this damned doctor-convict's present intention? If Easterling had been in case to board him he would have known no apprehension, for even his prize crew on the *Santa Barbara* outnumbered Blood's men by more than two to one. But the crippled *Santa Barbara* could never be laid board and board with the *Cinco Llagas* unless Blood desired it, and if Blood meant mischief as a result of what had happened with the *Bonaventure*, the *Santa Barbara* must lie at the mercy of his guns.

The reflection, vexatious enough in itself, was maddening to Easterling when he considered what he carried under hatches. Fortune, it now began to seem, had not favoured him at all. She had merely mocked him by allowing him to grasp something which he could not hold.

But this was by no means the end of his vexation. For now, as if the circumstances in themselves had not been enough to enrage a man, his prize crew turned mutinous. Led by a scoundrel named Gunning, a man almost as massive and ruthless as Easterling himself, they furiously blamed their captain and his excessive and improvident greed for the peril in which they found themselves – a peril of death or capture embittered by the thought of the wealth they held. With such a prize in his hands, Easterling should have taken no risks. He should have kept the *Bonaventure* at hand for protection, and paid no heed to the empty hulk of the *Cinco Llagas*. This they told him in terms of fiercest vituperation, whose very justice left him without answer other than insults, which he liberally supplied.

Whilst they wrangled, the *Cinco Llagas* drew nearer, and now Easterling's quartermaster called his attention to the signals she was flying. These demanded the immediate presence aboard her of the commander of the *Santa Barbara*.

Easterling was taken with panic. The high colour receded

from his cheeks, his heavy lips grew purple. He vowed that he would see Dr Blood in hell before he went.

His men assured him that they would see him in hell, and shortly, if he did not go.

Gunning reminded him that Blood could not possibly know what the *Santa Barbara* carried, and that therefore it should be possible to cozen him into allowing her to go her ways without further molestation.

A gun thundered from the *Cinco Llagas*, to send a warning shot across the bows of the *Santa Barbara*. That was enough. Gunning thrust the quartermaster aside, and himself seized the helm and put it over, so that the ship lay hove to, as a first intimation of compliance. After that the buccaneers launched the cockboat and a half dozen of them swarmed down to man her, whilst, almost at pistol point, Gunning compelled Captain Easterling to follow them.

When presently he climbed into the waist of the *Cinco Llagas* where she lay hove to, a cable's length away across the sunlit waters, there was hell in his eyes and terror in his soul. Straight and tall, in Spanish corselet and headpiece, the despised doctor stood forward to receive him. Behind him stood Hagthorpe and a half score of his followers. He seemed to smile.

"At last, Captain, ye stand where ye have so long hoped to stand: on the deck of the *Cinco Llagas*."

Easterling grunted ragefully for only answer to this raillery. His great hands twitched as if he would have them at his Irish mocker's throat. Captain Blood continued to address him.

"It's an ill thing, Captain, to attempt to grasp more than you can comfortably hold. Ye'll not be the first to find himself empty-handed as a consequence. That was a fine fast-sailing sloop of yours, the *Bonaventure*. Ye should have been content. It's a pity that she'll sail no more; for she's sunk, or will be entirely at high water." Abruptly he asked: "How many hands are with you?" and he had to repeat the question before he was sullenly answered that forty men remained aboard the *Santa Barbara*.

"What boats does she carry?"

"Three with the cockboat."

"That should be enough to accommodate your following. You'll order them into those boats at once if you value their lives, for in fifteen minutes from now I shall open fire on the ship and sink her. This because I can spare no men for a prize crew, nor can I leave her afloat to be repossessed by you and turned to further mischief."

Easterling began a furious protest that was mixed with remonstrances of the peril to him and his of landing on Hispaniola. Blood cropped it short.

"Ye're receiving such mercy as you probably never showed to any whom ye compelled to surrender. Ye'ld best profit by my tenderness. If the Spaniards on Hispaniola spare you when you land there, you can get back to your hunting and boucanning, for which ye're better fitted than the sea. Away with you now."

But Easterling did not at once depart. He stood with feet planted wide, swaying on his powerful legs, clenching and unclenching his hands. At last he took his decision.

"Leave me that ship, and in Tortuga, when I get there, I'll pay you fifty thousand pieces of eight. That's better nor the empty satisfaction of turning us adrift."

"Away with you!" was all that Blood answered him, his tone more peremptory.

"A hundred thousand!" cried Easterling.

"Why not a million?" wondered Blood. "It's as easily promised, and the promise as easily broken. Oh, I'm like to take your word, Captain Easterling, as like as I am to believe that ye command such a sum as a hundred thousand pieces of eight."

Easterling's baleful eyes narrowed. Behind his black beard his thick lips tightened. Almost they smiled. Since there was nothing to be done without disclosures, nothing should be done at all. Let Blood sink a treasure which in any case must now be lost to Easterling. There was in the thought a certain bitter negative satisfaction.

"I pray that we may meet again, Captain Blood," he said,

falsely, grimly unctuous. "I'll have something to tell you then that'll make you sorry for what you do now."

"If we meet again I've no doubt the occasion will be one for many regrets. Good day to you, Captain Easterling. Ye've just fifteen minutes, ye'll remember."

Easterling sneered and shrugged, and then abruptly turned and climbed down to the rocking boat that awaited him below.

When he came to announce Blood's message to his buccaneers they stormed and raged so fiercely at the prospect of thus being cheated of everything that they could be heard across the water aboard the *Cinco Llagas*, to the faintly scornful amusement of Blood, who was far from suspecting the true reason of all this hubbub.

He watched the lowering of the boats, and was thereafter amazed to see the decks of the *Santa Barbara* empty of that angry, vociferous mob. The buccaneers had gone below before leaving, each man intent upon taking as much of the treasure as he could carry upon his person. Captain Blood became impatient.

"Pass the word down to Ogle to put a shot into her forecastle. Those rogues need quickening."

The roar of the gun, and the impact of the twenty-four-pound shot as it smashed through the timbers of the high forward structure brought the buccaneers swarming upon deck again, and thence to the waiting boats with the speed of fear. Yet a certain order they preserved for their safety's sake, for in the sea that was running the capsizing of a boat would have been an easy matter.

They pushed off, their wet oars flashed in the sunlight, and they began to draw away towards the promontory not more than two miles to windward. Once they were clear, Blood gave the word to open fire, when Hagthorpe clutched his arm.

"Wait, man! Wait! Look! There's someone still aboard her!"

Surprised, Blood looked, first with his naked eye, then through his telescope. He beheld a bareheaded gentleman in corselet and thigh-boots, who clearly was no buccaneer of the kind that sailed with Easterling, and who stood on the poop frantically waving a scarf. Blood was quick to guess his identity.

"It'll be one of the Spaniards who were aboard when Easterling took the ship and whose throat he forgot to cut."

He ordered a boat to be launched, and sent six men with Dyke, who had some knowledge of Spanish, to bring the Spaniard off.

Don Ildefonso, who, callously left to drown in the doomed ship, had worked himself free of the thong that bound his wrists, stood in the forechains to await the coming of that boat. He was quivering with excitement at this deliverance of himself and the vessel in his charge with her precious freight – a deliverance which he regarded as little short of miraculous. For, like the guarda-costa, Don Ildefonso, even if he had not recognized the Spanish lines of this great ship which had come so unexpectedly to the rescue, must have been relieved of all doubt by the flag of Spain which had been allowed to remain floating at the masthead of the *Cinco Llagas*.

So with speech bubbling eagerly out of him in that joyous excitement of his, the Spanish commander poured into the ears of Dyke, when the boat brought up alongside, the tale of what had happened to them and what they carried. Because of this it was necessary that they should lend him a dozen men so that with the six now under hatches on the *Santa Barbara* he might bring his precious cargo safely into San Domingo.

To Dyke this was an amazing and exciting narrative. But he did not on that account lose grip of his self-possession. Lest too much Spanish should betray him to Don Ildefonso, he took refuge in curtness.

"Bueno," said he. "I'll inform my captain." Under his breath he ordered his men to push off and head back for the *Cinco Llagas*.

When Blood heard the tale and had digested his amazement, he laughed.

"So this is what that rogue would have told me if ever we met again. Faith, it's a satisfaction to be denied him."

Ten minutes later the *Cinco Llagas* lay board and board with the *Santa Barbara*.

In the distance Easterling and his men, observing the operation, rested on their oars to stare and mutter. They saw themselves cheated of even the meagre satisfaction for which they had looked in the sinking of an unsuspected treasure. Easterling burst into fresh profanity.

"It'll be that damned Spaniard I forgot in the cabin who'll ha' blabbed of the gold! Oh 'sdeath! This is what becomes o' being soft-hearted; if only I'd cut his throat, now . . ."

Meanwhile, to Don Ildefonso, who had been able to make nothing of this boarding manoeuvre, Captain Blood, save for the light eyes in his bronzed face, looking every inch a Spaniard, and delivering himself in the impeccable Castilian of which he was master, was offering explanations.

He was unable to spare a crew to man the *Santa Barbara*, for his own following was insufficient. Nor dared he leave her afloat, since in that case she would be repossessed by the abominable pirates whom he had constrained to abandon her. It remained, therefore, before scuttling her only to tranship the treasure with which Don Ildefonso informed him she was laden. At the same time he would be happy to offer Don Ildefonso and his six surviving hands the hospitality of the *Cinco Llagas* as far as Tortuga, or, if Don Ildefonso preferred it, as seemed probable, Captain Blood would seize a favourable moment for allowing them to take one of his boats and land themselves upon the coast of Hispaniola.

Now his speech was the most amazing thing that had yet happened to Don Ildefonso in that day of amazements.

"Tortuga!" he exclaimed. "Tortuga! You sail to Tortuga, do you say? But what to do there? In God's name who are you, then? What are you?"

"As for who I am, I am called Peter Blood. As for what I am, faith, I scarce know myself."

"You are English!" cried the Spaniard in sudden horror of partial understanding.

"Ah no. That, at least, I am not." Captain Blood drew himself up with great dignity. "I have the honour to be Irish."

"Ah, bah! Irish or English, it is all one."

51

"Indeed and it is not. There's all the difference in the world between the two."

The Spaniard looked at him with angry eyes. His face was livid, his mouth scornful. "English or Irish, the truth is you are just a cursed pirate."

Blood looked wistful. He fetched a sigh. "I'm afraid you are right," he admitted. "It's a thing I've sought to avoid. But what am I to do now, when Fate thrusts it upon me in this fashion, and insisted that I make so excellent a beginning?"

3

THE KING'S MESSENGER

O
N A BRILLIANT May morning of the year 1690 a gentleman stepped ashore at Santiago de Porto Rico, followed by a Negro servant shouldering a valise. He had been brought to the mole in a cockboat from the yellow galleon standing in the roadstead, with the flag of Spain floating from her maintruck. Having landed him, the cockboat went smartly about, and was pulled back to the ship, from which circumstances the gaping idlers on the mole assumed that this gentleman had come to stay.

They stared at him with interest, as they would have stared at any stranger. This, however, was a man whose exterior repaid their attention, a man to take the eye. Even the wretched white slaves toiling half naked on the fortifications, and the Spanish soldiery guarding them, stood at gaze.

Tall, straight, and vigorously spare, our gentleman was dressed with sombre Spanish elegance in black and silver. The curls of his black periwig fell to his shoulders, and his keen shaven face with its high-bridged nose and disdainful lips was shaded by a broad black hat about the crown of which swept a black ostrich plume. Jewels flashed at his breast, a foam of Mechlin almost concealed his hands, and there were ribbons to the long gold-mounted ebony cane he carried. A fop from the Alameda he must have seemed but for the manifest vigour of him and the air of assurance and consequence with which he bore himself. He carried his dark finery with an indifference to the broiling tropical heat which argued an iron constitution, and his glance was so imperious that the eyes of the inquisitive fell away abashed before it.

He asked the way to the Governor's residence, and the officer commanding the guard over the toiling white prisoners detached a soldier to conduct him.

Beyond the square, which architecturally, and saving for the palm trees throwing patches of black shadow on the dazzling white sundrenched ground, might have belonged to some little town in Old Spain, past the church with its twin spires and marble steps, they came, by tall, wrought-iron gates, into a garden, and by an avenue of acacias to a big white house with deep external galleries all clad in jessamine. Negro servants in ridiculously rich red-and-yellow liveries admitted our gentleman, and went to announce to the Governor of Porto Rico the arrival of Don Pedro de Queiroz on a mission from King Philip.

Not every day did a messenger from the King of Spain arrive in this almost the least of his Catholic Majesty's overseas dominions. Indeed, the thing had never happened before, and Don Jayme de Villamarga, whilst thrilled to the marrow by the announcement, knew not whether to assign the thrill to pride or to alarm.

A man of middle height, big of head and paunch, and of less than mediocre intelligence, Don Jayme was one of those gentlemen who best served Spain by being absent from her, and this no doubt had been considered in appointing him Governor of Porto Rico. Not even his awe of majesty, represented by Don Pedro, could repress his naturally self-sufficient manner. He was pompous in his reception of him, and remained unintimidated by the cold haughty stare of Don Pedro's eyes – eyes of a singularly deep blue, contrasting oddly with his bronzed face. A Dominican monk, elderly, tall and gaunt, kept his excellency company.

"Sir, I give you welcome." Don Jayme spoke as if his mouth were full. "I trust you will announce to me that I have the honour to meet with his majesty's approbation."

Don Pedro made him a deep obeisance, with a sweep of his plumed hat, which, together with his cane, he thereafter handed to one of the Negro lackeys. "It is to signify the royal approbation that I am here, happily, after some adventures. I have just landed from the *San Tomas*, after a voyage of many vicissitudes. She has gone on to San Domingo, and it may be three or four days before she returns to take me off again. For that brief while I must make free with your excellency's hospitality." He seemed to claim it as a right rather than ask it as a favour.

"Ah!" was all that Don Jayme permitted himself to answer. And with head on one side, a fatuous smile on the thick lips under his grizzled moustache, he waited for the visitor to enter into details of the royal message.

The visitor, however, displayed no haste. He looked about him at the cool spacious room with its handsome furnishings of carved oak and walnut, its tapestries and pictures, all imported from the Old World, and inquired, in that casual manner of the man who is at home in every environment, if he might be seated. His excellency, with some loss of dignity made haste to set a chair.

Composedly, with a thin smile which Don Jayme disliked, the messenger sat down and crossed his legs.

"We are," he announced, "in some sort related, Don Jayme."

Don Jayme stared. "I am not aware of the honour."

"That is why I am at the trouble of informing you. Your marriage, sir, established the bond. I am a distant cousin of Doña Hernanda."

"Oh! My wife!" His excellency's tone in some subtle way implied contempt for that same wife and her relations. "I had remarked your name: Queiroz." This also explained to him the rather hard and open accent of Don Pedro's otherwise impeccable Castilian. "You will, then, be Portuguese, like Doña Hernanda?" and again his tone implied contempt of Portuguese, and particularly perhaps of Portuguese who were in the service of the King of Spain, from whom Portugal had re-established her independence a half century ago.

"Half Portuguese, of course. My family—"

"Yes, yes." Thus the testy Don Jayme interrupted him. "But your message from his majesty?"

"Ah yes. Your impatience, Don Jayme, is natural." Don Pedro was faintly ironical. "You will forgive me that I should have intruded family matters. My message, then. It will be no

55

surprise to you, sir, that eulogistic reports should have reached his majesty, whom God preserve" – he bowed his head in reverence, compelling Don Jayme to do the same – "not only of the good government of this important island of Porto Rico, but also of the diligence employed by you to rid these seas of the pestilent rovers, particularly the English buccaneers who trouble our shipping and the peace of our Spanish settlements."

There was nothing in this to surprise Don Jayme. Not even upon reflection. Being a fool, he did not suspect that Porto Rico was the worst governed of any Spanish settlement in the West Indies. As for the rest, he had certainly encouraged the extirpation of the buccaneers from the Caribbean. Quite recently, and quite fortuitously, be it added, he had actually contributed materially to this desirable end, as he was not slow to mention.

With chin high and chest puffed out, he moved, strutting, before Don Pedro as he delivered himself. It was gratifying to be appreciated in the proper quarter. It encouraged endeavour. He desired to be modest. Yet in justice to himself he must assert that under his government the island was tranquil and prosperous. Frey Luis here could bear him out in this. The Faith was firmly planted, and there was no heresy in any form in Porto Rico. And as for the matter of the buccaneers, he had done all that a man in his position could do. Not perhaps as much as he could have desired to do. After all, his office kept him ashore. Had Don Pedro remarked the new fortifications he was building? The work was all but complete, and he did not think that even the infamous Captain Blood would have the hardihood to pay him a visit. He had already shown that redoubtable buccaneer that he was not a man with whom it was prudent to trifle. A party of this Captain Blood's men had dared to land on the southern side of the island a few days ago. But Don Jayme's followers were vigilant. He saw to that. A troop of horse was in the neighbourhood at the time. It had descended upon the pirates and had taught them a sharp lesson. He laughed as he spoke of it; laughed at the thought of it; and Don Pedro politely laughed with him, desiring with courteous and appreciative interest to know more of this.

"You killed them all, of course?" he suggested, his contempt of them implicit in his tone.

"Not yet." His excellency spoke with a relish almost fierce. "But I have them under my hand. Six of them, who were captured. We have not yet decided upon their end. Perhaps the rope. Perhaps an auto-da-fé and the fires of the Faith for them. They are heretics all, of course. It is a matter I am still considering with Frey Luis here."

"Well, well," said Don Pedro, as if the subject began to weary him. "Will your excellency hear the remainder of my message?"

The Governor was annoyed by this suggestion that his lengthy exposition had amounted to an interruption. Stiffly he bowed to the representative of majesty. "My apologies," he said in a voice of ice.

But the lofty Don Pedro paid little heed to his manner. He drew from an inner pocket of his rich coat a folded parchment, and a small flat leather case.

"I have to explain, your excellency, the condition in which this comes to you. I have said, although I do not think you heeded it, that I arrive here after a voyage of many vicissitudes. Indeed, it is little short of a miracle that I am here at all, considering what I have undergone. I, too, have been a victim of that infernal dog, Captain Blood. The ship on which I originally sailed from Cadiz was sunk by him a week ago. More fortunate than my cousin Don Rodrigo de Queiroz, who accompanied me and who remains a prisoner in that infamous pirate's hands, I made my escape. It is a long tale with which I will not weary you."

"It would not weary me," exclaimed his excellency, forgetting his dignity in his interest.

But Don Pedro waved aside the implied request for details. "Later! Later, perhaps, if you care to hear of it. It is not important. What is important on your excellency's account is that I escaped. I was picked up by the *San Tomas*, which has brought me here, and so I am happily able to discharge my mission." He held up the folded parchment. "I but mention it to explain how this has come to suffer by sea water, though not to the extent of being illegible. It is a letter from his majesty's Secretary of State informing you that our Sovereign, whom God preserve, has been graciously pleased to create you, in recognition of the services I have mentioned, a knight of the most noble order of St James of Compostella."

Don Jayme went first white, then red, in his incredulous excitement. With trembling fingers he took the letter and unfolded it. It was certainly damaged by sea water. Some words were scarcely legible. The ink in which his own surname had been written had run into a smear, as had that of his government of Porto Rico, and some other words here and there. But the amazing substance of the letter was indeed as Don Pedro announced, and the royal signature was unimpaired.

As Don Jayme raised his eyes at last from the document, Don Pedro, proffering the leather case, touched a spring in it. It flew open, and the Governor gazed upon rubies that glowed like live coals against their background of black velvet.

"And here," said Don Pedro, "is the insignia; the cross of the most noble order in which you are invested."

Don Jayme took the case gingerly, as if it had been some holy thing, and gazed upon the smouldering cross. The friar came to stand beside him, murmuring congratulatory words. Any knighthood would have been an honourable, an unexpected, reward for Don Jayme's services to the crown of Spain. But that of all orders this most exalted and coveted order of St James of Compostella should have been conferred upon him was something that almost defied belief. The Governor of Porto Rico was momentarily awed by the greatness of the thing that had befallen him.

And yet when, a few minutes later, the room was entered by a little lady, young and delicately lovely, Don Jayme had already recovered his habitual poise of self-sufficiency.

The lady, beholding a stranger, an elegant, courtly stranger, who rose instantly upon her advent, paused in the doorway, hesitating, timid. She addressed Don Jayme.

"Pardon. I did not know you occupied."

Don Jayme appealed, sneering, to the friar. "She did not know me occupied! I am the King's representative in Porto Rico, his majesty's Governor of this island, and my wife does not know that I am occupied, conceives that I have leisure. It is unbelievable. But come in, Hernanda. Come in." He grew more playful. "Acquaint yourself with the honours the King bestows upon his poor servant. This may help you to realize what his majesty does me the justice to realize, although you may have failed to do so: that my occupations here are onerous."

Timidly she advanced, obedient to his invitation. "What is it, Jayme?"

"What is it?" He seemed to mimic her. "It is merely this." He displayed the order. "His majesty invests me with the cross of Saint James of Compostella. That is all."

She grew conscious that she was mocked. Her pale, delicate face flushed a little. But there was no accompanying sparkle of her great, dark, wistful eyes to proclaim it a flush of pleasure. Rather, thought Don Pedro, she flushed from shame and resentment at being so contemptuously used before a stranger and at the boorishness of a husband who could so use her.

"I am glad, Jayme," she said, in a gentle, weary voice. "I felicitate you. I am glad."

"Ah! You are glad. Frey Alonso, you will observe that Doña Hernanda is glad." Thus he sneered at her without even the poor grace of being witty. "This gentleman, by whose hand the order came, is a kinsman of yours, Hernanda."

She turned aside, to look again at that elegant stranger. Her gaze was blank. Yet she hesitated to deny him. Kinship when claimed by gentlemen charged by kings with missions of investiture is not lightly to be denied in the presence of such a husband as Don Jayme. And, after all, hers was a considerable family, and must include many with whom she was not personally acquainted.

The stranger bowed until the curls of his periwig met across his face. "You will not remember me, Doña Hernanda. I am, nevertheless, your cousin, and you will have heard of me from our other cousin Rodrigo. I am Pedro de Queiroz."

"You are Pedro?" She stared the harder. "Why, then . . ."
She laughed a little. "Oh, but I remember Pedro. We played together as children. Pedro and I."

Something in her tone seemed to deny him. But he confronted her unperturbed.

"That would be at Santarem," said he.

"At Santarem it was." His readiness appeared now to bewilder her. "But you were a fat, sturdy boy then, and your hair was golden."

He laughed. "I have become lean in growing, and I favour a black periwig."

"Which makes your eyes a startling blue. I do not remember that you had blue eyes."

"God help us, ninny!" croaked her husband. "You never could remember anything."

She turned to look at him, and for all that her lip quivered, her eyes steadily met his sneering glance. She seemed about to speak, checked herself, and then spoke at last, very quietly. "Oh yes. There are some things a woman never forgets."

"And on the subject of memory," said Don Pedro, addressing the Governor with cold dignity, "I do not remember that there are any ninnies in our family."

"Faith, then, you needed to come to Porto Rico to discover it," his excellency retorted with his loud, coarse laugh.

"Ah!" Don Pedro sighed. "That may not be the end of my discoveries."

There was something in his tone which Don Jayme did not like. He threw back his big head and frowned. "You mean?" he demanded.

Don Pedro was conscious of an appeal in the little lady's dark, liquid eyes. He yielded to it, laughed, and answered:

"I have yet to discover where your excellency proposes to lodge me during the days in which I must inflict myself upon you. If I might now withdraw . . ."

The Governor swung to Doña Hernanda. "You hear? Your kinsman needs to remind us of our duty to a guest. It will not have occurred to you to make provision for him."

60

"But I did not know . . . I was not told of his presence until I found him here."

"Well, well. You know now. And we dine in half an hour."

At dinner Don Jayme was in high spirits, which is to say that he was alternately pompous and boisterous, and occasionally filled the room with his loud jarring laugh.

Don Pedro scarcely troubled to dissemble his dislike of him. His manner became more and more frigidly aloof, and he devoted his attention and addressed his conversation more and more exclusively to the despised wife.

"I have news for you," he told her, when they had come to the dessert, "of our Cousin Rodrigo."

"Ah!" sneered her husband. "She'll welcome news of him. She ever had a particular regard for her Cousin Rodrigo, and he for her."

She flushed, keeping her troubled eyes lowered. Don Pedro came to the rescue, swiftly, easily. "Regard for one another is common among the members of our family. Every Queiroz owes a duty to every other, and is at all times ready to perform it." He looked very straightly at Don Jayme as he spoke, as if inviting him to discover more in the words than they might seem to carry. "And that is at the root of what I am to tell you, cousin Hernanda. As I have already informed his excellency, the ship in which Don Rodrigo and I sailed from Spain together was set upon and sunk by that infamous pirate Captain Blood. We were both captured, but I was so fortunate as to make my escape."

"You have not told us how. You must tell us how," the Governor interrupted him.

Don Pedro waved a hand disdainfully. "It is no great matter, and I soon weary of talking of myself. But . . . if you insist . . . some other time. At present I am to tell you of Rodrigo. He remains a prisoner in the hands of Captain Blood. But do not be unduly alarmed."

There was need for his reassuring tone. Doña Hernanda, who had been hanging on his words, had turned deathly white.

"Do not be alarmed. Rodrigo is in good health, and his life

61

is safe. Also, from my own experience, I know that this Blood, infamous pirate though he be, is not without chivalrous ideals, and, piracy apart, he is a man of honour."

"Piracy apart?" Laughter exploded from Don Jayme. "On my soul, that's humorous! You deal in paradox, Don Pedro. Eh, Frey Alonso?"

The lean friar smiled mechanically. Doña Hernanda, pale and piteous, suffered in silence the interruption. Don Pedro frowned.

"The paradox is not in me, but in Captain Blood. An indemoniated robber, yet he practises no wanton cruelty, and he keeps his word. Therefore I say you need have no apprehension on the score of Don Rodrigo's face. His ransom has been agreed between himself and Captain Blood, and I have undertaken to procure it. Meanwhile he is well and courteously entreated, and, indeed, a sort of friendship has come to exist between himself and his pirate captor."

"Faith, that I can believe!" cried the Governor, whilst Doña Hernanda sank back in her chair with a sigh of relief. "Rodrigo was ever ready to consort with rogues. Was he not, Hernanda?"

"I ..." She bridled indignantly; then curbed herself. "I never observed it."

"You never observed it! I ask myself have you ever observed anything? Well, well, and so Rodrigo's to be ransomed. At what is his ransom fixed?"

"You desire to contribute?" cried Don Pedro with a certain friendly eagerness.

The Governor started as if he had been stung. His countenance became gravely blank. "Not I, by the Virgin! Not I. That is entirely a matter for the family of Queiroz."

Don Pedro's smile perished. He sighed. "True! True! And yet ... I've a notion you'll come to contribute something before all is ended."

"Dismiss it," laughed Don Jayme, "for that way lies disappointment."

They rose from table soon thereafter and withdrew to the noontide rest the heat made necessary.

They did not come together again until supper, which was served in that same room, in the comparative cool of eventide and by the light of a score of candles in heavy silver branches brought from Spain.

The Governor's satisfaction at the signal honour of which he was the recipient appeared to have grown with contemplation of it. He was increasingly jovial and facetious, but not on this account did he spare Doña Hernanda his sneers. Rather did he make her the butt of coarse humours, inviting the two men to laugh with him at the shortcomings he indicated in her. Don Pedro, however, did not laugh. He remained preternaturally grave, indeed almost compassionate, as he observed the tragic patience on that long-suffering wife's sweet face.

She looked so slight and frail in her stiff black satin gown, which rendered more dazzling by contrast the whiteness of her neck and shoulders, even as her lustrous, smoothly dressed black hair stressed the warm pallor of her gentle countenance. A little statue in ebony and ivory she seemed to Don Pedro's fancy, and almost as lifeless, until after supper he found himself alone with her in the deep jessamine-clad galleries that stood open to the cool night breezes blowing from the sea.

His excellency had gone off to indite a letter of grateful acknowledgement to the King, and had taken the friar to assist him. He had commended his guest to the attention of his wife, whilst commiserating with him upon the necessity. She had led Don Pedro out into the scented purple tropic night, and stepping now beside him came at last to life, and addressed him in a breathless anxiety.

"What you told us today of Don Rodrigo de Queiroz, is it true? That he is a prisoner in the hands of Captain Blood, but unhurt and safe, awaiting ransom?"

"Most scrupulously true in all particulars."

"You . . . you pledge your word for that? Your honour as a gentleman? For I must assume you a gentleman, since you bear commissions from the King."

"And on no other ground?" quoth he, a little taken aback.

"Do you pledge me your word?" she insisted.

"Unhesitatingly. My word of honour. Why should you doubt me?"

"You give me cause. You are not truthful in all things. Why, for instance, do you say you are my cousin?"

"You do not, then, remember me?"

"I remember Pedro de Queiroz. The years might have given you height and slenderness; the sun might have tanned your face, and under your black periwig your hair may still be fair, though I take leave to doubt it. But what, I ask myself, could have changed the colour of your eyes? For your eyes are blue, and Pedro's were dark brown."

He was silent a moment, like a man considering, and she watched his stern, handsome face, made plain by the light beating upon it from the windows of the house. He did not meet her glance. Instead his eyes sought the sea, gleaming under the bright stars and reflecting the twinkling lights of ships in the roadstead, watched the fireflies flitting among the bushes in pursuit of moths, looked anywhere but at the little figure at his side.

At last he spoke, quietly, almost humorously, in admission of the imposture. "We hoped you would have forgotten such a detail."

"We?" she questioned him.

"Rodrigo and I. He is at least my friend. He was hastening to you when this thing befell him. That is how we came to be on the same ship."

"And he desired you to do this?"

"He shall tell you so himself when he arrives. He will be here in a few days, depend on it. As soon as I can ransom him, which will be very soon after my departure. When I was escaping – for, unlike him, I had given no parole – he desired that if I came here I should claim to be your cousin, so as to stand at need in his place until he comes."

She was thoughtful, and her bosom rose and fell in agitation. In silence they moved a little way in step.

"You took a foolish risk," she said, thereby showing her acceptance of his explanation.

"A gentleman," said he sententiously, "will always take a risk to serve a lady."

"Were you serving me?"

"Does it seem to you that I could be serving myself?"

"No. You could not have been doing that."

"Why question further, then? Rodrigo wished it so. He will explain his motives fully when he comes. Meanwhile, as your cousin, I am in his place. If this boorish husband burdens you overmuch . . ."

"What are you saying?" Her voice rang with alarm.

"That I am Rodrigo's deputy. So that you remember it, that is all I ask."

"I thank you, cousin," she said, and left him.

Three days Don Pedro continued as the guest of the Governor of Porto Rico, and they were much as that first day, saving that daily Don Jayme continued to increase in consciousness of his new dignity as a knight of Saint James of Compostella, and became, consequently, daily more insufferable. Yet Don Pedro suffered him with exemplary fortitude, and at times seemed even disposed to feed the Governor's egregious vanity. Thus, on the third night at supper, Don Pedro cast out the suggestion that his excellency should signallize the honour with which the King had distinguished him by some gesture that should mark the occasion and render it memorable in the annals of the island.

Don Jayme swallowed the suggestion avidly. "Ah yes! That is an admirable thought. What do you counsel that I do?"

Don Pedro smiled with flattering deprecation. "Not for me to counsel Don Jayme de Villamarga. But the gesture should be worthy of the occasion."

"Indeed, yes. That is true." The dullard's wits, however, were barren of ideas. "The question now is what might be considered worthy?"

Frey Alonso suggested a ball at Government House, and was applauded in this by Doña Hernanda. Don Pedro, apologetically to the lady, thought a ball would have significance only for those who were bidden to it. Something was required that should impress all social orders in Porto Rico.

"Why not an amnesty?" he inquired at last.

"An amnesty?" The three of them looked at him in questioning wonder.

"Why not? It is a royal gesture, true. But is not a governor in some sort royal, a viceroy, a representative of royalty, the one to whom men look for royal gestures? To mark your accession to this dignity, throw open your gaols, Don Jayme, as do kings upon their coronation."

Don Jayme conquered his stupefaction as the magnitude of the act suggested, and smote the table with his fist, protesting that here was a notion worth adopting. Tomorrow he would announce it in a proclamation, and set all prisoners free, their sentences remitted.

"That is," he added, "all but six, whose pardon would hardly please the colony."

"I think," said Don Pedro, "that exceptions would stultify the act. There should be no exceptions."

"But these are exceptional prisoners. Can you have forgotten that I told you I had made captive six buccaneers out of a party that had the temerity to land on Porto Rico?"

Don Pedro frowned, reflecting. "Ah, true!" he cried at last. "I remember."

"And did I tell you, sir, that one of these men is that dog Wolverstone?" He pronounced it Volverstohn.

"Wolverstone?" said Don Pedro, who also pronounced it Volverstohn. "You have captured Wolverstone!" It was clear that he was profoundly impressed; as well he might be, for Wolverstone, who was nowadays the foremost of Blood's lieutenants, was almost as well known to Spaniards and as detested by them as Blood himself. "You have captured Wolverstone!" he repeated, and for the first time looked at Don Jayme with eyes of unmistakable respect. "You did not tell me that. Why, in that case, my friend, you have clipped one of Blood's wings. Without Wolverstone he is shorn of half his power. His own destruction may follow now at any moment, and Spain will owe that to you."

Don Jayme spread his hands in an affectation of modesty.

"It is something towards deserving the honour his majesty has bestowed upon me."

"Something!" echoed Don Pedro. "If the King had known this, he might have accounted the order of Saint James of Compostella inadequate."

Doña Hernanda looked at him sharply, to see whether he dealt in irony. But he seemed quite sincere, so much so that for once he had shed the hauteur in which he usually arrayed himself. He resumed after a moment's pause.

"Of course, of course; you cannot include these men in the amnesty. They are not common malefactors. They are enemies of Spain." Abruptly, with a hint of purpose, he asked: "How will you deal with them?"

Don Jayme thrust out a nether lip, considering. "I am still undecided whether to hang them out of hand or to let Frey Alonso hold his auto-da-fé upon them and consign them to the fire as heretics. I think I told you so."

"Yes, yes. But I did not then know that Wolverstone is one of them. That makes a difference."

"What difference?"

"Oh, but consider. Give this matter thought. With thought you'll see for yourself what you should do. It's plain enough."

Don Jayme considered awhile as he was bidden. Then shrugged his shoulders.

"Faith, sir, it may be plain enough to you. But I confess that I see no choice beyond that of rope or fire."

"Ultimately, yes. One or the other. But not here in Porto Rico. That is to smother the effulgence of your achievement. Send them to Spain, Don Jayme. Send them to his majesty, as an earnest of the zeal for which he has been pleased to honour you. Show him thus how richly you deserve that honour and even greater honours. Let that be your acknowledgement".

Don Jayme was staring at him with dilating eyes. His face glowed. "I vow to heaven I should never have thought of it," he said at last.

"Your modesty made you blind to the opportunity."

"It may be that," Don Jayme admitted.

"But you perceive it now that I indicate it?"

"Oh, I perceive it. Yes, the King of Spain shall be impressed."

Frey Alonso seemed downcast. He had been counting upon his auto-da-fé. Doña Hernanda was chiefly puzzled by the sudden geniality of her hitherto haughty and disdainful pretended cousin. Meanwhile Don Pedro piled Pelion upon Ossa.

"It should prove to his majesty that your excellency is wasted in so small a settlement as Porto Rico. I see you as governor of some more important colony. Perhaps as viceroy. . . . Who shall say? You have displayed a zeal such as has rarely been displayed by any Spanish governor overseas."

"But how and when to send them to Spain?" wondered Don Jayme, who no longer questioned the expediency of doing so.

"Why, that is a matter in which I can serve your excellency. I can convey them for you on the *San Tomas*, which should call for me at any moment now. You will write another letter to his majesty, offering him these evidences of your zeal, and I will bear it, together with these captives. Your general amnesty can wait until I've sailed with them. Thus there will be nothing to mar it. It will be complete and properly imposing."

So elated and so grateful to his guest for his suggestion was Don Jayme that he actually went the length of addressing him as cousin in the course of thanking him.

The matter, it seemed, had presented itself for discussion only just in time. For early on the following morning Santiago was startled by the boom of a gun, and turning out to ascertain the reason, beheld again the yellow Spanish ship which had brought Don Pedro coming to anchor in the bay.

Don Pedro himself sought the Governor with the information that this was the signal for his departure, expressing a polite regret that duty did not permit him longer to encroach upon Don Jayme's princely hospitality.

Whilst his Negro valet was packing his effects he went to take his leave of Doña Hernanda, and again assured that wistful little lady that she need be under no apprehension on the score of her cousin Rodrigo, who would soon now be with her.

After this Don Jayme, with an officer in attendance, carried

Don Pedro off to the town gaol, where the pirates were lodged.

In a dark, unpaved stone chamber, lighted only by a small, heavily barred, unglazed window set near the ceiling, they were herded with perhaps a score of other malefactors of all kinds and colours. The atmosphere of the place was so indescribably foul and noisome that Don Pedro recoiled as from a blow when it first assailed him. Don Jayme's loud, coarse laugh derided his fastidiousness. Nevertheless, the Governor flicked out a handkerchief that was sprayed with verbena, and thereafter at intervals held it to his nostrils.

Wolverstone and his five associates, heavily loaded with irons, were in a group a little apart from their fellow-prisoners. They squatted against the wall on the foul dank straw that was their bedding. Unshaven, dishevelled and filthy, for no means of grooming themselves had been allowed them, they huddled together there as if seeking strength in union against the common rogues with whom they were confined. Wolverstone, almost a giant in build, might from his dress have been a merchant. Dyke, that sometime petty officer in the King's Navy, had similarly been arrayed like a citizen of some consequence. The other four wore the cotton shirts and leather breeches which had been the dress of the boucan-hunters before they took to the sea, and their heads were swathed in coloured kerchiefs.

They did not stir when the door creaked on its ponderous hinges and a half dozen corseletted Spaniards with pikes entered to form a guard of honour as well as a protection for the Governor. When that august personage made his appearance attended by his officer and accompanied by his distinguished-looking guest, the other prisoners sprang up and ranged themselves in awe and reverence. The pirates stolidly sat on. But they were not quite indifferent. As Don Pedro sauntered in, languidly leaning on his beribboned cane, dabbing his lips with a handkerchief, which he, too, had deemed it well to produce, Wolverstone stirred on his foul bed, and his single eye (he had lost the other one at Sedgmoor) rolled with almost portentous ferocity.

Don Jayme indicated the group by a wave of his hand.

"There are your cursed pirates, Don Pedro, hanging together like a brood of carrion birds."

"These?" quoth Don Pedro haughtily, and pointed with his cane. "Faith, they look their trade, the villains."

Wolverstone glared more fiercely than ever, but was contemptuously silent. A stubborn rogue, it was plain.

Don Pedro advanced towards them, superb in his black and silver, seeming to symbolize the pride and majesty of Spain. The thick-set Governor, in pale green taffetas, kept pace with him, and presently, when they had come to a halt before the buccaneers, he addressed them.

"You begin to know, you English dogs, what it means to defy the might of Spain. And you'll know it better before all is done. I deny myself the pleasure of hanging you as I intended, so that you may go to Madrid, to feed a bonfire."

Wolverstone leered at him. "You are noble," he said, in execrable but comprehensible Spanish. "Noble with the nobility of Spain. You insult the helpless."

The Governor raged at him, calling him the unprintably foul names that came so readily to an angry Spaniard's lips. This until Don Pedro checked him with a hand upon his arm.

"Is this waste of breath worth while?" He spoke disdainfully. "It but serves to detain us in this noisome place."

The buccaneers stared at him in a sort of wonder. Abruptly he turned on his heel.

"Come, Don Jayme." His tone was peremptory. "Have them out of this. The *San Tomas* is waiting, and the tide is on the turn."

The Governor hesitated, flung a last insult at them, then gave an order to the officer, and stalked after his guest, who was already moving away. The officer transferred the order to his men. With the butts of their pikes and many foul words the soldiers stirred the buccaneers. They rose with clank of gyves and manacles, and went stumbling out into the clean air and the sunshine, herded by the pikemen. Hangdog, foul and weary, they dragged themselves across the square, where the palms waved in the sea breeze, and the islanders stood to

70

watch them pass, and so they came to the mole, where a wherry of eight oars awaited them.

The Governor and his guest stood by whilst they were being packed into the sternsheets, whither the pikemen followed them. Then Don Pedro and Don Jayme took their places in the prow with Don Pedro's Negro, who carried his valise. The wherry pushed off and was rowed across the blue water to the stately ship from whose masthead floated the flag of Spain.

They came bumping along her yellow side at the foot of the entrance ladder, to which a sailor hitched a boathook.

Don Pedro, from the prow of the wherry, called peremptorily for a file of musketeers to stand to order in the waist. A morioned head appeared over the bulwarks to answer him that it was done already. Then, with the pikemen urging them, and moving awkwardly and painfully in their irons, the buccaneer prisoners climbed the ladder and dropped one by one over the ship's side.

Don Pedro waved his black servant after them with the valise, and finally invited Don Jayme to precede him aboard. Himself Don Pedro followed close, and when at the ladder's head Don Jayme came to a sudden halt it was Don Pedro's continuing ascent that thrust him forward, and this so sharply that he almost tumbled headlong into the vessel's waist. There were a dozen ready hands to steady him, and a babble of voices to give him laughing welcome. But the voices were English, and the hands belonged to men whose garments and accoutrements proclaimed them buccaneers. They swarmed in the waist, and already some of them were at work to strike the irons from Wolverstone and his mates.

Gasping, livid, bewildered, Don Jayme de Villamarga swung round to Don Pedro, who followed. That very Spanish gentleman had paused at the head of the ladder and stood there steadying himself by a ratline, surveying the scene below him. He was calmly smiling.

"You have nothing to apprehend, Don Jayme. I give you my word for that. And my word is good. I am Captain Blood."

He came down to the deck under the stare of the bulging eyes of the Governor, who understood nothing. Before enlightenment finally came his dull, bewildered wits were to understand still less.

A tall, slight gentleman, very elegantly arrayed, stepped forward to meet the Captain. This, to the Governor's increasing amazement, was his wife's cousin, Don Rodrigo. Captain Blood greeted him in a friendly manner.

"I have brought your ransom, as you see, Don Rodrigo," and he waved a hand in the direction of the group of manacled prisoners. "You are free now to depart with Don Jayme. We'll cut short our farewells, for we take up the anchor at once. Hagthorpe, give the order."

Don Jayme thought that he began to understand. Furiously, he turned upon this cousin of his wife's.

"My God, are you in this? Have you plotted with these enemies of Spain to—?"

A hand gripped his shoulder, and a boatswain's whistle piped somewhere forward. "We are weighing the anchor," said Captain Blood. "You were best over the side, believe me. It has been an honour to know you. In future be more respectful to your wife. Go with God, Don Jayme."

The Governor found himself, as in a nightmare, bustled over the side and down the ladder. Don Rodrigo followed him after taking courteous leave of Captain Blood.

Don Jayme collapsed limply in the sternsheets of the wherry as it put off. But soon he roused himself furiously to demand an explanation whilst at the same time overwhelming his companion with threats.

Don Rodrigo strove to preserve his calm. "You had better listen. I was on that ship, the *San Tomas*, on my way to San Domingo, when Blood captured her. He put the crew ashore on one of the Virgin Islands. But me he retained for ransom because of my rank."

"And to save your skin and your purse you made this infamous bargain with him?"

"I have said that you had better listen. It was not so at all.

He treated me honourably, and we became in some sort friends. He is a man of engaging ways, as you may have discovered. In the course of our talks he gleaned from me a good deal of my private life and yours, which in a way, through my Cousin Hernanda, is linked with it. A week ago, after the capture of the men who had gone ashore with Wolverstone, he decided to use the knowledge he had gained; that and my papers, of which he had, of course, possessed himself. He told me what he intended to do, and promised me that if by the use of my name and the rest he succeeded in delivering those followers of his, he would require no further ransom from me."

"And you? You agreed?"

"Agreed? Sometimes, indeed often, you are fatuous. My agreement was not asked. I was merely informed. Your own foolishness and the order of Saint James of Compostella did the rest. I suppose he conferred it upon you, and so dazzled you with it that you were prepared to believe anything he told you?"

"You were bringing it to me? It was among your papers?" quoth Don Jayme, who thought he began to understand.

There was a grim smile on Don Rodrigo's long, sallow face. "I was taking it to the Governor of Hispaniola Don Jayme de Guzman, to whom the letter was addressed."

Don Jayme de Villamarga's mouth fell open. He turned pale. "Not even that, then? The order was not intended for me? It was part of his infernal comedy?"

"You should have examined the letter more attentively."

"It was damaged by sea water!" roared the Governor furiously.

"You should have examined your conscience, then. It would have told you that you had done nothing to deserve the cross of Saint James."

Don Jayme was too stunned to resent the gibe. Not until he was home again and in the presence of his wife did he recover himself sufficiently to hector her with the tale of how he had been bubbled. Thus he brought upon himself his worst humiliation.

"How does it come, madam," he demanded, "that you recognized him for your cousin?"

"I did not," she answered him, and dared at last to laugh at him, taking payment in that moment for all the browbeating she had suffered at his hands.

"You did not! You mean that you knew he was not your cousin?"

"That is what I mean."

"And you did not tell me?" The world was rocking about him.

"You would not allow me. When I told him that I did not remember that my Cousin Pedro had blue eyes, you told me that I never remembered anything, and you called me ninny. Because I did not wish to be called ninny again before a stranger I said nothing further."

Don Jayme mopped the sweat from his brow, and appealed in livid fury to her cousin Rodrigo, who stood by. "And what do you say to that?" he demanded.

"For myself, nothing. But I might remind you of Captain Blood's advice to you at parting. I think it was that in future you be more respectful to your wife."

4

THE WAR INDEMNITY

IF IT was incredibly gallant, it was no less incredibly foolish of the *Atrevida* to have meddled with the *Arabella*, considering the Spaniard's inferior armament and the orders under which she sailed.

The *Arabella* was that *Cinco Llagas* out of Cadiz of which Peter Blood had so gallantly possessed himself. He had so renamed her in honour of a lady in Barbados, whose memory was ever to serve him as an inspiration and to set restraint upon his activities as a buccaneer. She was going westward in haste to overtake her consorts, which were a full day ahead, and was looking neither to right nor to left, when somewhere about 19° of northern longitude and 66° of western latitude, the *Atrevida* espied her, turned aside to steer across her course, and opened the attack by a shot athwart her hawse.

The Spaniard's commander, Don Vicente de Casanegra, was actuated by a belief in himself that was tempered by no consciousness of his limitations.

The result was precisely what might have been expected. The *Arabella* went promptly about on a southern tack which presently brought her on to the *Atrevida*'s windward quarter, thus scoring the first tactical advantage. Thence, whilst still out of range of the Spaniard's sakers, the *Arabella* poured in a crippling fire from her demi-cannons, which went far towards deciding the business. At closer quarters she followed this up with cross-bar and langrel, and so cut and slashed the *Atrevida*'s rigging that she could no longer have fled, even had Don Vicente been prudently disposed to do so. Finally within pistol-range the *Arabella* hammered her with a broadside that converted the trim Spanish frigate into a staggering impotent hulk. When, after that, they grappled, the Spaniards avoided

75

death by surrender, and it was to Captain Blood himself that the grey-faced, mortified Don Vicente delivered up his sword.

"This will teach you not to bark at me when I am passing peacefully by," said Captain Blood. "I see that you call yourself the *Atrevida*. But it's more impudent than daring I'm accounting you."

His opinion was even lower when, in the course of investigating his capture, he found among the ship's papers a letter from the Spanish Admiral, Don Miguel de Espinosa y Valdez, containing Don Vicente's sailing orders. In these he was instructed to join the Admiral's squadron with all speed at Spanish Key off Bieque, for the purpose of a raid upon the English settlement of Antigua. Don Miguel was conveniently expressive in his letter.

Although [he wrote] *His Catholic Majesty is at peace with England, yet England makes no endeavour to repress the damnable activities of the pirate Blood in Spanish waters. Therefore it becomes necessary to make reprisals and obtain compensation for all that Spain has suffered at the hands of this indemoniated filibuster.*

Having stowed the disarmed Spaniards under hatches – all save the rash Don Vicente, who, under parole, was taken aboard the *Arabella* – Blood put a prize crew into the *Atrevida*, patched up her wounds, and set a south-easterly course for the passage between Anegada, and the Virgin Islands.

He explained the changed intentions which this implied at a council held that evening in the great cabin and attended by Wolverstone, his lieutenant, Pitt, his shipmaster, Ogle, who commanded on the main deck, and two representatives of the main body of his followers, one of whom, Albin, was a Frenchman. This because one-third of the buccaneers aboard the *Arabella* at the time were French.

He met with some opposition when he announced the intention of making for Antigua.

This opposition was epitomized by Wolverstone, who

76

banged the table with a fist that was like a ham before delivering himself. "To hell with King James and all who serve him! It's enough that we never make war upon English ships or English settlements. But I'll be damned if I account it our duty to protect folk whose hands are against us."

Captain Blood explained. "The impending Spanish raid is in the nature of reprisals for damage suffered by Spaniards at our hands. This seems to me to impose a duty upon us. We may not be patriots, as ye say, Wolverstone, and we may not be altruists. If we go to war and remain to assist, we do so as mercenaries, whose services are to be paid for by a garrison which should be very glad to hire them. Thus we reconcile duty with profit."

By these arguments he prevailed.

At dawn, having negotiated the passage, they hove to with the southernmost point of the Virgen Gorda on their starboard quarter, some four miles away. The sea being calm, Captain Blood ordered the boats of the *Atrevida* to be launched, and her Spanish crew to depart in them, whereafter the two ships proceeded on their way to the Leeward Islands.

Going south of Saba with gentle breezes, they were off the west coast of Antigua on the morning of the next day, and with the Union Jack flying from the maintruck they came to cast anchor in ten fathoms on the north side of the shoal that divides the entrance to Fort Bay.

A few minutes after noon, just as Colonel Courtney, the Captain-General of the Leeward Islands, whose seat of government was in Antigua, was sitting down to dinner with Mrs Courtney and Captain Macartney, he was astounded by the announcement that Captain Blood had landed at St John's and desired to wait upon him.

Colonel Courtney, a tall, dried-up man of forty-five, sandy and freckled, stared with pale, red-rimmed eyes at Mr Ives, his young secretary, who had brought the message. "Captain Blood, did you say? Captain Blood? What Captain Blood? Surely not the damned pirate of that name, the gallows-bird from Barbados?"

Mr Ives permitted himself to smile upon his excellency's excitement. "The same, sir."

Colonel Courtney flung his napkin amid the dishes on the spread table and rose, still incredulous. "And he's here? Here? Is he mad? Has the sun touched him? Stab me, I'll have him in irons for his impudence before I dine, and on his way to England before . . ." He broke off. "Egad!" he cried, and swung to his second-in-command. "We'd better have him in, Macartney."

Macartney's round face, as red as his coat, showed an amazement no less than the Governor's. That a rascal with a price on his head should have the impudence to pay a morning call on the Governor of an English settlement was something that left Captain Macartney almost speechless and more incapable of thought than usual.

Mr Ives admitted into the long, cool, sparsely furnished room a tall, spare gentlemen, very elegant in a suit of biscuit-coloured taffetas. A diamond of price gleamed amid the choice lace at his throat, a diamond buckle flashed from the band of the plumed hat he carried, a long pear-shaped pearl hung from his left ear and glowed against the black curls of his periwig. He leaned upon a gold-mounted ebony cane. So unlike a buccaneer was this modish gentleman that they stared in silence into the long, lean, sardonic countenance with its high-bridged nose, and eyes that looked startlingly blue and cold in a face that was burnt to the colour of a Red Indian's. More and more incredulous, the Colonel brought out a question with a jerk.

"You are Captain Blood?"

The gentleman bowed. Captain Macartney gasped and desired his vitals to be stabbed. The Colonel said "Egad!" again, and his pale eyes bulged. He looked at his pallid wife, at Macartney, and then again at Captain Blood. "You're a daring rogue. A daring rogue, egad!"

"I see you've heard of me."

"But not enough to credit this. Ye'll not have come to surrender?"

The buccaneer sauntered forward to the table. Instinctively Macartney rose.

"If you'll be reading this it will save a world of explanations," and he laid before his excellency the letter from the Spanish Admiral. "The fortune of war brought it into my hands together with the gentleman to whom it is addressed."

Colonel Courtney read, changed colour, and handed the sheet to Macartney. Then he stared again at Blood, who spoke as if answering the stare.

"It's here to warn you I am, and at need to serve you."

"To serve me?"

"Ye seem in need of it. Your ridiculous fort will not stand an hour under Spanish gunfire, and after that you'll have these gentlemen of Castile in the town. Maybe you know how they conduct themselves on these occasions. If not, I'll be after telling you."

"But – stab me!" spluttered Macartney. "We're not at war with Spain!"

Colonel Courtney turned in cold fury upon Blood. "It is you who are the author of all our woes. It is your rascalities which bring these reprisals upon us."

"That's why I've come. Although I think I am a pretext rather than a reason." Captain Blood sat down. "You've been finding gold in Antigua, as I've heard. Don Miguel will have heard it too. Your militia garrison is not two hundred strong, and your fort, as I've said, is so much rubbish. I bring you a strong ship very heavily armed, and two hundred of the toughest fighting-men to be found in the Caribbean, or any-where in the world. Of course I'm a damned pirate, and there's a price on my head, and if ye're fastidiously scrupulous ye'll have nothing to say to me. But if ye've any sense, as I hope ye have, it's thanking God ye'll be that I've come, and ye'll make terms with me."

"Terms?"

Captain Blood explained himself. His men did not risk their lives for the honour and glory of it, and there were in his following a number who were French, and who therefore lacked all patriotic feeling where a British colony was concerned. They would expect a trifle for the valuable services they were about to render.

"Also, Colonel," Blood concluded, "there's a point of honour for you. Whilst it may be difficult for you to enter into alliance with us, there's no difficulty about hiring us, and you may pursue us again without scruple once this job is done."

The Governor looked at him with gloomy eyes. "If I did my duty I would have you in irons and send you home to England to be hanged."

Captain Blood was unperturbed. "Your immediate duty is to preserve the colony of which ye're governor. Ye'll perceive its danger. And the danger is so imminent that even moments may count. We'd do well, faith, not to be wasting them."

The Governor looked at Macartney. Macartney's face was as blank as his mind. Then the lady, who had sat a scared and silent witness, suddenly stood up. Like her husband, she was tall and angular, and a tropical climate had prematurely aged her and consumed her beauty. Apparently, thought Blood, it had not consumed her reason.

"James, how can you hesitate? Think of what will happen to the women – the women and the children – if these Spaniards land. Remember what they did at Bridgetown."

The Governor stood with his chin upon his breast, frowning gloomily. "Yet I cannot enter into alliance with . . . I cannot make terms with outlaws. My duty here is clear. Quite clear." There was finality in his tone.

"Fiat officium, ruat coelum," said the classical-minded Blood. He sighed, and rose. "If that's your last word, I'll be wishing you a very good day. I've no mind to be caught unawares by the Caribbean Squadron."

"You don't leave," said the Colonel sharply. "There too my duty is clear. The guard, Macartney."

"Och, don't be a fool now, Colonel." Blood's gesture arrested Macartney.

"I'm not a fool, sir, I know what becomes me. I must do my duty."

"And is your duty demanding so scurvy a return for the valuable service I've already rendered you by my warning? Give it thought now, Colonel."

Again the Colonel's lady acted as Blood's advocate – and acted passionately in her clear apprehension of the only really material issue.

Exasperated, the Colonel flung himself down into his chair again. "But I cannot. I will not make terms with a rebel, an outlaw, a pirate. The dignity of my office ... I ... I cannot."

In his heart Captain Blood cursed the stupidity of governments that sent such men as this to represent them overseas.

"Will the dignity of your office restrain the Spanish Admiral, d'ye suppose?"

"And the women, James!" his lady again reminded him. "Surely, James, in this extreme need – a whole squadron coming to attack you – his majesty must approve your enlisting any aid."

Thus she began and thus continued, and now Macartney was moved to alliance with her against his excellency's narrow stubbornness, until in the end the Captain-General was brought to sacrifice dignity to expediency. Still reluctant, he demanded ill-humouredly to know the terms of the buccaneers.

"For myself," said Blood, "I ask nothing. I will organize your defences for the sake of the blood in my veins. But when the Spaniards have been driven off I shall require a hundred pieces of eight for each of my men. I have two hundred of them."

His excellency was scandalized. "Twenty thousand pieces!" He choked, and so far forgot his dignity as to haggle. But Blood was coldly firm, and in the end the price was agreed.

That afternoon he set to work upon the defences of St John's.

Fort Bay is an inlet some two miles in depth and a mile across its widest part. It narrows a little at the mouth, forming a slight bottleneck. In the middle of this neck ran a long, narrow spit of sand, partly uncovered at extreme low water, with a channel on either side. The southern channel was safe only for vessels of shallow draught; in the narrow, northern channel, however, at the entrance to which the *Arabella* now rode at anchor, there was never less than eight fathoms, at times slightly increased by the small tides of this sea, so that this was the only gateway to the bay.

The fort guarded this channel, occupying a shallow eminence on the northern promontory. It was a square, squat, machicolated structure of grey stone, and its armament consisted of a dozen ancient sakers and a half dozen faucons with an extreme range of two thousand yards – guns these which provoked Captain Blood's contempt. He supplemented them by twelve sakers of more modern fashion, which he brought ashore from the *Atrevida*.

Twelve more guns he landed from the Spanish ship, including two twelve-pounders. These, however, he reserved for another purpose. Fifty yards west of the fort on the extreme edge of the promontory he set about the construction of earthworks – and set about it at a rate which allowed Colonel Courtney some insight into buccaneer methods and the secret of their success.

He landed a hundred of his men for the purpose and had them toiling almost naked in the broiling sun. To these he added three hundred whites and as many Negroes from St John's – practically the whole of its efficient male population – and he had them digging, banking, and filling the wickerwork gabions into the making of which he impressed the women. Others were sent to cut turf and fell trees, and fetch one and the other to the site of these operations. Throughout the afternoon the promontory seethed and crawled like an antheap. By sunset all was done. It seemed a miracle to the Captain-General. In six hours, under Blood's direction and the drive of his will, another fort had been constructed which by ordinary methods could not have been built in less than a week.

And it was not only built and armed with the remaining twelve guns brought from the *Atrevida* and with a half dozen powerful demi-cannons landed from the *Arabella*; it was so effectively dissembled that from the sea no suspicion of its existence could be formed. Strips of turf faced it so that it merged into the background of shallow cliff; coconut palms topped it and rose about it; clumps of white acacia and arnotto trees masked the gun emplacements so effectively as to render them invisible at half a mile.

Colonel Courtney conceived that here was a deal of wasted labour. Why trouble to conceal fortifications whose display should have the effect of deterring an assailant?

Blood explained. "If he's intimidated, he'll merely be postponing attack until some time when I'm not here to defend you. I mean either to destroy him or so to maul him that he'll be glad to leave British settlements alone in future."

That night Blood slept aboard the *Arabella* at her anchorage under the bluff. In the morning St John's was awakened and alarmed by the sound of heavy gunfire. The Captain-General ran from his house in a bedgown, conceiving that the Spaniards were already here. The firing, however, proceeded from the new earthworks, and was directed upon the completely dismasted hull of the *Atrevida*, which had been anchored fore and aft athwart the narrow fairway, right in the middle of the channel.

The Captain-General dressed in haste, took horse, and rode out to the bluff with Macartney. As he reached it the firing ceased. The hulk, riddled with shot, was slowly settling down. She sank with a gurgle, as the now furious Governor flung himself from his horse beside the earthworks. Of Captain Blood, who with a knot of his rude followers was observing the end of the *Atrevida*, he stormily demanded to know in the name of heaven and of hell what folly this might be. Did Captain Blood realize that he had completely blocked the entrance to the harbour for all but vessels of the lightest draught?

"That was the aim," said Blood. "I've been at pains to find the shallowest part of the channel. She lies in six fathoms, reducing the depth to a bare two."

The Captain-General conceived that he was being mocked. Livid, he demanded why so insane a measure should have been taken, and this without consulting him. With a note of weariness in his voice Captain Blood explained what should have been obvious. It gave some pause to the Governor's anger. Yet the suspicions natural to a man of such limited vision were not quieted.

"But, if to sink the hulk there was your only object, why in the devil's name did you waste shot and powder on her? Why didn't you scuttle her?

Blood shrugged. "A little gunnery practice. We accomplished two objects in one."

"Gunnery practice? His excellency was savage. "At that range? What are you telling me, man?"

"You'll understand better when Don Miguel arrives."

"I'll understand now, if you please. I will so. Stab me! Ye'll observe that I command here in Antigua."

Blood was annoyed. He had never learned to suffer fools gladly. "Faith, then your command outstrips your understanding if my object isn't plain. Meanwhile, there are some other matters yet to be settled, and time may be short." With that he swung on his heel, and left the Captain-General spluttering.

Blood had surveyed the coast and found a snug inlet, known as Willoughby's Cove, not two miles away, where the *Arabella* could lie concealed and yet so conveniently at hand that he and all his men might remain aboard. This at least was good news to Colonel Courtney, who was in dread of having pirates quartered on the town. Blood demanded that his men should be victualled, and required fifty head of cattle and twenty hogs. The Captain-General would have haggled with him, but was overborne in terms which did not improve their relations. The beasts were duly delivered, and in the days that followed the buccaneers became buccaneers in earnest; the boucan fires were lighted on the shores of Willoughby's Cove, and there the flesh of the slaughtered animals was boucanned, together with a quantity of turtle which the adventurers captured thereabouts.

In these peaceful arts three days were consumed, until the Captain-General began to ask himself if the whole thing were not some evil game to cover nefarious ends of Captain Blood and his pirates. Blood, however, explained the delay. Not until Don Miguel had abandoned hope of being joined by Don Vicente de Casanegra with the *Atrevida* would he decide to sail without him.

Another four days of inactivity went by, on each of which the Captain-General rode out to Willoughby's Cove to vent his suspicions in searching questions. The interviews increased daily in acrimony. Daily Blood expressed more and more plainly to the Captain-General that he saw little hope for the colonial future of a country which exercised so little discrimination in the election of her overseas governors.

Don Miguel's squadron appeared off Antigua only just in time to avert an open rupture between the Captain-General and his buccaneer ally.

Word being brought of this to Willoughby's Cove, early one Monday morning, by one of the guards left in charge of the earthworks, Captain Blood landed a hundred of his men and marched them across to the bluff. Wolverstone was left in command aboard. Ogle, that formidable gunner, was already quartered at the fort with a gun-crew.

Six miles out at sea, standing directly for the harbour of St John's, with a freshening breeze from the north-west to temper the increasing heat of the morning sun, came four stately ships under full spread of sail, the banner of Castile afloat from the head of each mainmast.

From the parapet of the old fort Captain Blood surveyed them through his telescope. At his elbow, with Macartney in attendance, stood the Captain-General, perceiving at last that the Spanish menace was a reality.

Don Miguel commanded at the time the *Virgen del Pilar*, the finest and most powerful vessel in which he had yet sailed since Blood had sunk the *Milagrosa* some months before. She was a great black-hulled galleon of forty guns, including in her armament several heavy demi-cannon with a range of three thousand yards. Of the other three ships, two, if inferior, were still formidable thirty-gun frigates, whilst the last was really little better than a sloop of ten guns.

Blood closed his telescope and prepared for action in the old fort. The new one was for the moment left inactive.

Within a half hour battle was joined. Don Miguel's advance had all the rashness which Blood knew of old. He made no attempt to shorten sail until within two thousand yards. He conceived, no doubt, that he was taking the place entirely unawares, and that the antiquated guns of the fort would probably be inadequate. Nevertheless, he must dispose of them before attempting to enter the harbour. To be sure of making short work of it, he continued to advance until Blood computed him within a thousand yards.

"On my soul," said Blood, "he'll be meaning to get within pistol range, or else he thinks the fort of no account at all. Wake him up, Ogle. Let him have a salute."

Ogle's crew had been carefully laying their guns, and they had followed the advance with the twelve sakers from the *Atrevida*. Others stood at hand with linstocks, rammers and watertubs, to serve the gunners.

Ogle gave the word, and the twelve guns were touched off as one, with a deafening roar. Within that easy range even the five-pound shot of these comparatively small cannon did some little damage to two of the Spanish ships. The moral effect of thus surprising those who came to surprise was even greater. The Admiral instantly signalled them to go about. In doing so they poured broadside after broadside into the fort, and for some minutes the place was a volcano, smoke and dust rising in a dense column above the flying stones and crumbling masonry. Blinded by it, the buccaneers had no vision of what the Spaniards might be doing. But Blood guessed it, and cleared every man from the fort into shelter behind it during the brief respite before the second broadsides came.

When that was over he drove them back again into the battered fortress, which for a while now had nothing more to fear, and the original antiquated guns of St Johns' were brought into action. The faucons were fired at random through the cloud of dust that hid them merely as a display and to let the Spaniards know that the fort was still alive. Then, as the cloud lifted, the five-pounders spoke, in twos and threes, carefully aimed at the ships which were now beating to windward. They did little damage; but this was less important than to keep the Spaniards in play.

Meanwhile the gun-crews were busy with the sakers from the *Atrevida*. Watertubs had been emptied over them, and now with swabs and wads and rammers at work the reloading was proceeding.

The Captain-General, idle amid this terrific activity, required presently to know why powder was so ineffectively being wasted by these pop-guns, when in the earthworks there were cannon of long range which might be hammering the Spaniards with twenty-four and thirty-pound shot. When he was answered evasively, he passed from suggestion to command, whereupon he was invited not to interfere with carefully laid plans.

An altercation was saved by the return of the Spaniards to the attack and a repetition of all that had gone before. Again the fort was smashed and pounded, and this time two negroes were killed and a half dozen buccaneers were injured by flying masonry, despite Blood's precaution to get them out of the place before the broadsides came.

When the second attack had been beaten off and the Spaniards were again retiring to reload, Blood resolved to withdraw the guns from the fort in which another half dozen broadsides might completely bury them. Negroes and buccaneers and men of the Antiguan militia were indiscriminately employed on the business and harnessed to the guns. Even so it took an hour to get them all clear of the rubble and emplaced anew on the landward side of the fort, where Ogle and his men proceeded once more to load and carefully to lay them. The body of the fort meanwhile served to screen the operation from the Spaniards as they sailed in for the third time. Now the English held their fire whilst another storm of metal crashed upon those battered but empty ramparts. When it was over, the fort was a shapeless heap of rubble, and the little army lying concealed behind the ruins heard the Spanish cheer that announced their conviction that all was done, since no single shot had been fired to answer their bombardment.

Proudly, confidently, Don Miguel came on. No need now to stand off to reload. Already the afternoon was well advanced and he would house his men in St John's before nightfall. The haze of dust and smoke, whilst serving to screen the defenders and their new emplacements from the sight of the enemy, could yet be penetrated at close quarters by the watchful eyes of the buccaneers. The *Virgen del Pilar* was within five hundred yards of the harbour's mouth, when six sakers, charged now with langrel, chain and crossbar, swept her decks with murderous effect and some damage to her shrouds. Six faucons, similarly charged, followed after a moment's pause, and if their fire was less effective it yet served to increase the confusion and the alarm of so unexpected an attack.

In the pause they could hear the blare of a trumpet aboard the *Virgen*, screeching the Admiral's orders to the other ships of his squadron. Then, as in the haste of their manoeuvre to go about the Spaniards yawed a moment, broadside on, Blood gave the signal, and two by two the remaining sakers sent their five-pound round shot in search of Spanish timbers. Odd ones took effect, and one very fortunate cannon-ball smashed the mainmast of one of the frigates. In her crippled state and the desperate haste resulting from it, she fouled the sloop, and before the two vessels could disentangle themselves and follow the retreat of the others, their decks had been raked again and again by langrel and crossbar from water-cooled and hurriedly reloaded guns.

Blood, who had been crouching with the rest, stood up at last as the firing ceased, its work temporarily accomplished. He looked into the long, solemn face of Colonel Courtney and laughed.

"Faith! It's another slaughter of the innocents, so it is!"

The Captain-General smiled sourly back at him. "If you had done as I desired you—"

Blood interrupted without ceremony. "On my soul, now!

88

Are ye not content? If I'd done as you desired me, I'd have put all my cards on the table by now. It's saving my trumps I am until the Admiral plays as I want him to."

"And if the Admiral doesn't, Captain Blood?"

"He will, for one thing because it's in the nature of him; for another because there's no other way to play at all. And so ye may go home and sleep in peace, placing your trust in Providence and me."

"I do not care for the association, sir," said the Governor frostily.

"But you will. On my soul, you will. For we do fine things when we work together, Providence and I."

An hour before sunset the Spaniards were hove to a couple of miles out at sea, and becalmed. The Antiguans, white and black, dismissed by Blood, went home to sup – all but some two score whom he retained for emergencies. Then his buccaneers sat down under the sky to a generous supply of meat and a limited amount of rum.

The sun went down into the jade waters of the Caribbean, and darkness followed almost as upon the extinction of a lamp – the soft, purple darkness of a moonless night irradiated by a myriad stars.

Captain Blood stood up and nosed the air. The north-westerly breeze, which had died down towards evening, was springing up again. He ordered all fires and lights to be extinguished, so as to encourage that for which he hoped.

Out at sea in the fine cabin of the *Virgen del Pilar*, the proud, noble, brave, incompetent admiral of the Carribbean held a council of war which was no council, for he had summoned his captains merely so that he might impose his will upon them. At dead midnight, by when all in St John's should be asleep, in the conviction that no further attack would come until morning, they would creep past the fort under cover of darkness and with all lights extinguished. Daylight should find them at anchor a mile or more beyond it, in the bay, with their guns trained upon the town. That must be checkmate to the Antiguans.

Upon this they acted, and with sails trimmed to the favouring breeze, and shortened so as to lessen the gurgle of water at their prows, they nosed gently forward through the velvety gloom. With the *Virgen* leading they reached the entrance of the harbour and the darker waters between the shadowy bluffs on either side. Here all was deathly still. Not a light showed save the distant phosphorescent line where the waters met the shore; not a sound disturbed the stillness save the silken rustle of the sea against their sides.

Already within two hundred yards of the fort, and of the spot where the *Atrevida* had been sunk to block the channel, the *Virgen* crept on, her bulwarks lined with silent, watchful men, Don Miguel, leaning immovable as a statue upon the poop-rail. He was abreast of the fort and counting the victory already won, when suddenly his keel grated, and, grating ever harder, drove shuddering onwards for some yards, to be finally gripped and held as if by some monstrous hand in the depths below, whilst overhead, under pressure of a wind to which the vessel no longer yielded, the sails drummed loudly to an accompaniment of groaning cordage and clattering blocks.

And then, before the Admiral could even conjecture what had happened to him, the gloom to larboard was split by flame, the silence smashed by a roar of guns, the rending of timbers, and the crashing fall of spars, as the demi-cannons landed from the *Arabella*, and held in reserve until now in the dissembled earthworks, hurled their thirty-two-pounds shot into the Spanish flagship at merciless short range. The deadly accuracy of these guns might have revealed to Colonel Courtney precisely why Captain Blood had elected to sink the *Atrevida* by gunfire instead of scuttling her. Thus he had obtained the exact range which enabled him to fire so accurately through the darkness.

One frantic, wildly-aimed broadside the *Virgen* discharged in answer before, smashed and riddled and held above water only by the hulk on which she had stuck fast, the Admiral abandoned her. With his survivors he clambered aboard one of the frigates, the *Indiana*, which, unable to check her way in time, had crashed into him astern. Moving very slowly, the *Indiana* had suffered little damage beyond a smashed bowsprit, and her captain, acting promptly, had taken in what little sail he carried.

Mercifully at that moment the guns ashore were reloading. In that brief respite the *Indiana* received the fugitives from the flagship, whilst the sloop which had been next in line, perceiving the situation, took in all sail at once, and getting out her sweeps, warped the *Indiana* astern from her entanglement, and out into the open, where the other frigate lay hove to firing desultorily in the direction of the now silent earthworks on the bluff. The only effect of this was to betray her whereabouts to the buccaneers, and presently the demi-cannons were roaring again, though no longer collectively. A shot from one of them completed the crippling of the *Indiana* by smashing her rudder; so that having been warped out of the harbour she had to be taken in tow by her sister ship.

The firing ceased on both sides, and the peace and silence of the tropical night would again have descended on St John's but that all in the town were now afoot and hastening out to the bluff for information.

When daylight broke the only ship on the blue expanse of the Caribbean within the vision of Antigua was the red-hulled *Arabella* at anchor in the shadow of the bluff to receive the demi-cannons she had lent the enterprise, and the battered *Virgen del Pilar* listing heavily to starboard where she had stuck on the submerged hull of the *Atrevida*. About the wrecked flagship swarmed a fleet of small boats and canoes in which the buccaneers were salving every object of value to be found aboard her. They brought all ashore: arms and armour some of great price, a service of gold plate, vessels of gold and silver, two steel-bound coffers being, presumably, the treasury of the squadron and containing some six thousand pieces of eight, besides jewels, clothes, oriental carpets and rich brocades from the great cabin. All were piled up beside the fort for subsequent division as provided by the articles under which the buccaneers sailed.

A string of four packmules came along the shallow cliff as the salving was concluded and drew up beside the precious heap.

"What's this?" quoth Blood, who was present at the spot.

"From his excellency, the Captain-General," replied the Negro muleteer, "fo' dah conveying ob deh treasure."

Blood was taken aback. When he recovered: "Much obliged," said he, and ordered the mules to be laden and conducted to the end of the bluff, to the boats which were to carry the spoils aboard the *Arabella*.

After that he went to wait upon the Captain-General.

He was shown into a long, narrow room from one end of which a portrait of his late sardonic majesty King Charles II looked into a mirror on the other. There was a long, narrow table on which stood some books, a guitar, a bowl of heavily-scented white acacia, and there were some tall-backed chairs of black oak without upholstery.

The Captain-General came in, followed by Macartney. His face looked longer and narrower than ever.

Captain Blood, telescope under his arm and plumed hat in his hand, bowed low.

"I come to take my leave, your excellency."

"I was about to send for you." The Colonel's pale eyes sought to meet the Captain's steady gaze, but failed. "I hear of considerable treasure taken from the Spanish wreck. I am told your men have carried this aboard your ship. You are aware, sir – or are you not? – that these spoils are the property of the King?"

"I am not aware of it," said Captain Blood.

"You are not? Then I inform you of it now."

Captain Blood shook his head, smiling tolerantly. "It is a prize of war."

"Exactly. And the war was being waged on behalf of his majesty and in defence of this his majesty's colony."

"Save that I did not hold the King's commission."

"Tacitly, and temporarily, I granted you it when I consented to enlist you and your men in the defence of the island."

Blood stared at him in amused astonishment. "What were you, sir, before they made you Captain-General of the Leeward Islands? A lawyer?"

"Captain Blood, I think you mean to be insolent."

"You may be sure I do, and more. You consented to enlist me, did you? Here's condescension! Where should you be now if I hadn't brought you the assistance you consented to receive?"

"We will take one thing at a time, if you please." The Colonel was coldly prim. "When you entered the service of King James, you became subject to the laws that govern his forces. Your appropriation of treasure from the Spanish flagship is an act of brigandage contrary to all those laws and severely punishable under them."

Captain Blood found the situation increasingly humorous. He laughed.

"My clear duty," added Colonel Courtney, "is to place you under arrest."

"But I hope you're not thinking of performing it?"

"Not if you choose to take advantage of my leniency, and depart at once."

"I'll depart as soon as I receive the twenty thousand pieces of eight for which I hired you my services."

"You have chosen, sir to take payment in another fashion. You have committed a breach of the law. I have nothing more to say to you, Captain Blood."

Blood considered him with narrowing eyes. Was the man so utterly a fool, or was he merely dishonest?

"Oh, sharper than the serpent's tooth!" he laughed. "Sure now I must spend the remainder of my days in succouring British colonies in distress. Meanwhile, here I am and here I stay until I have my twenty thousand pieces." He flung his hat on the table, drew up a chair, sat down, and crossed his legs. "It's a warm day, Colonel, so it is."

The Colonel's eyes flashed. "Captain Macartney, the guard is waiting in the gallery. Be good enough to call it."

"Will ye be intending to arrest me?"

The Colonel's eyes gloomed at him. "Naturally, sir. It is my clear duty. It has been my duty from the moment that you landed here. You show me that I should have considered nothing else whatever my own needs." He waved a hand to the soldier who had paused by the door. "If you please, Captain Macartney."

"Oh, a moment yet, Captain Macartney. A moment yet, Colonel." Blood raised his hand. "This amounts to a declaration of war."

The Colonel shrugged contemptuously. "You may so regard it if you choose. It is not material."

Captain Blood's doubts about the man's honesty were completely dissipated. He was just a fool with a mental vision that could perceive one object only at a time.

"Indeed, and it's most material. Since you declare war on me, war you shall have; and I warn you that you'll find me as ruthless an opponent as the Spaniards found me yesterday when I was your ally."

"By God!" swore Macartney. "Here's fine talk from a man whose person we hold!"

"Others have held me before, Captain Macartney. Don't be attaching too much importance to that." He paused to smile, and then resumed. "It's fortunate now for Antigua that the war you have declared on me may be fought without bloodshed. Indeed, you may perceive at a glance that it has been fought already, that the strategic advantages lie with me, and, therefore, that nothing remains for you but capitulation."

"I perceive nothing of the kind, sir."

"That is because you are slow to perceive the obvious. I am coming to think that at home they regard this as a necessary qualification in a Colonial Governor. A moment's patience, Colonel, while I point out to you that my ship is off the harbour. She carries two hundred of the toughest fighting-men, who would devour your spineless militia at a gulp. She carries forty guns, the half of which could be landed on the bluff within an hour, and within another hour St John's would be a dustheap. If you think they would hesitate because this colony is English,

I'll remind you that a third of my following is French and the other two-thirds are outlaws like myself. They would sack this town with pleasure, firstly because it is held in the name of King James, a name detestable to all of them, and secondly because the gold you have been finding in Antigua should make it well worth the sacking."

Macartney, purple in the face, was fingering his swordhilt. But it was the Colonel, livid with passion, who answered, waving one of his bony freckled hands.

"You infamous pirate scoundrel! You damned escaped convict! You've forgot one thing: that until you can get back to your pestilential buccaneers none of this can happen."

"We have to thank him for the warning, sir," Captain Macartney jeered.

"Ah, bah! Ye've no imagination, as I suspected yesterday. Your muleteer gave me a glimpse of what to expect from you. I took my measures accordingly, so I did. I left orders with my lieutenant to assume at twelve o'clock that war had been declared, and to land the guns and haul them to the fort, whence they command the town. I left your mules with him for the purpose." He glanced at the timepiece on the overmantel. "It's nearly half past twelve already. From your windows here you can see the fort." He stood up and proffered his telescope. "Assure yourself that what I have said is happening."

There was a pause in which the Captain-General considered him with eyes of hate. Then in silence he took the telescope and went to the window. When he turned from it again he was fierce as a rattlesnake. "But you forget one thing still. That we hold you. "I'll send word to your pirate scum that at the first shot from them I'll hang you. The guard, Macartney. There's been talk enough."

"Oh, a moment yet," Blood begged. "Ye're so plaguily hasty in your conclusions. Wolverstone has my orders, and no threat to my life will swerve him from them by a hair's breadth. Hang me if you will." He shrugged. "If I set great score by life I should hardly follow the trade of a buccaneer. But when

95

you've hanged me be sure that not one stone of St John's will be left upon another, not man, woman or child will my buccaneers spare in avenging me. Consider that, and consider at the same time your duty to this colony and to your King – this duty by which you rightly set such store."

The Governor's pale eyes stabbed him as if they would reach his soul. Calm and intrepid he stood before them, intimidatingly calm.

The Colonel looked at Macartney as if for help. He found none there. Irritably he broke out at last: "Oh, stab me! I am well served for dealing with a pirate. To be rid of you, I'll pay you your twenty thousand pieces, and so farewell and be damned to you."

"Twenty thousand pieces!" Blood raised his eyebrows in surprise. "But that was whilst I was your ally; that was before ye declared war upon me."

"What the devil do you mean now?"

"That since ye admit defeat, we will pass to the discussion of terms."

"Terms! What terms?" The Captain-General's exasperation was swiftly mounting.

"You shall hear them. First, the twenty thousand pieces of eight that you owe my men for services rendered. Next, thirty thousand for the redemption of the town from the bombardment that is preparing."

"What! By God, sir! . . ."

"Next," Captain Blood pursued relentlessly, "ten thousand pieces for your own ransom, ten thousand for the ransom of your own family, and five thousand for that of other persons of consequence on St John's, including Captain Macartney here. That makes seventy-five thousand pieces of eight, and they must be paid within the next hour, since later will be too late."

The Captain-General looked unutterable things. He tried to speak. But speech failed him. He sat down heavily. At last he found his voice. It came thick and quavering.

"You . . . you abuse my patience. You surely . . . You think me mad?"

"Best hang him, Colonel, and have done," Macartney exploded.

"And thereby destroy the colony it is your duty at all costs – at all costs, mark you – to preserve."

The Captain-General passed a hand across his wet, pallid brow, and groaned.

They talked, of course, for some time yet; but ever within the circle of what had been said already, until in the end Colonel Courtney broke into a laugh that was almost hysterical.

"Stab me, sir! It only remains to marvel at your moderation. You might have asked seven hundred thousand pieces, or seven millions—"

"True," Blood interrupted him. "But then I am by nature moderate, and also I have a notion of the resources of your treasury."

"But the time!" cried the Governor desperately, to show that he had yielded. "How can I collect the sum within an hour?"

"I'll be reasonable. Send me the money to the bluff by sunset, and I'll withdraw. And now I'll take my leave at once, so as to suspend the operations. It's a very good day I'll be wishing you."

They let him go, perforce. And at sunset Captain Macartney rode out to the gun emplacements of the buccaneers, followed by a Negro leading a mule on which the gold was laden.

Captain Blood came forward alone to receive him.

"It isn't what you'd have got from me," said the choleric captain through his teeth.

"I'll remember that in case you should ever command a settlement. And now, sir, to business. What do these sacks hold?"

"You'll find five thousand pieces in each."

"Then set me down four of them: the twenty thousand pieces for which I agreed to serve Antigua. The rest you can take back to the Captain-General with my compliments. Let the experience teach him, and you too, Captain darling, that a man's first duty is less to his office than to his own honour, and that he cannot perform it unless he fulfils the engagements of his word."

Captain Macartney sucked in his breath. "Gadslife!" he exclaimed huskily. "And you're a pirate!"

Sternly came the vibrant metallic voice of the buccaneer. "I am Captain Blood."

5

BLOOD MONEY

CAPTAIN BLOOD was pleased with the world – which is but another way of saying that he was pleased with himself.

He stood on the mole at Cayona and surveyed the shipping in the rockbound harbour. With pride he considered the five great ships that now made up his fleet, every spar and timber of which had once been the property of Spain. There was his own flagship, the *Arabella*, of forty guns, her red bulwarks and gilded ports aflame in the evening sunlight, with the scarcely less powerful blue and white *Elizabeth* beside her. Beyond them rode the three smaller twenty-gun vessels captured in the great affair at Maracaybo from which Blood was lately returned. These ships, originally named the *Infanta*, the *San Felipe*, and the *Santo Nino*, Blood had renamed after the three Parcae, the *Clotho*, the *Lachesis*, and the *Atropos*, by which it was his intention playfully to convey that they were the arbiters of the fate of any Spaniard henceforth encountered by them upon the seas.

Captain Blood took satisfaction in his own delicate, scholarly humour. He was, as I have said, well pleased with himself. His following numbered close upon a thousand men, and he could double this number whenever he pleased. For his luck was passing into a proverb, and luck is the highest quality that can be sought in a leader of hazardous enterprises. Not the great Henry Morgan himself in his best days had wielded such authority and power. Not even Montbar – surnamed by Spain the Exterminator – had been more dreaded by Spaniards in his day than was now Don Pedro Sangre, as they translated Peter Blood's name, accounting it most apt.

Order, he knew, was being taken against him. Not only the King of Spain, of whose power he had made a mock, but also the King of England, whom he accounted, and with some reason, a contemptible fellow, were concerting measures for his destruction; and news had lately come to Tortuga that the Spanish Admiral, Don Miguel de Espinosa, who had been the latest and most terrible sufferer at his hands, had proclaimed that he would pay ten thousand pieces of eight to any man who should deliver up to him the person of Captain Blood alive. Don Miguel's was a vindictiveness that was not to be satisfied by mere death.

Peter Blood was not intimidated, or likely to mistrust his luck so much as to let himself run to rust in the security of Tortuga. For that which he had suffered – and he had suffered much – at the hands of man, he had chosen to make Spain the scapegoat. Thus he accounted that he served a twofold purpose. He took compensation, and at the same time served, not indeed the Stuart King, whom he despised – although himself born an Irishman and bred a Papist – but England, and, for that matter, all the rest of civilized mankind, which cruel, treacherous, greedy, bigoted Castile sought to debar from intercourse with the New World.

He was turning from the mole, almost deserted by now of its usual bustling, heterogeneous crowd, when the voice of Hayton, the boatswain of the *Arabella*, called after him from the boat that had brought him ashore.

"Back at eight bells, Captain?"

"At eight bells," said Blood over his shoulder, and sauntered on, swinging his long ebony cane, elegant and courtly in a suit of grey and silver.

He took his way up towards the town, saluted as he went by most of those whom he met, and stared at by the rest. He chose to go by way of the wide, unpaced Rue du Roi de France, which the townsfolk had sought to embellish by flanking it with rows of palm trees. As he approached the tavern of The King of France the little crowd about its portals drew to attention. From within came a steady drone of voices as a muffled accompaniment to foul exclamations, snatches of coarse songs, and the shrill, foolish laughter of women. Through all ran the rattle of dice and the chinkling of drinking-cans.

Blood realized that his buccaneers were making merry with the gold they had brought back from Maracaybo. The ruffians overflowing from that house of infamy hailed him with a ringing cheer. Was he not the king of all the ruffians that made up the great Brotherhood of the Coast?

He acknowledged their greeting by a lift of the hand that held the cane, and passed on. He had business with M. d'Oger-on, the Governor, and this business took him now to the handsome white house crowning the eminence to the east of the town.

The Captain was an orderly, provident man, and he was busily providing against the day when the death or downfall of King James II might make it possible for him to return home. For some time now it had been his practice to make over the bulk of his share of prizes to the Governor against bills of exchange on France, which he forwarded to Paris for collection and deposit. Peter Blood was ever a welcome visitor at the Governor's house, not only because these transactions were profitable to M. d'Ogeron, but in a still deeper measure because of a signal service that the Captain had once done him and his in rescuing his daughter Madeleine from the hands of a ruffianly pirate who had attempted to carry her off. By M. d'Ogeron, his son and his two daughters, Captain Blood had ever since been regarded as something more than an ordinary friend.

It was therefore nowise extraordinary that when, his business being transacted, he was departing on this particular evening, Mademoiselle d'Ogeron should choose to escort him down the short avenue of her father's fragrant garden.

A pale-faced, black-haired beauty, tall and statuesque of figure, and richly gowned in the latest mode of France, Mademoiselle d'Ogeron was as romantic of appearance as of temperament. And as she stepped gracefully beside the Captain in the gathering dusk she showed her purpose to be not without a certain romantic quality also.

"Monsieur," she said in French, hesitating a little, "I have come to implore you to be ever on your guard. You have too many enemies."

He halted and, half turning, hat in hand, he bowed until his long black ringlets almost met across his clear-cut, gipsy-tinted face.

"Mademoiselle, your concern is flattering; but so flattering." Erect again, his bold eyes, startlingly light under their black brows and in a face so burnt and swarthy, laughed into her own. "I do not want for enemies, true. It is the penalty of greatness. Only he who is without anything is without enemies. But at least they are not in Tortuga."

"Are you so very sure of that?"

Her tone gave him pause. He frowned, and considered her solemnly for an instant before replying.

"Mademoiselle, you speak as if from some knowledge."

"Hardly so much. My knowledge is but the knowledge of what a slave told me today. He says that the Spanish Admiral has placed a price upon your head."

"That is just the Spanish Admiral's notion of flattery, mademoiselle."

"And that Cahusac has been heard to say he will make you rue the wrong you did him at Maracaybo."

"Cahusac?"

The name revealed to him the rashness of his assertion that he had no enemy in Tortuga. He had forgotten Cahusac: but he realized that Cahusac would not be likely to have forgotten him. Cahusac had been with him at Maracaybo, and had been trapped with him there by the arrival of Don Miguel de Espinosa's fleet. The French rover had taken fright, had charged Blood with rashness in his conduct of the enterprise, had quarrelled with him and had made terms with the Spanish Admiral for himself and his own French contingent. Granted a safe-conduct by Don Miguel, he had departed empty-handed, leaving Captain Blood to his fate. But it proved not at all as the timorous Cahusac conceived it. Captain Blood had not only broken out of the Spanish trap, but he had sorely mauled the Admiral, captured three of his ships, and returned to Tortuga laden with rich spoils of victory.

To Cahusac this was gall and wormwood. With the faculty

for confusing cause and effect, which is the chief disability of stupid egoists, he came to account himself cheated by Captain Blood. And he was making no secret of his unfounded resentment.

"He is saying that, is he?" said Captain Blood. "Now, that is indiscreet of him. Besides, all the world knows he was not wronged. He was allowed to depart in safety as he wished when he thought the situation grew too dangerous.

"But by doing so he sacrificed his share of the prizes, and for that he and his companions have since been the mock of Tortuga. Can you not conceive what must be that ruffian's feelings?"

They had reached the gate.

"You will take precautions? You will guard yourself?" she begged him.

He smiled upon her friendly anxiety.

"If only so that I may live on to serve you." With formal courtesy he bowed low over her hand and kissed it.

Seriously concerned, however, by her warning he was not. That Cahusac should be vindictive he could well believe. But that Cahusac should utter threats here in Tortuga was an indiscretion too dangerous to be credible in the case of a cur who took no risk.

He stepped out briskly through the night that was closing down, soft and warm, and came soon within sight of the lights of the Rue du Roi de France. As he reached the head of that now deserted thoroughfare a shadow detached itself from the mouth of a lane on his right to intercept him.

Even as he checked, prepared to fall on guard, he made out the figure to be a woman's, and heard his name called softly in a woman's voice.

"Captain Blood!"

As he halted she came closer, and addressed him quickly, breathlessly. "I saw you pass two hours since. But I dursn't be seen speaking to you in daylight here in the street. So I have been on the watch for your return. Don't go on, Captain. You are walking into danger; walking to your death."

At last his puzzled mind recognized her; and before the eyes of his memory flashed a scene enacted a week ago at The King of France. Two drunken ruffians had quarrelled over a woman – a fragment of the human wreckage of Europe washed up on the shores of the New World – an unfortunate creature of a certain comeliness, which, however, like the cast-off finery she wore, was tarnished, soiled, and crumpled. The woman, arrogating a voice in a dispute of which she was the object, was brutally struck by one of her companions, and Blood, upon an impulse of chivalrous anger, had felled her assailant and escorted her from the place.

"They're lying in wait for you down yonder," she was saying, "and they mean to kill you."

"Who does?" he asked her, Mademoiselle d'Ogeron's words of warning sharply recalled.

"There's a score of them. And if they was to know – if they was to see me here a-warning you – my own throat would be cut before morning."

She peered fearfully about her through the gloom as she spoke, and fear quivered in her voice. Then she cried out huskily, as if with mounting terror.

"Oh, don't let us stand here! Come with me; I'll make you safe until daylight. Then you can go back to your ship, and if you're wise you'll stay on board after this, or else come ashore in company. Come!" she ended, and caught him by the sleeve.

"Whisht now! Whisht!" said he, resisting the pressure on his arm. "Whither will you be taking me!"

"Oh, what odds, so long as I make you safe?" She was dragging on him with all her weight. "You was kind to me, and I can't leave you to be killed. And we'll both be murdered unless you come."

Yielding at last, as much for her sake as his own, he allowed her to lead him from the wide street into the byway from which she had issued to intercept him. It was a narrow lane with little one-storeyed houses that were mostly timber standing at wide intervals along one side of it. Along the other ran a palisade enclosing a plantation.

At the second house she stopped. The little door stood open, and the interior was dimly lighted by the naked flame of a brass oil-lamp set upon a table.

"Go in," she bade him in a shuddering whisper.

Two steps led down to the floor of the house, which was below the level of the street. Down these went Captain Blood, and on into the room, whose air was rank with the reek of stale tobacco and the sickly odour of the little oil-lamp. The woman followed, and closed the door. And then, before Captain Blood could turn to inspect his surroundings in that dim light, he was struck over the head from behind with something heavy and hard-driven, which, if it did not stun him outright, at least stretched him sick and faint upon the grimy naked earth of the unpaved floor.

At the same moment a woman's scream, that ended abruptly in a stifled gurgle, cut sharply upon the silence.

In an instant, before Captain Blood could move to help himself, before he could even recover from his bewildered surprise, swift, sinewy, skilful hands had done their work upon him. Thongs of hide lashed his ankles and his wrists, which had been dragged behind him. Then he was rolled over on to his back, lifted, forced into a chair, and lashed by the waist to that.

A man of low stature and powerful, apelike build, long in the body and short in the legs, was leaning over him. The sleeves of his blue shirt were rolled to the elbows of his prodigious, long, muscular and hairy arms. Little black eyes twinkled wickedly in a broad face that was almost as flat and sallow as a mulatto's. A red and blue scarf swathed his head, completely concealing his hair; heavy gold rings hung in the lobes of the great ears.

Captain Blood considered him for a long moment, setting a curb upon the violent rage that rose in him in a measure as his senses cleared. Instinctively he realized that violence and passion would help him not at all, and that at all costs they must be suppressed. And he suppressed them.

"Cahusac!" he said slowly. And then added: "This is an unexpected pleasure entirely!"

"Ye've dropped anchor at last, Captain," said Cahusac, and he laughed softly with infinite malice.

Blood looked beyond him towards the door, where the woman was writhing in the grasp of Cahusac's companion.

"Will you be quiet, you slut, or must I quiet you?" the ruffian was threatening.

"What are you going to do with him, Sam?" she whimpered.

"No business of yours, my girl."

"Oh yes, it is! You told me he was in danger, and I believed you, you lying tyke!"

"Well, so he was. But he's safe and snug now. You go in there, Molly." He pointed across the room to the black entrance of an alcove.

"I'll not—" she was beginning angrily.

"Go in," he snarled, "or it'll be the worse for you!"

He seized her roughly again at neck and waist and thrust her, still resisting, across the room and into the alcove. He closed the door and bolted it.

"Stay you there, you drab, and keep quiet, or I'll quiet you once for all."

From behind the door he was answered by a moan. Then there was the creak of a bed as the woman flung herself violently upon it, and thereafter silence.

Captain Blood accounted her part in this business explained, and more or less ended. He looked up into the face of his sometime associate, and his lips smiled to simulate a calm he was far from feeling.

"Would it be an impertinence to inquire what ye're intending, Cahusac?" said he.

Cahusac's companion laughed, and lounged across the table, a tall, loose-limbed fellow, with a long face of an almost Indian cast of features. His dress implied the hunter. He answered for Cahusac, who glowered, morosely silent.

"We intend to hand you over to Don Miguel de Espinosa."

He stooped to give his attention to the lamp, pulling up the wick and trimming it, so that the light in the shabby little room was suddenly increased.

"C'est ça!" said Cahusac. "And Don Miguel, no doubt, 'll intend to hang you from the yardarm."

"So Don Miguel's in this, is he? Glory be! I suppose it's the blood-money that's tempted ye. Sure, now, it's the very work that ye're fitted for, devil a doubt. But have ye considered all? There are reefs ahead, my lad. Hayton was to have met me with a boat at the mole at eight bells. I'm late as it is. Eight bells was made an hour ago and more. Presently they'll take alarm. They knew where I was going. They'll follow and track me. To find me, the boys will be turning Tortuga inside out like a sack. And what'll happen to ye then, Cahusac? Have you thought of that? The pity of it is that ye're entirely without foresight. It was lack of foresight that sent ye away empty-handed from Maracaybo. And even then, but for me, ye'd be hauling at the oar of a Spanish galley this very minute. Yet ye're aggrieved, being a poor-spirited, cross-grained cur, and to vent your spite you're running straight upon destruction. If ye've a spark of sense you'll haul in sail, my lad, and heave-to, before it's too late."

Cahusac leered at him for only answer, and then in silence went through the Captain's pockets. The other, meanwhile, sat down on a three-legged stool of pine.

"What's o'clock, Cahusac?" he asked.

Cahusac consulted the Captain's watch.

"Near half past nine, Sam."

"Plague on it!" grumbled Sam. "Three hours to wait!"

"There's dice in the cupboard," said Cahusac, "and here's something to be played for."

He jerked his thumb towards the yield of Captain Blood's pockets, which made a little pile upon the table. There were some twenty gold pieces, a little silver, an onion-shaped gold watch, a gold tobacco box, a pistol, and, lastly, a jewel which Cahusac had detached from the lace at the Captain's throat, besides a sword and a rich balrick of grey leather heavily wrought in gold.

Sam rose, went to a cupboard, and fetched thence the dice. He set them on the table and, drawing up his stool, again resumed his seat. The money he divided into two equal halves. Then he added the sword and the watch to one pile, and the jewel, the pistol, and the tobacco box to the other.

Blood, very alert and watchful – so concentrated, indeed, upon the problem of winning free from this trap that he was hardly conscious of the pain in his head from the blow that had felled him – began to speak again. Resolutely he refused to admit the fear and hopelessness that were knocking at his heart.

"There's another thing ye've not considered," said he slowly, almost drawlingly, "and that is that I might be willing to ransom myself at a far more handsome price than the Spanish Admiral has offered for me."

But they weren't impressed. Cahusac merely mocked him.

"Tiens! And your certainty that Hayton will come to your rescue then? What of that?"

He laughed, and Sam laughed with him.

"It's probable," said Blood, "most probable. But not certain; nothing is, in this uncertain world. Not even that the Spaniard will pay you the ten thousand pieces of eight they tell me he has been after offering for me. You could make a better bargain with me, Cahusac."

He paused, and his keen, watchful glance observed the sudden gleam of covetousness in the Frenchman's eye, as well as the frown contracting the brow of the other ruffian. Therefore he continued.

"You might make such a bargain as would compensate you for what you missed at Maracaybo. For every thousand pieces that the Spaniard offers, sure now I'll offer two."

Cahusac's jaw fell, his eyes widened.

"Twenty thousand pieces!" he gasped in blank amazement.

And then Sam's great fist crashed down upon the rickety table, and he swore foully and fiercely.

"None of that!" he roared. "I've made my bargain, and I abides by it. It'll be the worse for me if I doesn't – ay, and for you, Cahusac. Besides, are you such a gull that you think this pretty hawk'll keep faith with you?"

"He knows that I would," said Blood; "he's sailed with me. He knows that my word is accounted good even by Spaniards."

"Maybe. But it's not accounted good by me." Sam stood over him, the long, evil face, with its sloping brows and heavy eyelids, grown dark and menacing. "I'm pledged to deliver you safely at midnight, and when I pledges myself to a job I does it. Understand?"

Captain Blood looked up at him, and actually smiled.

"Faith," said he. "You don't leave much to a man's imagination."

And he meant it literally; for what he had clearly gathered was that it was Sam who had entered into league with the Spanish agents, and dared not for his life's sake break with them.

"Then that's as well," Sam assured him. "If you want to be spared the discomfort of a gag for the next three hours, you'll just hold your plaguey tongue. Understand that?"

He thrust his long face forward into his captive's, sneering and menacing.

Understanding, Captain Blood abandoned his desperate clutch of the only slender straw of hope that he had discovered in the situation. He realized that he was to wait here, helpless in his bonds, until the time appointed for his delivery to someone who should carry him off to Don Miguel de Espinosa. Upon what would happen to him then he scarcely dared to dwell. He knew the revolting cruelties of which a Spaniard was capable, and he could guess what a spur of rage would be the Spanish admiral's. A sweat of horror broke upon his skin. Was he indeed to end his gloriously hazardous career in this mean way? Was he, who had so proudly sailed the seas of the Main as a conqueror, to founder thus in a dirty backwater? He could found no hope upon the search that Hayton and the others would presently be making. That, as he had said, they would turn the place inside out, he never doubted. But he never doubted, either, that they would come too late. They might hunt down his betrayers, and wreak a terrible vengeance upon them. But how should that avail him?

The fogs of passion thickened in his mind; despair smothered the power of thought. He had close upon a thousand devoted men here in Tortuga, almost within hail, and he bound and helpless, and so to be delivered to the vindictive justice of Castile! That insistent, ever-recurring thought beat backwards and forwards like a pendulum in his brain, distracting it.

And then, in a sense, he came to himself again. His mind grew clear once more, preternaturally clear and active. Cahusac he knew for a venal scoundrel, who would keep faith with none if he saw profit in treachery. And the other was probably no better; indeed, probably worse, since interest alone – that Spanish blood-money – had lured him to his present task. He concluded that he had too soon abandoned the attempt to outbid the Spanish admiral. That way he might yet throw a bone of contention to these mangy curs, over which they would perhaps end by tearing at each other's throats.

A moment he surveyed them, observing the evil greed in the eyes of each as they watched the fall of the dice over their trifling stakes from the gold and trinkets of which they had rifled him, and with which they were gaming to beguile the time of waiting.

And then he heard his own crisp voice breaking the silence.

"You gamble there for halfpence with a fortune within your reach."

"Are you beginning again?" growled Sam.

But the Captain went on undaunted.

"I'll outbid the Spanish admiral's blood-money by forty thousand pieces. I offer you fifty thousand pieces of eight for my life."

Sam, who had risen in anger, stood suddenly arrested by the mention of so vast a sum.

Cahusac had risen too, and now both men stood, one on each side of the table, tense with excitement, which, if unexpressed as yet, was none the less to be read in the sudden pallor of their faces and dilation of their eyes. At last the Frenchman broke the silence.

"God of God! Fifty thousand pieces of eight!" He uttered the words slowly, as if to impress the figure upon his own and his companion's mind. And he repeated: "Fifty thousand pieces of eight! Twenty-five thousand for each! Pardi! but that is worth some risk! Eh, Sam?"

"A mort of money, true," said Sam thoughtfully. And then he recovered. "Bah! What's a promise, anyhow? Who's to trust him? Once he's free, who's to make him pay, and he's—"

"Oh, I pay," said Blood. "Cahusac will tell you that I always pay." And he continued: "Consider that such a sum, even when divided, will make each of you wealthy enough to lead a life of ease and plenty. *Mucho viño, muchas mugeres!*" He laughed. "To be sure now, you'll be wise."

Cahusac licked his lips and looked at his companion. "It could be done," he muttered persuasively. "It's not yet ten, and between this and midnight we could put ourselves beyond the reach of your Spanish friends."

But Sam was not to be persuaded. He had been thinking; yet, tempting as he must find the lure, he dared not yield, discerning a double peril within it. Committed now by Spain to this venture, he dared neither draw back nor shift his course. Between the certain rage of the Spaniards should he play them false, and the probable resentment of Blood once he was restored to liberty, Sam saw himself inevitably crushed. Better an assured five thousand pieces to be enjoyed in comparative safety than a possible twenty-five thousand accompanied by such intolerable risks.

"It could not be done at all!" he cried angrily. "So let us hear no more about it. I've warned you once already."

"Mordieu!" cried Cahusac thickly. "But I say it could! And I say it's worth the risk."

"You say so, do you? And where's the risk for you? The Spaniards do not even know that you're in the business. It's easy for you, my lad, to talk about risks that you won't be called upon to run. But it's not quite the same for me. If I fail the Don, he'll want to know the reason. And, anyhow, I've pledged myself, and I'm a man of my word. So let's hear no more of it."

He towered there, fierce and determined, and Cahusac, after a scowling stare into that long, resolute face, uttered a sigh of exasperation, and sat down again.

Blood perceived quite clearly the inward rage that consumed the Frenchman. Vindictive though he might be towards the Captain, the venal scoundrel preferred his enemy's gold to his blood, and it was easy to guess the bitterness in which he saw himself compelled to forgo the more tangible satisfaction simply because of the risks with which acceptance would be fraught for his associate.

For a while there was no word spoken between the twain, nor did Blood judge that he could further serve his ends by adding anything to what he had already said. He took heart, meanwhile, from the clear perception of the mischief he had already made.

When at last he broke the brooding silence, his words seemed to have no bearing whatever upon the situation.

"Though you may mean to sell me to Spain, sure there's no reason why ye should let me die of thirst in the meantime. I've a throat that's like the salt ponds on Saltatudos, so I have."

Although he had a definite purpose to serve, to which he made his thirst a pretext, yet that thirst itself was real, and it was suffered by his captors in common with himself. The air of the room, whose door and window were tight-barred, was stifling. Sam passed a hand across his dank brow and swept away the moisture.

"Hell! The heat!" he muttered. "And now I thirst myself."

Cahusac licked his dry lips.

"Is there nothing in the house?" he asked.

"No. But it's only a step to The King of France." He rose. "I'll go fetch a jack of wine."

Hope soared wildly in the breast of Captain Blood. It was precisely for this that he had played. Knowing their drinking habit, and how easily suggestion must arouse their desire to indulge it, he had hoped to send one of them upon that errand,

and that the one to go would be Sam. With Cahusac he was sure he could make a deal at once.

And then Cahusac, the fool, ruined all by his excessive eagerness. He, too, was on his feet.

"A jack of wine! Yes, yes!" he cried. "Make haste. I, too, am thirsty."

Almost was there a quiver in his voice. Sam's ears detected it. He stood arrested, pondering his associate, and reading in his face the little rascal's treacherous intent.

He smiled a little.

"On second thoughts," said he, slowly, "it will be best if you go and I stays on guard."

Cahusac's mouth fell open; almost he turned pale. Inwardly Captain Blood cursed him for a triple fool.

"D'ye mean that ye don't trust me?" he demanded.

"It ain't that – not exactly," he was answered. "But it's me that stays."

Cahusac became really and vehemently angry. "Ah, ça! Name of God! If you don't trust me with him, I don't trust you neither."

"You don't need to. You know that I dursn't be tempted by his promises. That's why I'm the one to stay."

For a long moment the two ruffianly associates glowered at each other in angry silence. Then Cahusac's glance became sullen. He shrugged and turned aside, as if grudgingly admitting that Sam's reasoning was unanswerable. He stood pondering with narrowed eyes. Finally he bestirred himself as if upon sudden resolve.

"Ah, bah, I go!" he declared, and abruptly went.

As the door closed on the departing Frenchman, Sam resumed his seat at the table. Blood listened to the quickly receding footsteps until they had faded in the distance; then he broke the silence with a laugh that startled his companion.

Sam looked up sharply.

"What's amusing you now, Captain?"

Blood would have preferred, as we know, to deal with Cahusac. Cahusac was a certainty. Sam was hardly a possibility, obsessed as he obviously was by the fear of Spain. Still, this possibility must be exploited, however slender it might appear.

"Your rashness, bedad!" answered Captain Blood. "Ye'll not trust him to remain on guard, yet ye trust him out of your sight."

"And what harm can he do?"

"He might not return alone," said the Captain darkly.

"Blister me!" cried Sam. "If he tries any such tricks, I'll pistol him at sight. That's how I serves them that gets tricky with me."

"Ye'd be wise to serve him so in any case. He's a treacherous tyke, Sam, as I should know. Ye've baffled him tonight, and he's not the man to forgive. Ye should know that from his betrayal of me. But ye don't know. Ye've eyes, Sam, but no more sight than a blind puppy. And a head, Sam, but no more brains than are contained in a melon, or you'd never hesitate between Spain and me."

"Oh, that's it, is it?"

"Just that. Just fifty thousand pieces of eight that I offer, and that I pledge my honour to pay you, as well as pledging my honour to bear no malice and seek no vengeance. Even Cahusac assures you that my word is good, and was ready enough to accept it."

He paused. The rascally hunter was considering him silently, his face clay-coloured and the perspiration standing in beads upon his brow.

Presently he spoke hoarsely.

"Fifty thousand pieces, you said?" quoth he softly.

"To be sure. For where's the need to share with the French cur? D'ye dream he'd share with you if he could make it all his own by slipping a knife into your back? Come, Sam, make a bold bid for fortune. Damn your fears of Spain! Spain's a phantom! I'll protect you from Spain. You can lie safe aboard my flagship."

Sam's eyes flashed momentarily, then grew troubled again by thought.

"Fifty thousand. Ah, but the risk!"

"Sure, there's no risk at all," said Blood. "Not half the risk you run when it comes out that you sold me to Spain, as come out it will. Man, ye'll never leave Tortuga alive. And if ye did, my buccaneers would hunt ye to the end of the earth."

"But who's to tell?"

"There's always someone. Ye were a fool to undertake this job, a bigger fool to have taken Cahusac for partner. Hasn't he talked openly of vengeance? And won't he, therefore, be the first man suspected? And when they get him, as get him they will, isn't it as sure as judgment that he'll tell on you?"

"By Heaven, I believe you in that!" cried the man, presented with facts which he had never paused to consider.

"Faith, you may believe me in the rest as readily, Sam."

"Wait! Let me think!"

As once before, Captain Blood judged wisely that he had said enough for the moment. So far his success with Sam had been greater than he had dared to hope. The seed he had sown might now be left awhile to germinate.

The minutes sped, and Sam, elbows on the table and head in his hand, sat still and thoughtful. When at last he looked up, and the yellow light beat once more upon his face, Blood saw that it was pallid and gleaming. He tried to conjecture how far the poison he had dropped into Sam's mind might have done its work. Presently Sam plucked a pistol from his belt, and examined the priming. This seemed to Blood significant. But it was more significant still that he did not replace the pistol in his belt. He sat nursing it, his yellowish face firmly set, his coarse lips tight with purpose.

"Sam," said Captain Blood softly, "what have you decided?"

"I'll put it out of the power of that French mongrel to bubble me," said the ruffian.

"And nothing else?"

"The rest can wait."

With difficulty Captain Blood bridled his eagerness to force the pace.

Followed an apparently interminable time of waiting, in a silence broken only by the ticking of the Captain's watch where it lay upon the table. Then, faintly at first, but swiftly growing louder as it drew nearer, came a patter of steps in the lane outside. The door was pushed open, and Cahusac appeared carrying a great black jack.

Sam was already on his feet beyond the table, his right hand behind him.

"You've been a long time gone!" he grumbled. "What kept you?"

Cahusac was pale, and breathing rather hard, as if he had been running. Blood, whose mind was preternaturally alert, knowing that he had not run, looked elsewhere for a reason, and guessed it to lie in either fear or excitement.

"I made all haste," was the Frenchman's answer. "But I was athirst myself, and I stayed to quench it. Here's your wine."

He set the leathern jack upon the table.

And on the instant, almost at point-blank range, Sam shot him through the heart.

Through the rising cloud of smoke, whose acrid smell took him sharply in the throat and set him coughing, Blood saw a picture that he was to retain in his mind to the end of his days. Face downwards on the floor lay Cahusac with twitching limbs, whilst Sam leaned forward across the table to watch him, a grin on his long, animal face.

"I takes no risk with French swines like you," he explained himself, as if his victim could still hear him. Then he put down the pistol and reached for the jack. He raised it to his mouth, and poured a full draught down his parched throat. Noisily he smacked his lips as he set down the vessel. Then as a bitter aftertaste caught him in the throat he made a grimace, and apprehension charged suddenly through his mind and spread upon his countenance. He snatched up the jack again and thrust his nose into it, sniffing audibly like a questing dog. Next, with eyes dilating in horror, he stared at Blood out of a countenance that was leather-hued, and in an awful voice screamed a single word:

"Manzanilla!"

Then he swung round, and, uttering horrible, bloodcurdling

blasphemies, he hurled the jack and the remainder of its contents at the dead man on the floor.

A moment later he was doubled up by pain, and his hands were clawing and clutching at his stomach. When at last he mastered himself, without any thought now for Blood, or anything but the torment at work upon his vitals, he reeled across the room and pulled the door wide. The effort seemed to increase his agony. Again he was taken by a cramp that doubled him until his chest was upon his knees, and he howled the while, blaspheming at first, but presently uttering mere inarticulate, animal noises. He collapsed at length upon the floor, a raving, writhing lunatic.

Captain Blood considered him grimly, amazed but no whit intrigued. The riddle did not even require the key supplied by the single word that Sam had ejaculated. It was very plain to read.

Never had poetic retribution more fitly and promptly overtaken a pair of villains. Cahusac had loaded the wine with the poison of the manchineel apple, so readily procurable in Tortuga. With this, and so that he might be free to make a bargain with Captain Blood, and secure to himself the whole of the ransom the Captain offered, he had murdered his associate in the very moment in which, with the same intent, his associate had murdered him.

If Captain Blood had his own wits to thank for much, he had his luck to thank for more.

Gradually and slowly, as it seemed to the captive spectator, though in reality very quickly, the poisoned man's struggles grew fainter. Presently they were merely, and ever decreasingly sporadic; finally they ceased altogether, as did his breathing, which at the last had grown stertorous. He lay quite still in a cramped huddle against the open door.

By then Captain Blood was giving his attention to himself, and he had already wasted some moments and some strength in ineffectual straining at his bonds. A drumming on the door of the alcove reminded him of the presence of the woman who had been used unconsciously to decoy him. The shot and Sam's utterances had aroused her into activity. Captain Blood called to her.

"Break down the door! There's no one left here but myself."

Fortunately that door was but a feeble screen of slender planks, and it yielded quickly to the shoulder that she set against it. Wild-eyed and dishevelled, she broke at last into the room, then checked and screamed at what she beheld there.

Captain Blood spoke sharply to steady her.

"Now, don't be screeching for nothing, my dear. They're both as dead as the planks of the table, and dead men never harmed anyone. There's a knife yonder. Just be slipping it through these plaguey thongs."

In an instant he was free and on his feet, shaking out his ruffled plumage. He recovered his sword, his pistol, his watch, and his tobacco box. The gold and the jewels he pushed together in a little heap upon the table.

"Ye'll have a home somewhere in the world, no doubt. This will help you back to it, my girl."

She began to weep. He took up his hat, picked up his ebony cane from the floor, bade her good night, and stepped out into the lane.

Ten minutes later he walked into an excited, torchlit mob of buccaneers upon the mole, whom Hagthorpe and Wolverstone were organizing into search parties to scour the town. Wolverstone's single eye fiercely conned the Captain.

"Where the devil have you been?" he asked.

"Observing the luck that goes with blood-money," said Captain Blood.

6

THE GOLD AT SANTA MARIA

THE BUCCANEER fleet of five tall ships rode snugly at anchor in a sequestered creek on the western coast of the Gulf of Darien. A cable's length away, across gently heaving, pellucid waters, shot with opalescence by the morning sun, stretched a broad crescent of silver-grey sand; behind this rose the forest, vividly green from the rains now overpast, abrupt and massive as a cliff. At its foot, among the flaming rhododendrons thrusting forward like outposts of the jungle, stood the tents and rude log huts, palmetto-thatched, of the buccaneer encampment. They were careening there, refitting, and victualling with the fat turtles abounding thereabouts. This buccaneer host, some eight hundred strong, surged like a swarming hive, a motley mob, English and French in the main, but including odd Dutchmen and even a few West Indian half-castes. There were boucan-hunters from Hispaniola, lumbermen from Campeachy, vagrant seamen, runagate convicts from the plantations and proscribed outlaws from the Old World and the New.

Out of the jungle into their midst stepped, on that glowing April morning, three Darien Indians, the foremost of whom was of a tall, commanding presence, broad in the shoulder, and long in the arm. He was clad in drawers of hairy, untanned hide, and a red blanket served him for a cloak. His naked breast was streaked in black and red; in his nose he wore a crescent-shaped plate of beaten gold that hung down to his lip, and there were massive gold rings in his ears. A tuft of eagle's feathers sprouted from his sleek black hair, and he was armed with a javelin which he used as a staff.

He advanced calmly and without diffidence into their staring midst, and in primitive Spanish announced himself as the cacique Guanahani, called by the Spaniards Brazo Largo. He begged to be taken before their captain, to whom he referred also by his Hispanicized name of Don Pedro Sangre.

They conducted him aboard the flagship, the *Arabella*, and there, in the captain's cabin, the Indian cacique was courteously made welcome by a spare gentleman of a good height, very elegant in the Spanish fashion, whose resolute face, in cast of features and deep coppery tan, might, but for the eyes of a vivid blue, have been that of a Darien Indian.

Brazo Largo came to the point with a directness and economy of words to which his limited knowledge of Spanish constrained him.

"*Usted venir conmigo. Yo llevar usted mucho oro Español. Caramba!*" said he, in deep, guttural tones. Literally this may be rendered: "You come with me. I take you much Spanish gold," with the added vague expletive: "Caramba!"

The blue eyes flashed with interest. And, in the fluent Spanish acquired in less unregenerate days, Captain Blood answered him with a laugh:

"You are very opportune. Caramba! Where is this Spanish gold?"

"Yonder." The cacique pointed vaguely westward. "March ten days."

Blood's face grew overcast. Remembering Morgan's exploit across the isthmus, he leapt at a conclusion.

"Panama?" quoth he.

But the Indian shook his head, a certain impatience in his sternly wistful features.

"No. Santa Maria."

And he proceeded clumsily to explain that there, on the river of that name, was collected all the gold mined in the mountains of the district for ultimate transmission to Panama. Now was the time when the accumulations were heaviest. Soon the gold would be removed. If Captain Blood desired it – and Brazo Largo knew that there was a prodigious store – he must come at once.

Of the Indian's sincerity and goodwill towards himself

Captain Blood entertained no single doubt. The bitter hatred of Spain smouldering in the breast of all Indians under Spanish rule made them the instinctive allies of any enemy of Spain.

Captain Blood sat on the locker under the stern windows and looked out over the sunkissed water of the lagoon.

"How many men would be required?" he asked at last.

"Forty-ten, fifty-ten, perhaps," said Brazo Largo, from which the captain adduced that he meant four or five hundred.

He questioned him closely as to the nature of the country they would have to cross and the fortifications defending Santa Maria. Brazo Largo put everything in the most favourable light, smoothed away all difficulties, and promised not only himself to guide them, but to provide bearers to convey their gear. And all the time, with gleaming, anxious eyes, he kept repeating, to Captain Blood:

"Much gold. Much Spanish gold. Caramba!"

So often did he reiterate this parrot cry, and with such obvious intent to allure, that Blood began to ask himself did not this Indian protest too vehemently for utter honesty.

Pondering him, the Captain voiced his suspicion in a question.

"You are very eager that we should go, my friend?"

"Go. Yes. Go you," the Indian answered. "Spaniards love gold. Guanahani no love Spaniards."

"So that you want to spite them? Indeed, you seem to hate them very bitterly."

"Hate!" said Brazo Largo. His lips writhed, and he made guttural noises of emphatic affirmation. "Huh! Huh!"

"Well, well, I must consider."

He called the boatswain and delivered the cacique into his care for entertainment.

A council, summoned by bugle call from the quarterdeck of the *Arabella*, was held as soon thereafter as those concerned were come aboard.

Assembled about the oak table in the admiral's cabin, they formed a motley group, truly representative of the motley host encamped ashore. Blood, at the table's head, looking like a Grandee of Spain in the sombre richness of his black and silver, the long ringlets of his sable hair reaching to his collar of fine point; young Jerry Pitt, ingenuous of face, and in plain grey homespun, like the West of England Puritan that he had been; Hagthorpe, stiffly built, sternfaced, wearing showy clothes without grace, looked the simple, downright captain of fortune he was become; Wolverstone, herculean of build, bronzed of skin, and picturesquely untidy of person, with a single eye of a fierceness far beyond his nature, was perhaps the only one whose exterior really sorted with his trade; Mackett and James had the general appearance of mariners; lastly, Yberville, who commanded a French contingent, vying in elegance with Blood, had more the air and manner of a Versailles exquisite than of a leader of desperate and bloody pirates.

The admiral – for such was the title by now bestowed by his following upon Captain Blood – laid before them the proposal brought by Brazo Largo. He merely added that it came opportunely inasmuch as they were without immediate plans.

Opposition sprang naturally enough from those who were, first and foremost, seamen – from Pitt, Mackett, and James. Each in turn dwelt upon the hardships and the dangers attending long overland expeditions. Hagthorpe and Wolverstone, intent upon striking the Spaniard where he most would feel it, favoured the proposal, and reminded the council of Morgan's successful raid upon Panama. Yberville, a French Huguenot proscribed and banished for his faith, and chiefly intent upon slitting the throats of Spanish bigots wherever and whenever it might be done, proclaimed himself also for the venture in accents as mild and gentle as his words were hot and bloodthirsty.

Thus stood the council equally divided, and it remained for Blood to cast the vote that should determine the matter. But the Admiral hesitated, and in the end resolved to leave the decision to the men themselves. He would call for volunteers, and if their numbers reached the necessary, he would lead them across the isthmus, leaving the others with the ships.

The captains approving this, they went ashore at once,

taking the Indians with them. There Blood harangued the buccaneers, fairly expounding what was to be said for and what against the venture.

"I myself," he announced, "have resolved to go if so be that I am sufficiently supported." And then, after the manner of Pizarro on a similar occasion, he whipped out his rapier, and with the point of it drew a line in the sand. "Let those who choose to follow me across the isthmus step now to windward of this line."

A full half of them responded noisily to his invitation. They included to a man the boucan-hunters from Hispaniola – who were by now amphibious fighters, and the hardiest of all that hardy host – and most of the lumbermen from Campeachy, for whom swamp and jungle had no terrors.

Brazo Largo, his coppery face aglow with satisfaction, departed to collect his bearers; and he marched them, fifty stalwart savages, into the camp next morning. The adventurers were ready. They were divided into three companies, each commanded respectively by Wolverstone, Yberville – who had shed his fripperies and dressed himself in the leather garb of the hunter – and Hagthorpe.

In this order they set out, preceded by the Indian bearers, who carried their heavier gear: their tents, six small brass cannons of the kind known as sakers, cans for fireballs, good store of victuals – doughboys and strips of dried turtle – and the medicine-chest. From the decks of the fleet bugles called farewell, and, in pure ostentation, Pitt, who was left in charge, fired a salute from his guns as the jungle swallowed the adventurers.

Ten days later, having covered a distance of some 160 miles, they encamped within striking distance of their destination.

The first part of the journey had been the worst, when for six days their way lay over precipitous mountains, laboriously scaled on the one side and almost as laboriously descended on the other. On the seventh they rested in a great Indian village, where dwelt the king or chief cacique of the Indians of Darien, who, informed by Brazo Largo of their object, received and entreated them with all honour and consideration. Gifts were exchanged, knives, scissors, and beads on the one side, against plantains and sugar-cane on the other; and, reinforced here by scores of Indians, the buccaneers pushed on.

They came on the morrow to the river of Santa Maria, on which they embarked in a fleet of some seventy canoes of Indian providing. But it was a method of travelling that afforded at first little of the ease it had seemed to promise. All that day and the next they were constrained, at the distance of every stone's cast, to turn out, to haul the boats over shallows or rocks or over trees that had fallen across the channel. At last the navigation grew clearer, and presently, the river becoming broad and deep, the Indian's discarded the poles, with which hitherto they had guided the canoes, and took to paddles and oars.

And so they came at length by night within saker-shot of Santa Maria. The town stood on the river bank a half mile beyond the next bend.

The buccaneers proceeded to unload their arms, which were fast lashed to the insides of the canoes, the locks, as well as their cartridge boxes and powderhorns, well cased and waxed down. Then, not daring to make a fire lest they should betray their presence, they posted sentries, and lay down to rest until daybreak.

It was Blood's hope to take the Spaniards so completely by surprise as to seize their town before they could put themselves in posture of defence, and so snatch a bloodless victory. This hope, however, was dispelled at dawn, when a distant discharge of musketry, followed by a drum beating frenziedly à travailler within the town, warned the buccaneers that they had not stolen upon the Spaniards as unobserved as they imagined.

To Wolverstone fell the honour of leading the vanguard, and two score of his men were equipped with firepots – shallow cylindrical cans filled with resin and gunpowder – whilst others bore forward the sakers, which were under the special command of Ogle, the gunner from the *Arabella*. Next came Hagthorpe's company, whilst Yberville's brought up the rear.

They marched briskly through the woods to the very edge of the savannah, where, at a distance of perhaps two furlongs, they beheld their Eldorado.

Its appearance was disappointing. Here was no handsome city of New Spain such as they had been expecting, but a mere huddle of one-storeyed wooden buildings, thatched with wild cane and palmetto royal, clustering about a church, and defended by a fort. The place existed solely as a receiving station for the gold produced by the neighbouring mountains, and it numbered few inhabitants apart from the garrison and the slaves who worked in the goldfields. Fully half the area occupied by the town was taken up by the mud fort, which, whilst built to front the river, presented its flank to the savannah. For further defence against the very hostile Indians of Darien, Santa Maria was encircled by a stout palisade, some twelve feet high, pierced at frequent intervals by loopholes for musketry.

Within the town the drums had ceased, but a hum of human movement reached the buccaneers as they reconnoitred from the wood's edge before adventuring upon the open ground. On the parapet of the fort stood a little knot of men in morion and corselet. Above the palisade quivered a thin line of smoke to announce that Spanish musketeers were at their posts with matches ready lighted.

Blood ordered the sakers forward, having decided to breach the palisade towards the north-east angle, where a storming party would be least attainable by the gunners of the fort. Accordingly, Ogle mounted his battery at a point where a projecting spur of the forest on his left gave him cover. But now a faint easterly breeze beginning to stir carried forward the smoke of their fuses, to betray their whereabouts and invite the speculative fire of the Spanish musketeers. Bullets were already flicking and spattering through the branches about them when Ogle opened with his guns. At that short range it was an easy matter to smash a breach through wooden pales that had never been constructed to resist such weapons. Into that breach, to hold it, rushed the badly-captained Spanish troops.

A withering volley from the buccaneers scattered them, whereupon Blood ordered Wolverstone to charge.

"Fireballs to the van! Scatter as you advance, and keep low. God speed you, Ned! Forward!"

Forth they leapt at the double, and they were half way across the open before the Spaniards brought any considerable body of fire to bear upon them. They dropped, and lay supine in the short gamma grass until that frenzied musketry had slackened; then they leapt up again, and on at speed before the Spaniards could reload. And meanwhile Ogle had swung his sakers round to the right, and he was freely hurling his five-pound shot into the town on the flank of the advancing buccaneers.

Seven of Wolverstone's men lay on the ground where they had paused, ten more were picked off during that second forward rush, and now Wolverstone was at the breach. Over went a score of fireballs to scatter death and terror, and before the Spaniards could recover from the confusion caused by these, the dread enemy was upon them, yelling as they burst through the cloud of smoke and dust.

Nevertheless, the Spanish commander, a courageous if unimaginative officer named Don Domingo Fuentes, rallied his men so effectively that for a quarter of an hour the battle swayed furiously backwards and forwards in the breach.

But in a battle of cold steel there were no troops in the world that, in anything approaching equality of numbers, could have stood long against these hardy, powerful, utterly reckless fellows. Gradually, but relentlessly and inevitably, the cursing, screaming Spaniards were borne back by Wolverstone, supported now by the main host, with Blood himself in command.

Back and back they were thrust, fighting with a wild fury of despair, until the beaten-out line of their resistance suddenly snapped. They broke and scattered, to re-form again, and by a rearguard action gain the shelter of the fort, leaving the buccaneers in possession of the town.

Within the fort, with the two hundred demoralized survivors of his garrison of three hundred men, Don Domingo Fuentes took counsel, and presently sent a flag of truce to Captain Blood, offering to surrender with the honours of war.

But this was more than Blood could prudently concede. He knew that his men would probably be drunk before night, and he could not take the risk of having two hundred armed Spaniards in the neighbourhood at such a time. Being, however, averse to unnecessary bloodshed, and eager to make an end without further fighting, he returned a message to Don Domingo, pledging his word that if he would surrender at discretion, no violence should be done to the life or ultimate liberty of the garrison or the inhabitants of Santa Maria.

The Spaniards piled arms in the great square within the fort, and the buccaneers marched in with banners flying and trumpets blaring. The commander stood forward to make formal surrender of his sword. Behind him were ranged his two hundred disarmed men, and behind these again the scanty inhabitants of the town, who had sought refuge with them. They numbered not more than sixty, amongst whom were perhaps a dozen women, a few Negroes, and three friars in the black-and-white habit of Saint Dominic. The black slave population, it was presently ascertained, were at the mines in the mountains, whither they had just returned.

Don Domingo, a tall, personable man of thirty, in corselet and headpiece of black steel, with a little peaked beard that added length to his long, narrow face, addressed Captain Blood almost contemptuously.

"I have accepted your word," he said, "because, although you are a pirate scoundrel and a heretic in every other way dishonourable, you have at least the reputation of observing your pledges."

Captain Blood bowed. He was not looking his best. Half the coat had been torn from his back, and he had taken a scalp wound in the battle. But, however begrimed with blood and sweat, dust and gunpowder, his grace of deportment remained unimpaired.

"You disarm me by your courtesy," said he.

"I have no courtesies for pirate rogues," answered the

uncompromising Castilian. Whereupon Yberville, that fierce hater of all Spaniards, thrust himself forward, breathing hard, but was restrained by Captain Blood.

"I am waiting," Don Domingo intrepidly continued, "to learn your detestable purpose here; to learn why you, the subject of a nation at peace with Spain, dare to levy war upon Spaniards."

Blood laughed.

"Faith, now, it's just the lure of gold, which is as potent with pirates as with more respectable scoundrels all the world over – the very lure that has brought you Spaniards to plant this town conveniently near the goldfields. To be plain, Captain, we've come to relieve you of the season's yield, and as soon as ye've handed it over we'll relieve you also of our detestable presence."

The Spaniard laughed, and looked round at his men as if inviting them to laugh with him.

"To be sure, you conceive me a fool!" he said.

"I'm hoping, for your own sake, that ye're not."

"Do you think that, forewarned as I was of your coming, I kept the gold at Santa Maria?" He was derisive. "You are too late, Captain Blood. It is already on its way to Panama. We embarked it in canoes during the night, and sent a hundred men to guard it. That is how my garrison comes to be depleted, and that is why I have not hesitated to surrender."

He laughed again, observing Blood's rueful countenance.

A gust of rage swept through the ranks of the buccaneers pressing behind their leader. The news had run as swiftly as flame over gunpowder, and with similar effect in the explosion it produced. With yells of execration and sinister baring of weapons, they would have flung thmselves upon the Spanish commander, who – in their view – had cheated them, and they would have torn him there and then to pieces, had not Blood swung round and made of his own body a shield for Don Domingo.

"Hold!" he commanded, in a voice that blared like a trumpet. "Don Domingo is my prisoner, and I have pledged my word that he shall suffer no violence!"

Yberville it was who fiercely voiced the common thought.

"Will you keep faith with a Spanish dog who has cheated us? Let him be hanged!"

"It was his duty, and I'll have no man hanged for doing no more than that!"

For a moment Blood's voice was drowned in uproar. But he stood his ground impassively, his light eyes stern, his hand upheld, imposing some measure of restraint upon them.

"Silence, there, and listen! You are wasting time. The harm is far from being beyond repair. The gold has but a few hours' start. You Yberville, and you, Hagthorpe, re-embark your companies at once, and follow. You should come up with them before they reach the Gulf, but even if you don't, it is still a far cry to Panama, and you'll overtake them long before they're in sight of it. Away with you! Wolverstone's company will await your return here with me."

It was the only thing that could have stayed their fury and prevented a massacre of the unarmed Spaniards. They did not wait to be told a second time, but poured out of the fort and out of the town faster than they had poured into it. The only grumblers were the six score men of Wolverstone's company who were bidden to remain behind. They locked up the Spaniards, all together, in one of the long penthouses that made up the interior of the fort. Then they scattered about the little town in quest of victuals and such loot as there might be.

Blood turned his attention to the wounded. These, both his own men and the Spaniards, had been carried into another of the penthouses, where beds of hay and dried leaves had been improvised. There were between forty and fifty of them in all, of which number one quarter were buccaneers. In killed and wounded the Spanish loss had been upwards of a hundred men; that of the buccaneers between thirty and forty.

With a half dozen assistants, of whom one was a Spaniard who had some knowledge of medicine, Blood went briskly to work to set limbs and patch up wounds. Absorbed in his task, he paid no heed to the sounds outside, where the Indians, who had gone to earth during the fighting, were now encamped, until suddenly a piercing scream disturbed him.

Before he could move or speak, the door of the hut was wrenched open, and a woman, hugging an infant to her breast, reeled in, calling him wildly by his Hispanicized name.

"Don Pedro! Don Pedro Sangre!" Then, as he stepped forward, frowning, she gasped for breath, clutched her throat, and fell on her knees before him, crying agonizedly in Spanish: "Save him! They are murdering him – murdering him!"

She was a lithe young thing that has scarcely yet crossed the threshold of womanhood, whom at a casual glance you might, from her apparel and general appearance, have supposed a Spaniard of the peasant class. Her blue-black hair and liquid black eyes were such as you might see in many an Andalusian, nor was her skin much swarthier. Only the high cheekbones and peculiar, dusky lips proclaimed, upon a closer inspection, her real race.

"What is it?" said Blood. "Whom are they murdering?"

A shadow darkened the sunlit doorway, and Brazo Largo entered dignified and grimly purposeful.

Overmastering terror of the advancing Indian froze the crouching woman's tongue.

Now he was standing over her. He stooped and set his hand upon her shrinking shoulder. He spoke to her swiftly in the guttural tongue of Darien, and though Blood understood no word of it, yet he could not mistake the note of stern command.

Wildly, a mad thing, she looked up at Captain Blood.

"He bids me go to see them roasting him alive! Mercy, Don Pedro! Save him!"

"Save whom?" barked the Captain, almost in exasperation.

Brazo Largo answered him, explaining:

"She to be my daughter – this. Captain Domingo, he come village, one year now, and carry her away with him. Caramba! Now I roast him, and take her home." He turned to the girl. "Vamos," he commanded, continuing to use his primitive

Spanish, "you to come with me. You see him roast, then you come back village."

Captain Blood found the explanation ample. In a flash he recalled Guanahani's excessive eagerness to conduct him to the Spanish gold at Santa Maria, and how that eagerness had momentarily awakened suspicion in him. Now he understood. In urging this raid on Santa Maria, Brazo Largo had used him and his buccaneers to exploit a private vengeance and to recover an abducted daughter from Domingo Fuentes. But however deserving of punishment that abduction might appear, it was also revealed that, whether the girl had gone off willingly or not with the Spanish captain, his subsequent treatment of her had been such that she now desired to stay with him, and was concerned to the point of madness for his life and safety.

"Is it true what he says – that Don Domingo is your lover?" the Captain asked her.

"He is my husband, my married husband, and my love," she answered, a passion of entreaty in her liquid eyes. "This is our little baby. Do not let them kill him, Don Pedro! Oh, if they do," she moaned, "I shall kill myself!"

Captain Blood looked across at the grim-faced Indian.

"You hear? The Spaniard has been good to her. She desires his life. And his offence being as you say, it is her will that decides his fate. What have you done with him?"

Both clamoured at once, the father in angry, almost incoherent remonstrance, the girl in passionate gratitude. She sprang up and caught Blood's arm to drag him thence.

But Brazo Largo, still protesting, barred the way. He conveyed that in his view Captain Blood was violating the alliance between them.

"Alliance!" snorted Blood. "You have been using me for purposes of your own. You should have been frank with me and told me of your quarrel with Don Domingo before I pledged myself that he should suffer no violence. As it is . . ."

He shrugged, and went out quickly with the young mother. Brazo Largo stalked after them, glowering and thoughtful.

Outside, Blood ran into Wolverstone and a score of men who were returning from the town. He ordered them to follow him telling them that the Indians were murdering the Spanish captain.

"Good luck to them!" quoth Wolverstone, who had been drinking

Nevertheless, he followed, and his men with him, being in reality less bloody in deed than in speech.

Beyond the breach in the palisade they came upon the Indians – some forty of them – kindling a fire. Near at hand lay the helpless Don Domingo, bound with leather thongs. The girl sped to him, crooning soft Spanish endearments. He smiled in answer out of a white face that yet retained something of scornful calm. Captain Blood, more practical, followed with a knife and slashed away the prisoner's bonds.

There was a movement of anger among the Indians, instantly quelled by Brazo Largo. He spoke to them rapidly, and they stood disappointed but impassive. Wolverstone's men were there, musket in hand, blowing on their fuses.

They escorted Don Domingo back to the fort, his little wife tripping between him and the buccaneer captain, whom she enlightened on the score of the Indian's ready obedience to her father.

"He told them that you must have your way since you had pledged your word that Domingo's life should be safe. But that presently you would depart. Then they would return and deal with him and the other few Spaniards left here."

"We must provide against it," said Captain Blood, to reassure her.

When they got back to the fort they found that, in their absence, the remainder of the Indians, numbering rather more than a score, had broken into the shed where the Spaniards were confined. Fortunately the business had only just begun, and the Spaniards, although unarmed, were sufficiently numerous to offer a resistance, which, so far, had been effective. Nevertheless, Captain Blood came no more than in time to prevent a general massacre.

When he had driven off his savage allies, the Spanish commander desired a word with him.

"Don Pedro," he said, "I owe you my life. It is difficult to thank you."

"Pray don't give yourself the trouble," said Captain Blood. "I did what I did, not for your sake, but for the sake of my pledged word, though concern for your little Indian wife may have had some part in it."

The Spaniard smiled almost wistfully as his glance rested on her standing near him, her fond eyes devouring him.

"I was discourteous to you this morning. I beg your pardon."

"That is an ample amend."

The Captain was very dignified.

"You are generous. May I ask, sir, what is your intention regarding us – myself and the others?"

"Nothing against your liberty, as I promised. So soon as my men return, we shall march away and leave you."

The Spaniard sighed.

"It is what I feared. You will leave us, weakened in strength, our defences wrecked, at the mercy of Brazo Largo and his Indians, who will butcher us the moment your backs are turned. For don't imagine that they will leave Santa Maria until that is done."

Captain Blood considered, frowning.

"You have certainly stirred up a personal vengeance, which Brazo Largo will prosecute without pity. But what can I do?"

"You could suffer us to depart for Panama at once, whilst you are here to cover our retreat from your Indian allies."

Captain Blood made a gesture of impatience.

"Ah, wait, Don Pedro! I would not propose it did I not deem you, from what I have seen, to be a man of heart, a gallant gentleman, pirate though you may be. Also you will observe that, since you have disavowed any intention of retaining us as prisoners, I am really not asking for anything at all."

It was quite true, and, upon turning it over in his mind, Captain Blood came to the conclusion that they would be much better off at Santa Maria without these Spaniards, who had to be guarded on the one hand and protected on the other. Therefore he consented. Wolverstone demurred. But when Blood asked him what possible purpose could be served by keeping the Spaniards at Santa Maria, Wolverstone confessed that he did not know. All that he could say was that he trusted no living Spaniard, which did not seem to have any bearing on the question.

So Captain Blood went off to find Brazo Largo, who was sulking on the wooden jetty below the fort.

The Indian rose at his approach, an exaggerated impassivity on his countenance.

"Brazo Largo," said the Captain, "your men have set my word at naught and put my honour in danger."

"I not understand," the Indian answered him. "You make friends with Spanish thieves?"

"Make friends! No. But when they surrendered to me I promised, as the condition of their surrender; that no harm should come to them. Your men would have murdered them in violation of that promise had I not prevented it."

The Indian was contemptuous.

"Huh! Huh! You not my friend. I bring you to Spanish gold, and you turn against me."

"There is no gold," said Blood. "But I am not quarrelling on that. You should have told me, my friend, before we came this journey, that you were using me so that we might deliver up to you your Spanish enemy and your daughter. Then I should not have passed my word to Don Domingo that he would be safe, and you could have drunk the blood of every Spaniard in the place. But you deceived me, Brazo Largo."

"Huh! Huh!" said Brazo Largo. "I not say anything more."

"But I do. They are your men. After what has happened, I cannot trust them. And my pledged word compels me to defend the Spaniards so long as I am here."

The Indian bowed.

"Perfectamente! So long as you here. What then?"

"If there is trouble again, there may be shooting, and some of your braves may be hurt. I should regret that more than the loss of the Spanish gold. It must not happen, Brazo Largo. You must summon your men, and let me consign them to one of the huts in the fort for the present – for their own sakes."

Brazo Largo considered. Then he nodded. He was a very reasonable savage. And so the Indians were assembled, and Brazo Largo, smiling the smile of the man who knows how to wait, submitted to confinement with them in one of the penthouses.

The assembled buccaneers murmured a little among themselves, and Wolverstone ventured to express the general disapproval.

"Ye're pushing matters rather far, Captain, to risk trouble with the Indians for the sake of those Spanish dogs!"

"Oh, not for their sake. For the sake of my pledged word, and that bit of an Indian girl with her baby. The Spanish commander has been good to her, and he's a gallant fellow."

"God help us!" said Wolverstone, and swung away in disgust.

An hour later the Spaniards were embarking from the jetty, under the eyes of the buccaneers, who, from the mud wall of the fort, watched their departure with some misgivings. The only weapons Blood allowed the voyagers were half a dozen fowling-pieces. They took with them, however, a plentiful supply of victuals, and Don Domingo, like the prudent captain, was very particular in the matter of water. Himself he saw the casks stowed aboard the canoes. Then he took his leave of Captain Blood.

"Don Pedro," he said. "I have no words in which to praise your generosity. I am proud to have had you for my enemy."

"Let us say that you are fortunate."

"Fortunate, too. I shall tell it wherever there are Spaniards to hear me that Don Pedro Sangre is a very gallant gentleman."

"I shouldn't," said Captain Blood. "For no one will believe you."

Protesting still, Don Domingo stepped aboard the piragua that carried his Indian wife and their half-caste baby. His men pushed the vessel off into the current, and he started on his journey to Panama, armed with a note in Captain Blood's hand, ordering Yberville and Hagthorpe to pass him unscathed in the event of his coming up with them.

In the cool of the evening the buccaneers sat down to a feast in the open square of the fort. They had found great stores of fowls in the town, and some goats, besides several hogsheads of excellent wine in the house of the Dominican fathers. Blood, with Wolverstone and Ogle, supped in the departed commander's well-equipped quarters, and through the open windows watched with satisfaction the gaiety of his feasting followers. But his satisfaction was not shared by Wolverstone, whose humour was pessimistic.

"Stick to the sea in future, Captain, says I," he grumbled between mouthfuls. "There's no packing off a treasure there when we come within saker-shot. Here we are, after ten days' march, with another ten days' march in front of us! And I'll thank God if we get back as light as we came, for as likely as not we shall have differences to settle with old Brazo Largo, and we'll be lucky if we get back at all, ever. Ye've bungled it this time, Captain."

"Ye're just a foolish heap of brawn, Ned," said the Captain. "I've bungled nothing at all. And as for Brazo Largo, he's an understanding savage, so he is, who'll keep friends with us if only because he hates the Spaniards."

"And ye behave as if ye loved 'em," said Wolverstone. "Ye're all smirks and bows for this plaguey commander who cheated us out of the gold, and ye—"

"Sure, now, he was a gallant fellow, Spaniard or no Spaniard," said Blood. "In packing off the gold when he heard of our approach he did his duty. Had he been less gallant, he would have gone off with it himself, instead of remaining here at his post. Gallantry calls to gallantry; and that's all I have to say about it."

And then, before Wolverstone could make answer, sharp and clear above the noise the buccaneers were making rang the note of a bugle from the side of the river. Blood leapt to his feet.

"It will be Hagthorpe and Yberville returning!" he cried.

"Pray God they've got the gold at last!" said Wolverstone.

They dashed out into the open and made for the parapet, to which the men were already swarming. As Blood reached it, the first of the returning canoes swung alongside the jetty, and Hagthorpe sprang out of it.

"Ye're soon returned," cried Blood, leaping down to meet him. "What luck?"

Hagthorpe, tall and square, his head swathed in a yellow kerchief, faced him in the dusk.

"Certainly not the luck that you deserve, Captain." His tone was curious.

"Do you mean that you didn't overtake them?"

Yberville, stepping ashore at that moment, answered for his fellow-leader.

"There was nobody to overtake, Captain. He fooled you, that treacherous Spaniard; he lied when he told you that he had sent off the gold; and you – you believed him – you believed a Spaniard!"

"If ye'd come to the point now!" said Captain Blood. "Did I hear ye say he had not sent off the gold? D'ye mean that it is still here?"

"No," said Hagthorpe. "What we mean is that, after he had so fooled you with his lies that ye didn't even trouble to make search, you allowed them to go off scot-free, taking the gold with them."

"What!" the Captain barked at him. "How do you know this?"

"A dozen miles or so from here we came upon an Indian village; and we had the wit to stop and inquire how long it might be since a Spanish fleet of canoes had gone that way. They answered that no such fleet had passed today, or yesterday, or any day since the last rains. That's how we knew that your gallant Spaniard had lied. We put about at once to return, and midway back we ran into Don Domingo's party. The meeting took him by surprise. He had not reckoned that we'd seek information so soon. But he was as smooth and specious as ever, and a deal more courteous. He confessed quite frankly that he had lied to you, adding that subsequently, after our departure, he had purchased his liberty, and that of all who accompanied him, by surrendering the gold to you. He was instructed by you, he said, to order us to return at once; and he showed us your note of hand, which made him safe."

And then Yberville took up the tale.

"But we being not quite so trustful of Spaniards, and arguing that he who lies once will lie again, took them ashore and subjected them to a search."

"And d'ye tell me that you found the gold?" cried Blood, aghast.

Yberville paused a moment and smiled.

"You had permitted them to victual themselves generously against that journey. Did you observe at what spring Don Domingo filled his water-casks?"

"His water-casks?" quoth Blood.

"Were casks of gold – there's six or seven hundredweight of it at the least. We've brought it with us."

By the time the joyous uproar excited by that announcement had settled down, Captain Blood had recovered from his chagrin. He laughed.

"I give you best," he said to Hagthorpe and Yberville. "And the least I can do, by way of amends for having suffered myself to be so utterly fooled, is to forgo my share of the booty." And then, on a graver note: "What did you do with Don Domingo?"

"I would have shot him for his perfidy!" said Hagthorpe fiercely. "But Yberville here – Yberville, of all men – turned mawkish, and besought me to let him go."

Shamefacedly the young Frenchman hung his head, avoiding the Captain's glance of questioning surprise.

"Oh, but after all," he flung out, defiant almost in self-defence, "what would you? There was a lady in the case – his little Indian wife."

"Faith, now, it was of her that I was thinking," said Blood. "And for her sake and his – oh, and also for our own – it will be best to tell Brazo Largo that Don Domingo and his wife were slain in the fight for the gold. The sight of the recovered water-casks will amply confirm the story. Thus there should be peace for all concerned, himself included."

And so, although they brought back that rich booty from Santa Maria, Blood's part in that transaction was rated as one of his few failures. Not so, however, did he himself account it.

7

THE LOVE-STORY OF JEREMY PITT

THE LOVE-STORY of Jeremy Pitt, the young Somersetshire
shipmaster, whose fate had been likened with Peter Blood's
since the disastrous night of Sedgmoor, belongs to those great
days of Blood's career when he commanded a fleet of five ships
and over a thousand men of mixed nationality, held in a
discipline to which his skill and good fortune made them willing
to submit.

He had lately returned from a very successful raid upon the
Spanish pearling fleet in the Rio de la Hache. He had come
back to Tortuga to refit, and this not before it was necessary.
There were several other buccaneer vessels in the harbour of
Cayona at the time, and the little town was boisterous with
their revelry. Its taverns and rum-shops throve, whilst the
taverners and the women, white and half-castes, as mixed in
origin and nationality as the buccaneers themselves, eased the
rovers of a good deal of the plunder of which they had eased
the Spaniards, who, again, were seldom better than robbers.

Usually these were unquiet times for Monsieur d'Ogeron,
the agent of the French West India Company and Governor
of Tortuga.

M. d'Ogeron himself, as we know, did very well out of the
buccaneers in the percentages on their prizes which they very
readily paid as harbour dues, and in other ways. But M.
d'Ogeron, you will remember, had two daughters, the dark
and stately Madeleine and the slight and joyous brunette
Lucienne. Now Madeleine, for all her stateliness, had once
succumbed to the wooing of a ruffianly buccaneer named
Levasseur. To abstract her from this danger her father had
shipped her off to France. But Levasseur, getting wind of it
in time, had followed, seized the ship that carried her, and the

worst might have befallen her but for the timely intervention of Captain Blood, who delivered her, unscathed, from his clutches and restored her, sobered by the experience, to her father.

Since then M. d'Ogeron had sought to practise discretion in the guests he received in the big white house set in its fragrant garden just above the town.

Captain Blood, by the service he had rendered the family on that occasion, had come to be regarded almost as a member of it. And since his officers, all of them driven to their trade as a consequence of transportation suffered for a political offence, were men of a different stamp from the ordinary buccaneer, they, too, were well received.

Now this in itself created a difficulty. If Monsieur d'Ogeron's house was open to the captains who followed Blood, he could not without offence close it to other buccaneer commanders. Therefore he was constrained to tolerate the visits of some whom he neither liked nor trusted, and this despite the pro-tests of a guest from France, the fastidious and delicate Monsieur de Mercoeur, who cared little for the society of any of them.

Monsieur de Mercoeur was the son of one of the governors of the French West India Company, sent by his father on a voyage of instruction to the settlements in which the company was interested. The frigate *Cygne*, which had brought him a week ago, had been at anchor since in Cayona Bay, and would continue there until the young gentleman should see fit to de-part again. From this his social consequence may be inferred. Obviously he was a person whose wishes a colonial governor would do his utmost to respect. But how was he to respect them, for instance, where such a truculent, swaggering fellow as Captain Tondeur of the *Reine Margot* was concerned? Monsieur d'Ogeron did not quite see how he could forbid him the house, as Monsieur de Mercoeur would have desired, not even when it became apparent that the rascal was attracted thither by Mademoiselle Lucienne.

Another who was yielding to the same attraction was young

Jeremy Pitt. But Pitt was a fellow of a very different stamp, and if his courtship of Lucienne occasioned Monsieur d'Ogeron some distress, at least it caused him no such uneasiness as that begotten by Tondeur.

If ever there was a man designed by nature for a lover, that man was Jeremy Pitt, with his frank, smooth, comely face, his ingenuous blue eyes, his golden locks and his neatly-apparelled, graceful figure. With the vigour of a man he combined the gentleness of a woman. Anything less like a conspirator, which he had been, and a buccaneer, which he was, it would be impossible to conceive. He had, too, ingratiating ways and a gift of almost poetical expression to complete his equipment as the ideal lover.

His instincts – or it may have been his hopes – and perhaps something in the lady's kindly manner, led him to believe that Lucienne was not indifferent to him; and so one evening, under the fragrant pimento trees in her father's garden, he told her that he loved her, and whilst she was still breathless from the effects of that avowal he kissed her lips.

Quivering and troubled, she stood before him after that operation. "Monsieur Jeremy . . . you . . . you should not . . . you should not have done that." In the fading light Mr Pitt saw that there were tears in her eyes. "If my father knew—"

Jeremy interrupted her with emphasis:

"He shall. I mean him to know. He shall know now." And as Monsieur de Mercoeur and Madeleine were at that moment approaching, Jeremy departed at once in quest of the Governor of Tortuga.

Monsieur d'Ogeron, that slight, elegant gentleman who had brought with him to the New World the courtliness of the Old, could scarcely dissemble his distress. Monsieur d'Ogeron, grown wealthy in his governorship, had ambitions for his motherless daughters, whom he contemplated removing before very long to France.

He said so, not crudely, or bluntly, but with an infinite delicacy calculated to spare Mr Pitt's feelings; and he added that she was already promised in marriage.

Jeremy's face was overspread with blank astonishment.

"Promised! But she told me nothing of this!" He forgot that he had never really given her an opportunity.

"It may be that she does not realize. You know how these things are contrived in France."

Mr Pitt began an argument upon the advantages of natural selection, nipped by Monsieur d'Ogeron before he had properly developed it.

"My dear Mr Pitt, my friend, consider, I beg, your position in the world. You are a filibuster – in short, an adventurer. I do not use the term offensively. I merely mean that you are a man who lives by adventure. What prospect of security, of domesticity, could you offer a delicately-nurtured girl? If you, yourself, had a daughter, should you gladly give her to such a man?"

"If she loved him," said Mr Pitt.

"Ah! But what is love, my friend?"

Although perfectly aware of what it was from his late rapture and present misery, Jeremy found a difficulty in giving expression to his knowledge. Monsieur d'Ogeron smiled benignly upon his hesitation.

"To a lover, love is sufficient, I know. To a parent, more is necessary so as to quiet his sense of responsibility. You have done me an honour, Monsieur Pitt. I am desolated that I must decline it. It will be better that we do not trouble our mutual esteem by speaking of this again."

Now, when a young man discovers that a certain young woman is necessary to his existence, and when he believes with pardonable egotism that he is equally necessary to hers, he does not abandon the quest at the first obstacle.

At the moment, however, the matter could be pursued no further because of the interruption afforded by the entrance of the stately Madeleine accompanied by Monsieur de Mercoeur. The young Frenchman's eyes and voice sought Lucienne. He had charming eyes and a charming voice, and was altogether a charming person, impeccable as to dress and manners. In build he was almost tall, but so slight and frail that he looked as if a strong wind might blow him over; yet he possessed an assurance of address oddly at variance with his almost valetudinarian air.

He seemed surprised not to find Lucienne with her father. He desired, he announced, to persuade her to sing again some of those Provençal songs with which last night she had delighted them. His gesture took in the harpsichord standing in a corner of the well-appointed room. Madeleine departed to seek her sister. Mr Pitt rose to take his leave. In his present mood he did not think he could bear to sit and hear Lucienne singing Provençal songs for the delight of Monsieur de Mercoeur.

He went off with his woes to Captain Blood, whom he found in the great cabin of the *Arabella*.

The Captain laid down his well-thumbed copy of Horace to lend an ear to the plaint of his young friend and shipmaster. Lounging on the cushioned locker under the sternports, Captain Blood thereafter delivered himself, as sympathetic in manner as he was uncompromising in matter. Monsieur d'Ogeron was entirely right, the Captain opined, when he said that Jeremy's occupation in life did not justify him in taking a wife.

"And that's only half the reason for abandoning this notion. The other is that Lucienne, charming and seductive child though she may be, is a thought too light to promise any peace and security to a husband not always at hand to guard and check her. That fellow Tondeur goes daily to the Governor's house. It hasn't occurred to you, now, to ask yourself what is attracting him? And why does this frail French dandy, Monsieur de Mercoeur, linger in Tortuga? Oh, and there are others I could name who have had, no doubt, your own delectable experience with a lady who's never reluctant to listen to a tale of love."

"Now devil take your lewdness!" roared out Pitt, with all a lover's unbounded indignation. "By what right do you say such a thing as that?"

"By the right of sanity and an unclouded vision. Ye'll not be

144

the first to have kissed Mademoiselle Lucienne's lips; and ye'll not be the last neither, not even if ye marry her. She has a beckoning eye, so she has, and it's the uneasy husband I should be at sea if she were my wife. Be thankful ye're not the husband of her father's choice. Lovely things like Lucienne d'Ogeron were created just to trouble the world.''

Jeremy would listen to no more of this blasphemy. It was like Blood, whom he bitterly denounced as without faith and without ideals, to think so vilely of the sweetest, purest saint in all the world. On that he flung out of the cabin, and left the Captain free to return to his Horace.

Blood, however, had planted a rankling seed in our young lover's heart. The clear perception of grounds for jealousy is a sword that can slay love at a stroke; but the mere suspicion of their existence is a goad to drive a lover on. Feverishly, then, on the morrow, and utterly oblivious of Monsieur d'Ogeron's rejection of his suit, Mr Pitt made his way betimes to the white house above the town. It was earlier than his wont, and he came upon the lady of his dreams walking in the garden. With her walked Captain Tondeur, that man of sinister reputation. It was said of him that once he had been a fencing master in Paris, and that he had taken to the sea so as to escape the justice it was desired to mete out to him by the family of a gentleman he had killed in a duel. He was a man of middle height and deceptive slimness, for he was as tough as whipcord. He dressed with a certain raffish elegance and moved with agile grace. His countenance was undistinguished save for the eyes, which, if small and round and black, were singularly penetrating. They were penetrating Mr Pitt now with an arrogant stare that seemed to invite him to depart again. The Captain's right arm was about the waist of Mademoiselle Lucienne. It remained there notwithstanding Mr Pitt's appearance, until presently, after a moment's surprised pause, the lady disengaged herself in some embarrassment.

"It is Monsieur Jeremy!" she cried, and added, quite needlessly, thought Mr Pitt: "I was not expecting you."

Jeremy took the hand she proffered and bore it to his lips,

more or less mechanically, whilst mumbling a greeting in his indifferent French. Followed an exchange of commonplaces, and then an awkward pause, at the end of which said Tondeur with a scowl:

"When a lady tells me that I am unexpected, I understand her to mean that I am inopportune."

"No doubt a common experience in your life."

Captain Tondeur smiled. Your practised duellist is always self-possessed.

"At least not a subject for pertness. It is not always wise to be pert. The moment's glitter may lead to painful instruction."

Lucienne intervened. She was a little breathless. Her eyes were scared.

"But what is this? What are you saying? You are wrong, Monsieur le Capitaine, to assume Monsieur Jeremy inopportune. Monsieur Jeremy is my friend, and my friends are never inopportune."

"Not perhaps to you, mademoiselle. But to other friends of yours they can be monstrously so."

"Again you are mistaken." Her manner was frigid. "He is no friend of mine to whom other friends of mine are unwelcome in my presence."

The Captain bit his lip, and Jeremy took a fragment of comfort, for all that he still hotly remembered that arm about the waist of the woman whose lips he had kissed last night and also Captain Blood's condemnation of her.

The elements of a very pretty quarrel were shattered by the sudden appearance of Monsieur d'Ogeron and Monsieur de Mercoeur. Both were out of breath as if they had been hurrying. They checked, however, and seemed relieved when they saw who was present. It was as if Monsieur d'Ogeron found not quite what he had expected, and relief upon the safety for Lucienne which is believed to reside in numbers. Their advent put an end to acrimony, and perhaps because he was in the humour for little else, Captain Tondeur presently took his leave. A smile of disquieting significance accompanied his parting words to Jeremy.

146

"I shall look forward, monsieur, to an early opportunity of continuing our interesting discussion."

Anon, when Jeremy, too, would have departed, Monsieur d'Ogeron detained him. "Remain yet a moment, Monsieur Pitt."

He took the young man by the arm in a friendly manner and drew him away from Monsieur de Mercoeur and Lucienne. They moved up the avenue and entered a tunnel fashioned of overarching orange trees imported from Europe; a cool place this, where the ripe fruit glowed like lamps against the dusky green.

"I did not like the parting words of Captain Tondeur, nor yet his smile. That is a very dangerous man. You would be wise to beware of him."

Jeremy bridled a little. "Do you suppose I fear him?"

"I suppose you would be prudent to do so. A very dangerous man. A canaille. He comes here too much."

"Regarding him as you do, why do you permit it?"

Monsieur d'Ogeron made a grimace. "Regarding him as I do, how shall I deny him?"

"You are afraid of him?"

"I confess it. Oh, not for myself, Monsieur Pitt. But there is Lucienne. He pays his court to her."

Jeremy quivered with fury. "Could you not forbid him your house?"

"Of course." Monsieur d'Ogeron smiled crookedly. "I did something of the kind once before, in the case of Levasseur. You know the story."

"Oh, but . . . Oh, but . . ." Jeremy encountered a difficulty. Finally he surmounted it. "Mademoiselle Madeleine was so misguided as to lend herself to the scheme of Levasseur. You do not dream that Mademoiselle Lucienne—"

"Why should I not dream it? This Tondeur, canaille though he be, is not without attraction, and he has over Levasseur the advantage that he was once a gentleman and can still display the manners of one when it suits him. An inexperienced child like Lucienne is easily allured by your bold, enterprising wooer."

Mr Pitt was a little sick at heart and bewildered. "Yet what good can temporizing do? Sooner or later you will have to reject him. And then . . . What then?"

"It is what I ask myself," said Monsieur d'Ogeron almost lugubriously. "Yet an evil that is postponed may ultimately be removed by chance." And then, suddenly, his manner changed. "Oh, but your pardon, my dear Mr Pitt. Our talk is taking a turn very far from what I intended. A father's anxiety! I meant to do no more than utter a warning, and I beg that you will heed it."

Mr Pitt thought he understood. What was in Monsieur d'Ogeron's mind was that Tondeur scented a rival in Jeremy and that such a man would take prompt means to eliminate a rival.

"I am obliged to you, Monsieur d'Ogeron. I can take care of myself."

"I trust so. Sincerely I trust so." And on that they parted.

Jeremy went back to dine on board the *Arabella*, and after dinner, pacing the poop with Blood, he told him what had passed.

Captain Blood was thoughtful. "There is cause enough to warn you. Though why the Governor should be troubling to do so is just a trifle odd. I'll pay him a visit, so I will. I may be able to help him, though I don't yet see how. Meanwhile, Jerry, if ye're prudent, ye'll be keeping the ship. Devil a doubt but Tondeur will be looking for you."

"And I am to avoid him, am I?" snorted Jeremy.

"If ye're wise."

"If I'm a coward."

"Now isn't a live coward better than a dead fool, which is what ye'll be if ye come to grips with Master Tondeur? Ye'll not be forgetting the man's a fencing master: whilst you . . . Pshaw! It would be just murder, so it would. And where's the glory of suffering that?"

Pitt knew it in his heart and yet would not admit the humiliating knowledge. Therefore, neglecting Blood's advice, he went ashore on the morrow, and was sitting with Hagthorpe and Wolverstone in the tavern of The King of France when Tondeur found him.

It was in the neighbourhood of noon, and the common room was thronged with buccaneers, a few ordinary seamen from the *Cygne*, beachcombers and the landsharks of both sexes who prey upon seafaring men, and particularly upon buccaneers, who are ever prodigal of their broad pieces of eight. The air of the ill-lighted place was heavy with the reek of rum, tobacco, spunyarn and humanity.

Tondeur came forward leisurely, his left hand resting on his hilt, exchanging nods and bringing up at last before Jeremy's table.

"You permit?" quoth he, and without waiting for an answer, he drew up a stool and sat down. "I am fortunate so soon to be able to resume the little discussion that yesterday was interrupted."

Jeremy, understanding perfectly what was coming, stared at him uneasily. His two companions, understanding nothing, stared with him.

"We discussed inopportuneness, I think, and your sluggishness in perceiving that your presence was not required."

Jeremy leaned forward. "What we discussed is no matter. You are here, I think, to pick a quarrel with me."

"I?" Captain Tondeur stared and frowned. "Why should you suppose that? You do me no harm. It is not in your power to do me harm. You are not even in my way. If you were, I should crack you like a flea." He laughed contemptuously, offensively, and by that laugh flung Jeremy, as he intended, into a passion.

"I am no flea for your cracking."

"Are you not?" Tondeur got up. "Then be careful not to pester me again, or you may find yourself under my thumbnail. You have your warning." He spoke loudly, so that all might hear him, and his tone brought a hush upon the crowded room.

He was turning away contemptuously when Jeremy's answer arrested him.

"You insolent dog!"

Captain Tondeur checked. He raised his brows. A snarling smile lifted an end of his little moustache. And meanwhile the burly Wolverstone, still understanding nothing, sought instinctively to restrain Jeremy, who had also risen.

"Dog?" said the Captain slowly. "Dog, eh? It is apt enough. the dog and the flea. All the same, I do not like dog. You will be so good as to retract dog. You will retract it at once. I am not a patient man, Monsieur Pitt."

"Certainly I will retract it," said Jeremy. "I'll not insult an animal."

"Meaning me?"

"Meaning the dog. I'll substitute instead—"

"Substitute rat," said a sharp voice from the background, which made Tondeur spin round where he stood.

Just within the doorway lounged Captain Blood, tall and elegant, in his black and silver, leaning upon his ebony cane. The intensely blue eyes in his clear-cut suntanned face met and held the stare of Captain Tondeur. He sauntered forward, speaking easily and without stress as he came.

"Rat, I think, describes you better, Captain Tondeur." And he stood waiting for the Frenchman's answer.

It came presently in the wake of a sneering laugh. "I see. I see. The little shipmaster here is to be protected. Papa Blood intervenes to save the little coward."

"Certainly he is to be protected. I will not have my shipmaster murdered by a bully-swordsman. That is why I intervene. You might have foreseen it, Captain Tondeur. As for cowardice, you paltry rascal, that is the attribute of the rat to which I liken you. You trade upon a certain skill with the sword; but you are careful to employ it only against those you have reason to believe unskilled. That is the coward's way. Oh, and the murderer's, which is, I believe, what they call you in France."

"That's a lie, anyway," said Tondeur, livid.

Captain Blood was unperturbed. He was deliberately playing Tondeur's own game of baiting an opponent into fury. "You may proceed to prove it upon me, in which case I shall retract, either before or after killing you. Thus you will die in honour, having lived in dishonour. The inner room there is spacious and empty. We can—"

But Tondeur interrupted him, sneering. "I am not so easily distracted. My affair is with Mr Pitt."

"Let it wait until you have settled mine."

Tondeur contained himself. He was white with passion and breathing hard.

"Look you, Captain Blood: I have been insulted by this shipmaster of yours, who called me dog in the presence here of these. You deliberately seek to thrust yourself into a quarrel that does not concern you. It is not to be tolerated. I appeal me to the company."

It was a shrewd move and the result justified it. The company was on his side. Such of Captain Blood's own men who were present kept silent, whilst the remainder loudly gave the Frenchman reason. Not even Hagthorpe and Wolverstone could do more than shrug, and Jeremy made matters utterly hopeless by declaring himself on the side of the enemy.

"Captain Tondeur is in the right, Peter. You are not concerned in this affair."

"You hear?" cried Tondeur.

"I am concerned, whatever may be said. You mean murder, you scum, and I mean to prevent it." Captain Blood abandoned his cane, and carried his hand to his sword.

But a dozen sprang to restrain him, protesting so forcibly and angrily that, finding himself without even the support of his own followers, Captain Blood was forced to give way.

Even the staunch and loyal Wolverstone was muttering in his ear: "Nay, Peter! A God's name! Ye'll provoke a riot for naught. Ye were just too late. The lad had committed himself."

"And what were you doing to let him? Well, well! There he goes, the rash fool."

Pitt was already leading the way to the inner room: a lamb not merely going to the slaughter, but actually conducting the butcher. Hagthorpe was with him. Tondeur followed closely, and others brought up the rear.

Captain Blood, with Wolverstone at his side, went with the crowd, controlling himself now with difficulty.

The inner room was spacious and almost bare. What few chairs and tables it contained were swiftly thrust aside. The place was little more than a shed or penthouse built of wood, and open from the height of some three feet along the whole of one side. Through this opening the afternoon sun was flooding the place with light and heat.

Sword in hand, stripped to the waist, the two men faced each other on the bare earthen floor, Jeremy, the taller of the two, sturdy and vigorous; the other, light, sinewy and agile as a cat. The taverner and the drawers were among the press of onlookers ranged against the inner wall; two or three young viragos were in the crowd, but most of the women had remained in the common room.

Captain Blood and Wolverstone had come to stand towards the upper end of the room at a table on which there were various objects cleared from the others: some drinking cans, a couple of flagons, a jack and a pair of brass candlesticks with wide saucer-like stands. In the moments of waiting, whilst preliminaries were being settled, Blood, pale under his tan and with a wicked look in his blue eyes, had glanced at these objects, idly fingering one or two of them as if he would have employed them as missiles.

Hagthorpe was seconding Jeremy. Ventadour, the lieutenant of the *Reine Margot*, stood by Tondeur. The antagonists faced each other along the length of the room, with the sunlight on their flank. As they took up their positions, Jeremy's eyes sought Blood's. The lad smiled to him. Blood, unsmiling, answered by a sign. For a moment there was inquiry in Jeremy's glance, then understanding followed.

Ventadour gave the word: "*Allez, messieurs!*" and the blades rang together.

Instantly, obeying that signal which he had received from his captain, Jeremy broke ground, and attacked Tondeur on his left. This had the effect of causing Tondeur to veer to that side, with the result that he had the sun in his eyes. Now was

Jeremy's chance if he could take it, as Blood had forseen when he had signalled the manoeuvre. Jeremy did his best and by the assiduity of his endeavours kept his opponent pinned in that position of disadvantage. But Tondeur was too strong for him. The practised swordsman never lost touch of the opposing blade, and presently, venturing a riposte, availed himself of the ensuing disengage to break ground in his turn, and thus level the position, the antagonists having now completely changed places.

Blood ground his teeth to see Jeremy lose the only advantage he possessed over the sometime fencing master who was bent on murdering him. Yet the end did not come as swiftly as he expected. Jeremy had certain advantages of reach and vigour. But these did not account for the delay, nor yet did the fact that the fencing master may have been a little rusty from lack of recent practice. Tondeur played a closely circling blade, which found openings everywhere in the other's wide and clumsy guard. Yet he did not go in to finish. Was he deliberately playing with his victim as cat with mouse, or was it perhaps that, standing a little in awe of Blood and of possible consequences should he kill Pitt outright, he aimed merely at disabling him?

The spectators, beholding what they beheld, were puzzled by the delay. They were puzzled still more when Tondeur again broke ground, so as to place his back to the sun and turn his helpless opponent into the position of disadvantage in which Tondeur had erstwhile found himself. To the onlookers this seemed a refinement of cruelty.

Blood, who now directly faced Tondeur, picked up in that moment one of the brass candlesticks from the table beside him. None observed him, every eye being upon the combatants. Blood alone appeared entirely to have lost interest in them. His attention was bestowed entirely upon the candlestick. So as to examine the socket intended for the candle, he raised the object until its broad saucerlike base was vertical. At that moment, for no apparent reason, Tondeur's blade faltered in its guard, and failed to deflect a clumsy thrust with which

Jeremy was mechanically in the act of countering. Meeting no opposition, Jeremy's blade drove on until some inches of it came out through Tondeur's back.

Almost before the amazed company had realized this sudden and unexpected conclusion, Captain Blood was on his knees beside the prostrate man. He called for water and clean linen, the surgeon in him now paramount. Jeremy – the most amazed in that amazed crowd – stood foolishly looking on beside him.

Whilst Blood was dressing the wound, Tondeur recovered from his momentary swoon; he stared with eyes that slowly focused the man who was bending over him.

"Assassin!" he said through his teeth, and then his head lolled limply on his shoulder once more.

"On the contrary," said Blood, his fingers deftly swathing the body which Ventadour was supporting, "I'm your preserver." And to the company he announced: "He will not die of this, for all that it went through him. With luck he'll be ruffling it again within the month. But he'd best not be moved from here for some days, and he'll need care."

Jeremy never knew how he found himself once more aboard the *Arabella*. The events of the afternoon were dim to him as the transactions of a dream. He had looked, as he conceived, into the grim face of death, and yet he had survived. That evening at supper in the great cabin he made philosophy upon it.

"It serves," he said, "to show the advantages of never losing heart or admitting defeat in an encounter. I might so easily have been slain today; and it would have been simply and solely by a preconception: the preconception that Tondeur was the better swordsman."

"It is still possible that he was," said Blood.

"Then how came I to run him through so easily?"

"How indeed, Peter?" demanded Wolverstone, and the other half dozen present echoed the question, whilst Hagthorpe enlarged upon the theme.

"The fact is the rascal's reputation for swordsmanship rested solely upon his own boasting. It's the source of many a reputation." And there the discussion was allowed to drop.

In the morning, Captain Blood suggested that they should pay a visit to Monsieur d'Ogeron, and render their account to him of what had taken place. As Governor of Tortuga, some formal explanation was due to him, even though his acquaintance with the combatant should render it almost unnecessary. Jeremy, at all times ready to visit the Governor's house on any pretext, was this morning more than willing, the events having set about him a heroic halo.

As they were being rowed ashore Captain Blood observed that the *Cygne* was gone from her moorings in the bay, which would mean, Jeremy opined with faint interest, that Monsieur de Mercoeur had at last departed from Tortuga.

The little Governor gave them a very friendly welcome. He had heard of the affair at The King of France. They need not trouble themselves with any explanations. No official cognizance would be taken of the matter. He knew but too well the causes which had led to it.

"Had things gone otherwise," he said quite frankly, "it would have been different. Knowing who would be the aggressor – as I warned you, Monsieur Pitt – I must have taken some action against Tondeur, and I might have had to call upon you, Captain Blood, to assist me. Order must be preserved even in such a colony as this. But as it is, why, the affair could not have had a more fortunate conclusion. You have made me very happy, Monsieur Pitt."

This augured so well that Mr Pitt presently asked leave to pay his homage to Mademoiselle Lucienne.

Monsieur d'Ogeron looked at him as if surprised by the request.

"Lucienne? But Lucienne has gone. She sailed for France this morning on the *Cygne* with her husband."

"Her ... her husband?" echoed Jeremy, with a sudden feeling of nausea.

"Monsieur de Mercoeur. Did I not tell you she was promised? They were married at cockcrow by Father Benoit. That

155

is why I say you have made me very happy, Monsieur Pitt. Until Captain Tondeur was laid by the heels I dared not permit this thing to take place. Remembering Levasseur, I could not allow Lucienne to depart before. Like Levasseur, it is certain that Tondeur would have followed, and on the high seas would have dared that which he dared not here in Tortuga."

"Therefore," said Captain Blood, in his driest tone, "you set the other two by the ears, so that whilst they were quarrelling over the bone, the third dog might make off with it. That, Monsieur d'Ogeron, was more shrewd than friendly."

"You are angry with me, Captain!" Monsieur d'Ogeron appeared genuinely distressed. "But I had to think of my child, and besides, I had no doubt of the issue. This dear Monsieur Pitt could not fail to prevail against a man like Tondeur."

"This dear Monsieur Pitt," said Captain Blood, "might very easily have lost his life for love of your daughter so as to forward your marriage schemes for her. There's a pretty irony in the thought." He linked his arm through that of his young shipmaster, who stood there white and hangdog. "You see, Jerry, the pitfalls injudicious loving can dig for a man. Let's be going, my lad. Good day to you, Monsieur d'Ogeron."

He almost dragged the boy away. Then, because he was very angry, he paused when they had reached the door, and there was an unpleasant smile on the face he turned to the Governor.

"Why do you suppose that I should not do on Mr Pitt's behalf what you feared Tondeur might do? Why shouldn't I go after the *Cygne* and capture your daughter for my shipmaster?"

"My God!" ejaculated Monsieur d'Ogeron, suddenly appalled by the prospect of so merited a vengeance. "You would never do that!"

"No, I would not. But do you know why?"

"Because I've trusted you. Because you are a man of honour."

"Honour! Bah! I'm just a pirate. It's because I don't think she is good enough for Mr Pitt, as I told him from the outset, and as I hope he now believes."

That was all the revenge he took of Monsieur d'Ogeron for his foxy part in the affair. Having taken it, he departed, and the stricken Jeremy suffered himself to be led away.

But by the time they had reached the mole the lad's numbness had given place to rage. He had been duped and tricked, his very life had been put in pawn to serve the schemes of those others, and somebody must pay.

"If ever I meet Monsieur de Mercoeur . . ." he was raging.

"You'll do fine things," the Captain mocked him.

"I'll serve him as I served that dog Tondeur."

And now Captain Blood stood still that he might laugh.

"Oh! It's the fine swordsman y've become all at once, Jerry. The very butcher of a silk button. I'd best be disillusioning you, my young Tybalt, before ye swagger into mischief."

"Disillusioning me?" Jeremy stared at him, a frown darkening that fair, honest face. "Did I, or did I not, lay low that French duellist yesterday?"

And Blood, still laughing, answered him: "You did not!"

"I did not? I did not?" Jeremy set his arms akimbo. "Will ye tell me, then, who did?"

"I did," said the Captain, and on that grew serious. "I did it with the bright bottom of a brass candlestick. I flashed enough reflected sunlight into his eyes to blind him whilst you were doing the business."

He saw Jeremy turn pale, and added the reminder: "He would have murdered you else." Then there was a whimsical twist of his firm lips, a queer flash from his vivid eyes, and he added on a note of conscious pride: "I am Captain Blood."

8

THE EXPIATION OF
MADAME DE COULEVAIN

ON A daybed under the wide square sternports of the
luxurious cabin of the *Estremadura* lounged Don Juan de
la Fuente, Count of Mediana, twanging a beribboned guitar
and singing in a languorous baritone voice an indelicate song
that was well known in Malaga at the time.

He was a young man of thirty, graceful and elegant, with
soft dark eyes and full red lips that were half veiled by small
moustaches and a little peaked black beard. Face, figure, dress
and posture advertised the voluptuary, and the setting afforded
him by the cabin of the great forty-gun galleon he commanded
was proper to its tenant. From bulkheads painted an olive
green detached gilded carvings of cupids and dolphins, fruit
and flowers, whilst each stanchion was in the shape of a fish-
tailed caryatid. Against the forward bulkhead a handsome
buffet was laden with gold and silver plate; between the doors
of two cabins on the larboard side hung a painting of Aphro-
dite; the floor was spread with a rich Eastern carpet; a finer
one covered the quadrangular table, above which was suspended a ponderous lamp of chiselled silver. There were books
in a rack: the Ars Amatoria of Ovid, the Satiricon, a Boccaccio
and a Poggio, to bear witness to the classico-licentious character
of this student. The chairs, like the daybed on which Don Juan
was sprawling, were of Cordovan leather, painted and gilded,
and although the sternports stood open to the mild airs that
barely moved the galleon, the place was heavy with ambergris
and other perfumes.

Don Juan's song extolled life's carnal joys and, in particular,
bewailed the Pope's celibacy amid opulence.

"Vida sin niña no es vida, es muerte,
Y del Padre Santo muy triste es la suerte."

That was its envoy and at the same time its mildest ribaldry.
You conceive the rest.

Don Juan was singing this song of his to Captain Blood, who
sat with an elbow leaning on the table and a leg thrown across
a second chair. On his dark aquiline face there was a set
mechanical smile, put on like a mask, to dissemble his weariness and disgust. He wore a suit of grey camlett with silver lace,
which had come from Don Juan's wardrobe, for they were
much of the same height and shape as they were akin in age;
and a black periwig, that was likewise of Don Juan's providing,
framed his countenance.

A succession of odd chances had brought about this incredible situation, in which that detested enemy of Spain came
to find himself an honoured guest aboard a Spanish galleon
crawling north across the Caribbean, with the Windward
Islands some twenty miles abeam. Let it be explained at once
that the languorous Don who entertained him was very far
from suspecting whom he entertained.

The tale of how he came there, set forth at great and almost
tedious length by Pitt in his chronicle, must here be briefly
summarized.

A week ago, on Margarita, in a secluded cove of which his
own great ship the *Arabella* was careened to clear her keel of
accumulated foulness, word had been brought him by some
friendly Carib Indians of a Spanish pearling fleet at work in
the Gulf of Cariaco, which had already collected a rich harvest.

The temptation to raid it proved irresistible to Captain
Blood. In his left ear he wore a great pear-shaped pearl of
enormous price that was part of the magnificent haul they had
once made from a similar fleet in the Rio de la Hacha. So with
three piraguas and forty men carefully picked from his crew of
close upon two hundred Blood slipped one night across the
narrow sea between Margarita and the Main, and lay most of
the following day under the coast, to creep towards evening

into the Gulf of Cariaco. There, however, they were surprised by a Spanish guarda-costa whose presence they had been far from suspecting.

They put about in haste and ran for the open. But the guardship gave chase in the brief dusk, opened fire, and shattered the frail boats that bore the raiders. Of the forty buccaneers, some must have been shot, some drowned, and others picked up to be made prisoners. Blood himself had spent the night clinging to a stout piece of wreckage. A stiffish southerly breeze had sprung up at sunset, and, driven by this, and borne by the currents, he had miraculously been washed ashore at dawn, exhausted, benumbed, and almost pickled by the long briny immersion, on one of the diminutive islands of the Hermanos group.

It was an island not more than a mile and a half in length and less than a mile across, sparsely grown with coconut palms and aloes, and normally uninhabited save by seabirds and turtles. But at the time of Blood's arrival there it happened to be tenanted in addition by a couple of castaway Spaniards. These unfortunates had escaped in a sailing pinnace from the English settlement of Saint Vincent, where they had been imprisoned. Ignorant of navigation, they had entrusted themselves to the sea, and with water and provisions exhausted, and at the point of death from thirst and hunger, they had fortuitously made their landfall a month ago. Not daring after that experience to venture forth again, they had subsisted there on shell-fish taken from the rocks and on coconuts, yams, and berries.

Since Captain Blood could not be sure that Spaniards, even when in these desperate straits would not slit his throat if they guessed his real identity, he announced himself as shipwrecked from a Dutch brig which had been on its way to Curaçao, gave himself the name of Peter Vandermeer, and attributed to himself a mixed parentage of Dutch father and Spanish mother, thus accounting for the fluent Castilian which he spoke.

Finding the pinnace in good order, he provisioned her with a store of yams and of turtle, which he himself boucanned, filled her water-casks, and put to sea with the two castaways.

By sun and stars he trusted to steer a course due east for Tobago, whose Dutch settlers were sufficiently neutral to give
them shelter. He deemed it prudent, however, to inform his
trusting companions that he was making for Trinidad.

But neither Trinidad nor Tobago was to prove their destination. On the third day out they were picked up by the
Spanish galleon *Estremadura*, to the jubilation of the two Spaniards and the dismay at first of Captain Blood. However, he
put a bold face on the matter and trusted to fortune and to
the ragged condition in which he went aboard the galleon to
escape recognition. When questioned he maintained the fictions
of his shipwreck, his Dutch nationality and his mixed parentage, and conceiving that since he was plunging he might as
well plunge deeply, and that since he claimed a Spanish mother
he might as well choose one amongst the noblest Spain could
afford, he announced her a Trasmiera of the family of the
Duke of Arcos, who, therefore, was his kinsman.

The authoritative bearing, which not even his ragged condition could diminish, his intrepid aquiline countenance, dark
skin and black hair, and, above all, his fluent, cultured Castilian, made credible the imposture. And, anyway, since he
desired no more than to be set ashore on some Dutch or French
settlement, whence he could resume his voyage to Curaçao,
there seemed no reason why he should not magnify his
identity.

The sybaritic Don Juan de la Fuente, who commanded the
Estremadura, impressed by this shipwrecked gentleman's tale
of high connections, treated him generously, placed a choice
and extensive wardrobe at his disposal, gave him a stateroom
off the main cabin, and used him in every way as one person of
distinction should use another. It contributed to this that Don
Juan found in Peter Vandermeer a man after his own heart.
He insisted upon calling him Don Pedro, as if to stress the
Spanish part in him, swearing that his Vandermeer blood had
been entirely beneaped by that of the Trasmieras. It was a
subject on which the Spanish gentleman made some ribaldries.
Indeed, ribaldry flowed from him naturally and copiously on

all occasions, and infected his officers, four of whom, young gentlemen of lineage, dined and supped with him daily in the great cabin.

Proclivities which in a raw lad of eighteen Blood might have condoned, trusting to time to correct them, he found frankly disgusting in this man of thirty. Under the curtly elegant exterior he perceived the unclean spirit of the rakehell. But he was far indeed from betraying his contempt. His own safety, resting precariously as it did upon maintaining the good impression he had made at the outset, compelled him to adapt himself to the company, to represent himself as a man of their own licentious kidney.

Thus it came about that during those days when, almost becalmed on the tropical sea, they crawled slowly north under a mountain of canvas that was often limp, something akin to a friendship sprang up between Don Juan and this Don Pedro. Don Juan found much to admire in him: his obvious vigour of body and of spirit, the deep knowledge of men and of the world which he displayed, his ready wit and the faintly cynical philosophy which his talk revealed. Spending long hours together daily, their intimacy grew at the rate peculiar to growths in that tropical region.

And that, briefly, is how you come to find these two closeted together on this the sixth day of Blood's voyage as a guest of honour in a ship in which he would have been travelling in irons had his identity been so much as suspected. Meanwhile her commander wearied him with lascivious songs, whilst Blood pondered the amusing side of the situation, which, nevertheless, it would be well to end at the earliest opportunity.

So presently, when the song had ceased and the Spaniard was munching Peruvian sweetmeats from a silver box beside him, Captain Blood approached the question. The pinnace in which he had travelled with the castaway Spaniards had been taken in tow by the *Estremadura*, and the time, he thought, had come to use it.

"We should now be abeam of Martinique," he said. "It cannot be more than six or seven leagues to land."

"Very true, thanks to this cursed lack of wind. I could blow harder from my own lungs."

"You cannot, of course, put in for me," said Blood. There was war at the time between France and Spain, which Blood understood to be one of the reasons of Don Juan's presence in these waters. "But in this calm sea I could easily pull myself ashore in the boat that brought me. Suppose, Don Juan, I take my leave of you this evening."

Don Juan looked aggrieved. "Here's a sudden haste to leave us! Was it not agreed that I carry you to Saint Martin?"

"True. But, thinking of it, I remember that ships are rare there, and I may be delayed some time in finding a vessel for Curaçao; whereas from Martinique—"

"Ah, no," he was peevishly interrupted. "You shall land, if you please, at Mariegalante, where I myself have business, or at Guadeloupe if you prefer it, as I think you may. But I vow I do not let you go just yet."

Captain Blood had checked in the act of filling himself a pipe of finest Sacerdotes tobacco from a jar of broken leaf upon the table. "You have business at Mariegalante?" So surprised was he that he abandoned for that question the matter more personal to himself. "What business is possible at present between you and the French?"

Don Juan smiled darkly. "The business of war, my friend. Am I not a man of war?"

"You are going to raid Mariegalante?"

The Spaniard was some time in answering. Softly he stirred the chords of his guitar into sound. The smile still hovered about his full red lips, but it had assumed a faintly cruel character and his dark eyes glowed.

"The garrison at Basseterre is commanded by a dog named Coulevain with whom I have an account to settle. It is over a year old, but at last we are approaching payday. The war gives me my opportunity. I serve Spain and myself at a single stroke."

Blood kindled a light, applied it to his pipe, and fell to smoking. It did not seem to him to be a very commendable service to Spain to risk one of her ships on an attack upon so negligible a settlement as Mariegalante. When presently he spoke, however, it was to utter the half of his thought upon another subject, and he said nothing more of landing on Martinique.

"It will be something to add to my experience, to have been aboard a ship in action. It will be something not easily forgotten – unless we are sunk by the guns of Basseterre."

Don Juan laughed. For all his profligacy, the fellow seemed of a high stomach, not easily disturbed at the imminence of a fight. Rather did the prospect fill him now with glee. This increased when that evening, at last, the breeze freshened and they began to make better speed, and that night in the cabin of the *Estremadura* spirits ran high, boisterously led by Don Juan himself. There was deep drinking of heady Spanish wines and a deal of easily excited laughter.

Captain Blood conjectured that heavy indeed must be the account of the French commander of Mariegalante with Don Juan if the prospect of a settlement could so exhalt the Spaniard. His own sympathies went out freely to the French settlers who were about to suffer one of those revolting raids by which the Spaniards had rendered themselves so deservedly detested in the New World. But he was powerless to raise a finger or utter a word in their defence, compelled to join in this brutal mirth at the prospect of French slaughter, and to drink damnation to the French in general and to Colonel de Coulevain in particular.

In the morning, when he went on deck, Captain Blood beheld the long coastline of Dominica, ten or twelve miles away on the larboard quarter, and in the distance ahead a vague grey mass which he knew to be the mountain that rises in the middle of the round Island of Mariegalante. They had come south of Dominica in the night, and so had passed out of the Caribbean Sea into the open Atlantic.

Don Juan, in high spirits and apparently none the worse for last night's carouse, came to join him on the poop and to inform him of that which he already knew, but of which he was careful to betray no knowledge.

For a couple of hours they held to their course, driving

straight before the wind with shortened sail. When within ten miles of the island, which now seemed to rise from the turquoise sea like a wall of green, the crew became active under sharp words of command and shrill notes from the boatswain's pipe. Nettings were spread above the *Estremadura*'s decks to catch any spars that might be brought down in action; the shot-racks were filled; the leaden aprons were cleared from the guns, and buckets for sea-water were distributed beside them.

From the carved poop rail, at Don Juan's side, Captain Blood looked on with interest and approval as the musketeers in corselet and peaked headpiece were marshalled in the waist. And all the while Don Juan was explaining to him the significance of things with which no man afloat was better acquainted than Captain Blood.

At eight bells they went below to dine, Don Juan less boisterous now that action was imminent. His face had lost some of its colour, and there was a restlessness about his long slender hands, a feverish glitter in his velvet eyes. He ate little, and this little quickly; but he drank copiously, and he was still at table when one of his officers, a squat youngster named Veraguas, who had remained on duty, came to announce that it was time for him to take command.

He rose, and, with the aid of his Negro steward Absolom, armed himself quickly in back and breast and steel cap; then went on deck. Captain Blood accompanied him, despite the Spaniard's warning that he should not expose himself without body armour.

The *Estremadura* had come within three miles of the port of Basseterre. She flew no flag, from a natural reluctance to advertise her nationality more than it was advertised already by her lines and rig. Within a mile Don Juan could, through his telescope, survey the whole of the wide-mouthed harbour, and he announced that at least no ships of war were present. The fort would be the only antagonist in the preliminary duel.

A shot just then across the *Estremadura*'s bows proclaimed that at least the commandant of the fort was a man who understood his business. Despite that definite signal to heave to, the

Estremadura raced on and met the roar of a dozen guns. Un-scathed by the volley, she held to her course, reserving her fire. Thus Don Juan earned the unspoken approval of Captain Blood. He ran the gauntlet of a second volley, and still held his fire until almost at point-blank range. Then he loosed a broad-side, went smartly about, loosed another, and then ran off, close-hauled, to reload, offering only the narrow target of his stern to the French gunners.

When he returned to the attack he trailed astern the three boats that hitherto had been on the booms amidships, in addition to the useful pinnace in which Captain Blood had travelled.

He suffered now some damage to the mizzen yards, and the tall deck structures of his ornate forecastle were heavily bat-tered. But there was nothing in this to distress him, and, handling his ship with great judgment, he smashed at the fort with two more heavy broadsides of twenty guns each, so well delivered that he effectively silenced it for the moment.

He was off again, and when next he returned the boats in tow were filled with his musketeers. He brought them to within a hundred yards of the cliff, to seaward of the fort and at an angle at which the guns could hardly reach him, and sending the boats ashore, he stood there to cover their landing. A party of French that issued from the half ruined fortress to oppose them were mown down by a discharge of langrel and case shot. Then the Spaniards were ashore and swarming up the gentle slope to the attack whilst the empty boats were being rowed back for reinforcements.

Whilst this was happening, Don Juan moved forward again and crashed yet another broadside at the fort to create a diver-sion and further to increase the distress and confusion there. Four or five guns answered him, and a twelve-pound shot came to splinter his bulwarks amidships; but he was away again without greater harm, and going about to meet his boats. He was still loading them with a further contingent when the musketry ashore fell silent. Then a lusty Spanish cheer came over the water, and soon thereafter the ring of hammers upon metal to announce the spiking of the fort's now undefended guns.

Hitherto Captain Blood's attitude had been one of dispassionate criticism of proceedings in which he was something of an authority. Now, however, his mind turned to what must follow, and from his knowledge of the ways of Spanish soldiery on a raid, and his acquaintance with the rakehell who was to lead them, he shuddered, hardened buccaneer though he might be, at the prospective sequel. To him war was war, and he could engage in it ruthlessly against men as ruthless. But the sacking of towns with the remorselessness of a brutal inflamed soldiery towards peaceful colonists and their women was something he had never tolerated.

That Don Juan de la Fuente, delicately bred gentleman of Spain though he might be, shared no particle of Blood's scruples was evident. For Don Juan, his dark eyes aglow with expectancy, went ashore with his reinforcements, personally to lead that raid. At the last, with a laugh, he invited his guest to accompany him, promising him rare sport and a highly diverting addition to his experiences of life. Blood commanded himself and remained outwardly cold.

"My nationality forbids it, Don Juan. The Dutch are not at war with France."

"Why, who's to know you're Dutch? Be entirely a Spaniard for once, Don Pedro, and enjoy yourself. Who is to know?"

"I am," said Blood. "It is a question of honour."

Don Juan stared at him as if he were ludicrous. "You must be the victim of your scruples, then"; and still laughing he went down the accommodation ladder to the waiting boat.

Captain Blood remained upon the poop, whence he could watch the town above the shore, less than a mile away; for the *Estremadura* now rode at anchor in the roadstead. Of the officers, only Veraguas remained aboard, and of the men not more than fourteen or fifteen. But they kept a sharp watch, and there was a master gunner amongst them for emergencies.

Don Sebastian Veraguas bewailed his fate that he should have been left out of the landing party, and spoke wistfully of the foul joys that might have been his ashore. He was a sturdy, bovine fellow of five-and-twenty, prominent of nose and chin, and he chattered self-sufficiently whilst Blood kept his glance upon the little town. Even at that distance they could hear the sounds of the horrid Spanish handiwork, and already more than one house was in flames. Too well Blood knew what was taking place at the instigation of a gentleman of Spain, and as grim-faced he watched, he would have given much to have had a hundred of his buccaneers at hand with whom to sweep this Spanish rubbish from the earth. Once before he had witnessed at close quarters such a raid, and he had sworn then that never thereafter would he show mercy to a Spaniard. To that oath he had been false in the past; but he vowed now that he would not fail to keep it in the future.

And meanwhile the young man at his elbow, whom he could gladly have strangled with his hands, was calling down the whole heavenly hierarchy to witness his disappointment at being absent from that Hell.

It was evening when the raiders returned, coming, as they had gone, by the road which led to the now silent fort, and there taking boat to cross a hundred yards of jade-green water to the anchored ship. They sang as they came, boisterous, and hilarious, a few of them with bandaged wounds, many of them flushed with wine and rum, and all of them laden with spoils. They made vile jests of the desolation they had left behind and viler boasts of the abominations they had practised. No buccaneers in the world, thought Blood, could ever have excelled them in brutality. The raid had been entirely successful and they had lost not more than a half dozen men, whose deaths had been terribly avenged.

And then in the last boat came Don Juan. Ahead of him up the accommodation ladder went two of his men bearing a heaving bundle, which Blood presently made out to be a woman whose head and shoulders were muffled in a cloak. Below the black folds of this he beheld a petticoat of flowered silk and caught a glimpse of agitated legs in silken hose and dainty high-heeled shoes. In mounting horror he judged from this that the woman was a person of quality.

Don Juan, with face and hands begrimed with sweat and powder, followed closely. From the head of the ladder he uttered a command: "To my cabin."

Blood saw her borne across the deck, through the ranks of men who jeered their ribaldries, and then she vanished in the arms of her captors down the gangway.

Now, whatever he may have been towards men, towards women Blood had never been other than chivalrous. This, perhaps, for the sake of that sweet lady in Barbados to whom he accounted himself nothing, but who was to him an inspiration to more honour than would be thought possible in a buccaneer. That chivalry arose in him now full-armed. Had he yielded to it completely and blindly he would there and then have fallen upon Don Juan, and thus wrecked at once all possibility of being of service to his unfortunate captive. Her presence here could be no mystery to any. She was the particular prize that the profligate Spanish commander reserved to himself, and Blood felt his flesh go crisp and cold at the thought.

Yet when presently he came down the companion and crossed the deck to the gangway he was calm and smiling. In that narrow passage he joined Don Juan's officers, the three who had been ashore with him as well as Veraguas. They were all talking at once and laughing boisterously, and the subject of their approving mirth was their captain's vileness.

Together they burst into the cabin, Blood coming last. The Negro servant had laid the table for supper with the usual six places, and had just lighted the great silver lamp, for with sunset the daylight faded almost instantly.

Don Juan was emerging at that moment from one of the larboard cabins. He closed the door, and stood for a dozen heartbeats with his back to it, surveying that invasion almost mistrustfully. It determined him to turn the key in the lock, draw it out and put in his pocket. From that lesser cabin, in which clearly the lady had been bestowed, there came no sound.

"She's quiet at last, God be praised," laughed one of the officers.

"Worn out with screeching," explained another. "Lord! Was there ever such a wildcat? A woman of spirit that, from the way she fought; a little devil worth the taming. It's a task I envy you, Juan."

Veraguas hailed the prize as well-deserved by such brilliant leadership, and then whilst questionable quips and jests were still being bandied, Don Juan, smiling grimly, introspectively, ordered them to table.

"We'll sup briefly, if you please," he announced, as he unbuckled his harness, and by the remark produced a fresh storm of hilarity on the subject of his haste and at the expense of the poor victim beyond that door.

When at last they sat down Captain Blood thrust himself upon Don Juan's notice with a question: "And Colonel de Coulevain?"

The handsome face darkened. "A malediction on him! He was away from Basseterre, organizing defences at Les Carmes."

Blood raised his brows, adopted a tone of faint concern. "Then the account remains unsettled in spite of all your brave efforts."

"Not quite. Not quite."

"By Heaven, no!" said another with a laugh. "Madame de Coulevain should give an ample quittance."

"Madame de Coulevain?" said Blood, although the question was unnecessary, as were the glances that travelled towards the locked cabin door to answer him. He laughed. "Now that . . ." – he paused – ". . . that is an artistic vengeance, Don Juan, whatever the offence." And, with Hell in his soul, he laughed again, softly, in admiring approval.

Don Juan shrugged and sighed. "Yet I would I had found him and made him pay in full."

But Captain Blood would not leave it there. "If you really

hate the man, think of the torment to which you have doomed him, always assuming that he loves his wife. Surely by comparison with that the peace of death would be no punishment at all."

"Maybe, maybe." Don Juan was short. Disappointment seemed to have spoiled his temper, or perhaps impatience fretted him. "Give me wine, Absolom. God of my life! How I thirst!"

The Negro poured for them. Don Juan drained his bumper at a draught. Blood did the same, and the goblets were replenished.

Blood toasted the Spanish commander in voluble terms. He was no great judge, he declared, of an action afloat; but he could not conceive that the one he had witnessed that day would have been better fought by any commander living.

Don Juan smiled his gratification; the toast was drunk with relish, and the cups were filled again. Then others talked, and Blood lapsed into thought.

He reflected that soon now, supper being done, Don Juan would drive them all to their quarters. Captain Blood's own were on the starboard side of the great cabin. But would he be suffered to remain there now, so near at hand? If so, he might yet avail that unhappy lady, and already he knew precisely how. The danger lay in that he might be sent elsewhere tonight.

He roused himself and broke in upon the talk, called noisily for more wine, and after that for yet more, in which the others who had sweated profusely in that day's action kept him company gladly enough. He broke into renewed eulogies of Don Juan's skill and valour, and it was presently observed that his speech was slurred and indistinct, and that he hiccoughed and repeated himself foolishly.

Thus he provoked ridicule, and when it was forthcoming he displayed annoyance, and appealed to Don Juan to inform these merry and befuddled gentlemen that he at least was sober; but his speech grew thicker even whilst he was protesting.

When Veraguas taxed him with being drunk he grew almost

violent, spoke of his Dutch origin to remind them that he came of a nation of great drinkers, and offered to drink any man in the Caribbean under the table. Boastfully, to prove his words, he called for more wine, and having drunk it lapsed gradually into silence. His eyelids drooped heavily, his body sagged, and presently, to the hilarity of all who beheld here a boaster confounded, he slid from his chair and came to rest upon the cabin floor, nor attempted to rise again.

Veraguas stirred him contemptuously and ungently with his foot. He gave no sign of life. He lay inert as a log, breathing stertorously.

Don Juan got up abruptly. "Put the fool to bed. And get you gone too; all of you."

Don Pedro was borne, insensible, amid laughter and some rude handling, to his cabin. His neckcloth was loosed, and so they left him, closing the door upon him.

Then, in compliance with Don Juan's renewed command they all departed noisily, and the commander locked the door of the now empty great cabin.

Alone, he came slowly back to the table, and stood a moment listening to the uncertain steps and the merry voices retreating down the gangway. His goblet stood half full. He picked it up and drank. Then, setting it down, and proceeding without haste, he drew from his pocket the key of the cabin in which Madame de Coulevain had been bestowed. He crossed the floor, thrust the key into the lock and turned it. But before he could throw open the door a sound behind him made him turn again.

His drunken guest was leaning against the bulkhead beside the open door of his stateroom. His clothes were in disorder, his face vacuous, and he stood so precariously that it was a wonder the gentle heave of the ship did not pitch him off his balance. He moved his lips like a man nauseated, and parted them with a dry click.

"Wha's o'clock?" was his foolish question.

Don Juan relaxed his stare to smile, although a thought impatiently.

The drunkard babbled on: "I . . . I don't . . . remember . . ." He broke off. He lurched forward. "Thousand devils! I . . . I thirst!"

"To bed with you! To bed!" cried Don Juan.

"To bed? Of . . . of course to bed. Whither . . . else? Eh? But first . . . a cup."

He reached the table. He lurched round it, a man carried forward by his own impetus, and came to rest opposite to the Spaniard, whose velvet eyes watched him with angry contempt. He found a goblet and a jug, a heavy, encrusted silver jug, shaped like an amphora with a handle on either side of its long neck. He poured himself wine, drank, and set down the cup; then he stood swaying slightly, and put forth his right hand as if to steady himself. It came to rest on the neck of the silver jug.

Don Juan, watching him ever with impatient scorn, may have seen for the fraction of a second the vacuity leave that countenance, and the vivid blue eyes under their black brows grow cold and hard as sapphires. But before the second was spent, before the brain could register what the eyes beheld, the body of that silver jug had crashed into his brow, and the commander of the *Estremadura* knew nothing more.

Captain Blood, without a trace now of drunkenness in face or gait, stepped quickly round the table, and went down on one knee beside the man he had felled. Don Juan lay quite still on the gay Eastern carpet, his handsome face clay coloured with a trickle of blood across it from the wound between the half closed eyes. Captain Blood contemplated his work without pity or compunction. If there was cowardice in the blow, which had taken the Spaniard unawares from a hand which he supposed friendly, that cowardice was born of no fear for himself, but for the helpless lady in that larboard cabin. On her account he could take no risk of Don Juan's being able to give the alarm; and, anyway, this cruel, soulless profligate deserved no honourable consideration.

He stood up briskly, then stooped and placed his hands under the inert Spaniard's armpits. Raising the limp body, he dragged it with trailing heels to the stern window, which stood open to the soft, purple, tropical night. He took Don Juan in his arms, and, laden with him, mounted the daybed. A moment he steadied his heavy burden upon the sill; then he thrust it forth, and, supporting himself by his grip of a stanchion, leaned far out to observe the Spaniard's fall.

The splash he made in the phosphorescent wake of the gently moving ship was merged into the gurgle of water about the vessel. For an instant as it took the sea the body glowed, sharply defined in an incandescence that was as suddenly extinguished. Phosphorescent bubbles arose and broke in the luminous line astern; then all was as it had been.

Captain Blood was still leaning far out, still peering down, when a voice in the cabin behind him came to startle him. It brought him instantly erect, but he did not yet turn round. Indeed, he checked himself in the very act, and remained stiffly poised, his left hand still supporting him against the stanchion, his back turned squarely upon the speaker.

For the voice was the voice of a woman. Its tone was tender, gentle, inviting. The words it had uttered in French were:

"Juan! Juan! Why do you stay? What do you there? I have been waiting. Juan!"

Speculation treading close upon amazement, he continued to stand there, waiting for more that should help him to understand. The voice came again, more insistently now.

"Juan! Don't you hear me? Juan!"

He swung round at last, and beheld her near the open door of her cabin, from which she had emerged: a tall, handsome woman, in the middle twenties, partly dressed, with a mantle of unbound golden tresses about her white shoulders. He had imagined this lady cowering, terror-stricken, helpless, probably pinioned, in the cabin to which the Spanish ravisher had consigned her. Because of that mental picture, intolerable to his chivalrous nature, he had done what he had done. Yet there she stood, not merely free, not merely having come forth of her own free will, but summoning Don Juan in accents that are used to a lover.

Horror stunned him: horror of himself and of the dreadful murderous blunder he had committed in his haste to play at knight-errantry: to usurp the place of Providence.

And then another deeper horror welled up to submerge the first: horror of this woman as she stood suddenly revealed to him. That dreadful raid on Basseterre had been no more than a pretext to cloak her elopement, and must have been undertaken at her invitation. The rest, her forcible conveyance aboard, her bestowal in the cabin, had all been part of a loathly comedy she had played – a comedy set against a background of fire and rape and murder, by all of which she remained so soullessly unperturbed that she could come forth to coo her lover's name on that seductive note.

It was for this harpy, who waded complacently through blood and the wreckage of a hundred lives to the fulfilment of her desires, that he had soiled his hands. The situation seemed to transmute his chivalrously-inspired deed into a foulness.

He shivered as he regarded her, and she, confronted by that stern aquiline face and those ice-cold blue eyes, that were certainly not Don Juan's, gasped, recoiled, and clutched her flimsy silken body garment closer to her generous breast.

"Who are you?" she demanded. "Where is Don Juan de la Fuente?"

He stepped down from the daybed, and something bodeful in his countenance changed her surprise to incipient alarm.

"You are Madame de Coulevain?" he asked, using her own language. He must make no mistake.

She nodded. "Yes, yes." Her tone was impatient, but the fear abode in her eyes. "Who are you? Why do you question me?" She stamped her foot. "Where is Don Juan?"

He knew that truth is commonly the shortest road, and he took it. He jerked a thumb backwards over his shoulder. "I've just thrown him through the window."

She stared and stared at this cold, calm man about whom she perceived something so remorseless and terrifying that she could not doubt his incredible words.

Suddenly she loosed a scream. It did not disconcert or even

move him. He began to speak again, and, dominated by those brilliant, intolerable eyes, which were like points of steel, she controlled herself to listen.

"You are supposing me one of Don Juan's companions; perhaps even that, covetous of the noble prize he took today at Basseterre, I have murdered him to possess it. This is far indeed from the truth. Deceived like the rest by the comedy of your being brought forcibly aboard, imagining you the unhappy victim of a man I knew for a profligate vuluptuary, I was moved to unutterable compassion on your behalf, and to save you from the horror I foresaw for you I killed him. And now," he added with a bitter smile, "it seems that you were in no need of saving, that I have thwarted you no less than I have thwarted him. This comes of playing Providence."

"You killed him!" she said. She staggered where she stood and, ashen-faced, looked as if she would swoon. "You killed him! Killed him! Oh, my God! My God! You've killed .my Juan!" Thus far she had spoken dully, as if she were repeating something so that she might force it upon her own understanding. But now she wrought herself to frenzy. "You beast! You assassin!" she screamed. "You shall pay! I'll rouse the ship! You shall answer, as God's in Heaven!"

She was already across the cabin hammering on the door; already her hand was upon the key when he came up with her. She struggled like a wildcat in his grip, screaming the while for help. At last he wrenched her away, swung her round and hurled her from him. Then he withdrew, and pocketed the key.

She lay on the floor, by the table, where he had flung her, and sent scream after scream to alarm the ship.

Captain Blood surveyed her coldly. "Aye, aye, breathe your lungs, my child," he bade her. "It will do you good and me no harm."

He sat down to await the exhaustion of her paroxysm. But his words had already quieted her. Her round eyes asked a question. He smiled sourly as he answered it.

"No man aboard this ship will stir a foot for all your cries, or even heed them, unless it be as matter for amusement. That is the kind of men they are who follow Don Juan de la Fuente."

He saw by her stricken expression how well she understood. He nodded with that faint sardonic smile which she found hateful. "Aye, madame. That's the situation. You were best bring yourself to a calm contemplation of it."

She got to her feet, and stood leaning heavily against the table, surveying him with rage and loathing. "If they do not come tonight, they will come tomorrow. Some time they must come. And when they come it will be very ill for you, whoever you may be."

"Will it not also be very ill for you?" quoth Blood.

"For me? I did not murder him."

"You'll not be accused of it. But in him you've lost your only protector aboard this ship. What will betide you, do you suppose, when you are alone and helpless in their power, a prisoner of war, the captive of a raid, in the hands of these merry gentleman of Spain?"

"God in Heaven!" She clutched her breast in terror.

"Quiet you," he bade her, almost contemptuously. "I did not rescue you, as I supposed, from one wolf, merely to fling you to the pack. That will not happen – unless you yourself prefer it to returning to your husband."

She grew hysterical.

"To my husband? Ah, that, no! Never that! Never that!"

"It is that or . . ." – he pointed to the door – ". . . the pack. I perceive no choice for you save between those alternatives."

"Who are you?" she asked abruptly. "What are you, you devil, who have destroyed me and yet torment me?"

"I am your saviour, not your destroyer. Your husband, for his own sake, shall be left to suppose, as all have been led to suppose, that you were violently carried off. He will receive you back with relief of his own anguish and with tenderness, and make amends to you for all that the poor fool will fancy you have suffered."

She laughed on a note of hysteria.

"Tenderness! Tenderness in my husband! If he had ever been tender I should not be where I now am." And suddenly, to his surprise, she was moved to explain, to exculpate herself. "I was married to a cold, gross, stupid, cruel animal. That is Monsieur de Coulevain, a fool who has squandered his possessions and is forced to accept a command in these raw barbarous colonies to which he has dragged me. Oh, you think the worst of me, of course. You account me just a light woman. But you shall know the truth."

"At the height of my disillusion some few months after my marriage, Don Juan de la Fuente came to us at Pau, where we lived, for my husband is a Gascon. Don Juan was travelling in France. We loved each other from our first meeting. He saw my unhappiness, which was plain to all. He urged me to fly to Spain with him, and I would to Heaven I had yielded then, and so put an end to my misery. Foolishly I resisted. A sense of duty kept me faithful to my vows. I dismissed him. Since then my cup of misery and shame has overflowed, and when a letter from him was brought to me here at Basseterre on the outbreak of war with Spain, to show me that his fond, loyal, noble heart had not forgotten, I answered him, and in my despair I bade him come for me whenever he would."

She paused a moment, looking at Captain Blood with tragic eyes from which the tears were flowing.

"Now, sir, you know precisely what you have done, what havoc you have made."

Blood's expression had lost some of its sternness. His voice, as he answered her, assumed a gentler note.

"The havoc exists only in your mind, madame. The change which you conceived to be from Hell to Heaven would have been from Hell to deeper Hell. You did not know this man, this loyal, noble heart, this Don Juan de la Fuente. You were taken by the external glitter of him. But this glitter was the incandescence of decay, for at the core of him the man was rotten, and in his hands your fate would have been infamy."

"Do you mend your case or mine by maligning the man you've murdered?"

"Malign him? Nay, madame. Proof of what I say is under my hand. You were in Basseterre today. You know something of the bloodshed, the slaughter of almost defenceless men, the dreadful violence to women—"

Faintly she interrupted him. "These things . . . in the way of war . . ."

"The way of war?" he roared. "Madame, undeceive yourself. Look truth boldly in the face, though it condemn you both. Of what consequence Mariegalante to Spain? And, having been taken, is it held? War served your lover as a pretext. He let loose his dreadful soldiery upon that ill-defended place solely so that he might answer your invitation. Men who today have been wantonly butchered, and unfortunate women who have suffered brutal violence, would now be sleeping tranquilly in their beds but for you and your evil lover. But for you—"

She interrupted him. She had covered her face with her hands while he was speaking, and sat rocking herself and moaning feebly. Now suddenly she uncovered her face again, and he saw that her eyes were fierce.

"No more!" she commanded, and stood up. "I'll hear no more. It's false! False what you say! You distort things to justify your own wicked deed."

He considered her grimly with those cold, penetrating eyes of his.

"Your kind," he said slowly, "will always believe what it chooses to believe. I do not think that I need pity you too much. But since I know that I have distorted nothing, I am content that expiation now awaits you. You shall choose the form of it, madame. Shall I leave you to these Spanish gentlemen, or will you come with me to your husband?"

She looked at him, her eyes distraught, her bosom in tumult. She began to plead with him. Awhile he listened; then he cut her short.

"Madame, I am not the arbiter of your fate. You have shaped it for yourself. I but point out the only two roads it leaves you free to tread."

"How . . . how can you take me back to Basseterre?" she asked him presently.

He told her, and without waiting for her consent, which he knew could not be withheld, he made swift preparation. He flung some provisions into a napkin, took a skin of wine, and a little cask of water, and by a rope which he fetched from his stateroom lowered these things to the pinnace, which was again in tow, and which he drew under the counter of the galleon.

Next he lashed the shortened towrope to a cleat on one of the stanchions, then summoned her to make with him the airy passage down that rope.

It appalled her. But he conquered her fears, and when she had come to stand beside him, he seized the rope and swung out on it and slid down a little way to make room for her above him. At his command, although almost sick with terror, she grasped the rope and placed her feet on his shoulders. Then she slid down between the rope and him, until his hold embraced her knees and held her firmly.

Gently now, foot by foot, they began to descend. From the decks above came the sound of voices raised in song. The men were singing some Spanish scrannel in chorus.

At last his toe was on the gunwale of the pinnace. He worked her nose forward with one foot, sufficiently to enable him to plant the other firmly on the foresheets. After that it was an easy matter to step backwards, drawing her after him whilst still she clung to the rope. Thus he hauled the boat a little farther under the counter until he could take his companion about the waist and gently lower her.

After that he attacked the tow-rope with a knife and hacked it swiftly through. The galleon with its glowing sternport and three great golden poop-lamps sped serenely on close-hauled to the breeze, leaving them gently oscillating in her wake.

When he had recovered breath he bestowed Madame de Coulevain in the sternsheets, then, hoisting the sail and trimming it, he broached to, and with his eyes on the brilliant stars in the tropical sky he steered a course which, with the wind astern, should bring them to Basseterre before sunrise.

In the sternsheets the woman was now gently weeping. With her, expiation had begun, as it does when it is possible to sin no more.

9

THE GRATITUDE OF
MONSIEUR DE COULEVAIN

A LL THROUGH the tepid night the pinnace, gently driven by
the southerly breeze, ploughed steadily through a calm
sea, which after moonrise became like liquid silver.

At the tiller sat Captain Blood. Beside him in the sternsheets
crouched a woman, who between silences was now whimpering,
now vituperative, now apologetic. Of the gratitude which he
accounted due to him he perceived no sign. But he was a
tolerant, understanding man, and he did not, therefore, account
himself aggrieved. Madame de Coulevain's case, however
regarded, was a hard one; and she had little, after all, for which
to be thankful to Fate or to Man.

Her mixed and alternating emotions did not surprise him.

He perceived quite clearly the sources of the hatred that
rang in her voice whenever in the darkness she upbraided him
and that glared in her pallid face when the dawn at last began
to render it visible.

They were then within a couple of miles of land: that green
flat coast with the single great mountain towering in the background. To larboard a tall ship was sweeping past them,
steering for the bay ahead, and in her lines and rig Captain
Blood read her English nationality. From her furled topsails
he assumed that her master, evidently strange to these waters,
was cautiously groping his way in. And this was confirmed by
the seaman visible on the starboard forechains, leaning far out
to take soundings. His chanting voice reached them across the
sunlit waters as he told the fathoms.

Madame de Coulevain, who latterly had fallen into a drowsy
stupor, roused herself to stare at the frigate, aglow in the
golden glory of the risen sun.

"No need for fear, madame. She is not Spanish."

"Fear?" She glared at him, blear-eyed from sleeplessness and weeping. Her full lips writhed into bitterness. "What have I to fear more than the fate you thrust upon me?"

"I, madame? I thrust no fate upon you. You are overtaken by the fate your own actions have invited."

Fiercely she interrupted him. "Have I invited this? That I should return to my husband?"

Captain Blood sighed in weariness. "Are we to have the argument all over again? Must I remind you that yourself you refused the only alternative, which was to remain at the mercy of those Spanish gallants on the Spanish ship? For the rest, your husband shall be left to suppose that you were carried off against your will."

"If it had not been for you, you assassin . . ."

"If it had not been for me, madame, your fate would have been even worse than you tell me that it is going to be."

"Nothing could be worse! Nothing! This man who has brought me out to these savage lands because, discredited and debtridden as he is, there was no longer a place for him at home, is . . . Oh, but why do I talk to you? Why do I try to explain to one who obstinately refuses to understand, to one who desires only to blame?"

"Madame, I do not desire to blame. I desire that you should blame yourself, for the horror you brought upon Basseterre. If you will accept whatever comes as an expiation, you may find some peace of mind."

"Peace of mind! Peace of mind!" Her scorn was fulminating.

He became sententious. "Expiation cleanses conscience. And when that has happened calm will return to your spirit."

"You preach to me! You! A filibuster, a sea robber! And you preach of things you do not understand. I owe no expiation. I have done no wrong. I was a desperate woman, hard-driven by a man who is a beast, a cruel drunken beast, a broken gamester without honour; not even honest. I took my only chance to save my soul. Was I to know that Don Juan was what you say he is? Do I know it even now?"

"Do you not?" he asked her. "Did you see the ruin and desolation wantonly wrought in Basseterre, the horrors that he loosed his men to perpetrate, and do you still doubt his nature? And can you contemplate that havoc wrought so as to give you to your lover's arms, and still protest that you did no wrong? That, madame, is the offence that calls for expiation; not anything that may lie between yourself and your husband, or yourself and Don Juan."

Her mind refused admission to a conviction which it dared not harbour. Therefore she ranted on. Blood ceased to listen. He gave his attention to the sail; hauled it a little closer, so that the craft heeled over and headed straight for the bay.

It was an hour later when they brought up at the mole. A long-boat was alongside, manned by English sailors from the frigate, which in the meantime had come to anchor on the roadstead.

Odd groups of men and women, white and black, idling, cowed at the waterside, with the horror of yesterday's events still heavy upon them, stared round-eyed at Madame de Coulevain as she was handed from the boat by her stalwart, grim-faced escort, in his crumpled coat of silver-laced grey camlett and black periwig that was rather out of curl.

The little mob moved forward in wonder, slowly at first, then with quickening steps, to crowd about the unsuspected author of their woes with questions of welcome and thanksgiving for this miracle of her return, of her deliverance, as they accounted it.

Blood waited, grim and silent, his eyes upon the sparse town which showed yesterday's ugly wounds as yet unscarred. Houses displayed shattered doors and broken windows, whilst here and there a heap of ashes smouldered where a house had stood. Pieces of broken furniture lay about in the open. From the belfry of the little church standing amid the acacias in the open square came the mournful note of a passing-bell. Within the walled enclosure about it there was an ominous activity, and Negroes could be seen at work there with pick and shovel.

Captain Blood's cold blue eyes played swiftly over all this

and more. Then, almost roughly, he extricated the lady from that little mob of stricken, questioning sympathizers, who little guessed to what extent she was the author of their woes. At once conducted and, conducting, he made his way up the gently rising ground. They passed a party of British sailors filling water-casks at a fountain which had been contrived by the damming of a brook. They passed the church with its busy graveyard. They passed a company of militia at drill: men in blue coats with red facings who had been hurriedly brought over by Colonel de Coulevain from Les Carmes after the harm was done.

Delayed on the way by others whom they met and who must stop to cry out in wonder at sight of Madame de Coulevain accompanied by this tall, stern stranger, they came at last by a wide gateway into a luxuriant garden, and by an avenue of palms to a long, low house of stone and timber.

There were no signs of damage here. The Spaniards who had yesterday invaded the place, if, indeed, they had invaded it, had wrought no other mischief than to carry off the Governor's lady. The elderly Negro who admitted them broke into shrill cries upon beholding his dishevelled mistress in her crumpled gown of flowered silk. He laughed and wept at once. He uttered scraps of prayer. He capered like a dog. He caught her hand and slobbered kisses on it.

"You appeared to be loved, madame," said Captain Blood when at last they stood alone in the long dining-room.

"Of course that must surprise you," she sneered, with that twist of her full lips which he had come to know.

The door of a connecting-room was abruptly flung open, and a tall, heavily built man with prominent features and sallow, deeply lined cheeks stood at gaze. His militia coat, of blue with red facings, was stiff with tarnished gold lace. His dark bloodshot eyes opened wide at sight of her. He turned pale under his tan.

"Antoinette!" he ejaculated. He came forward unsteadily and took her by the shoulders. "Is it really you? They told me ... But where have you been since yesterday?"

"Where they told you I was, no doubt." There was little in her tone besides weariness. "Fortunately, or unfortunately, this gentleman delivered me, and he has brought me safely back."

"Fortunately or unfortunately?" he echoed, and scowled. His lip curled. The dislike of her in his eyes was not to be mistaken. He took his hands from her shoulders, and half turned to consider her companion. "This gentleman?" Then his glance darkened further. "A Spaniard?"

Captain Blood met the frown with a smile. "A Dutchman, sir," he lied. But the rest of his tale was true. "By great good-fortune I was aboard that Spanish ship the *Estremadura*. I had been picked up by her at sea a few days before. I had access to the great cabin in which the Spanish commander had locked himself with Madame your wife. I interrupted his amorous intentions. In fact, I killed him with my hands." And he added a brief account of how, thereafter, he had conveyed her from the galleon.

Monsieur de Coulevain swore profoundly to express his wonder; stood silently pondering the thing he had been told; then swore again. Blood accounted him a dull, brutish fellow whom any woman would be justified in leaving. If the Colonel felt any tenderness towards his wife, or thankfulness for her delivery from the dreadful fate to which he must suppose her to have been exposed, he kept the emotions to himself. He showed presently, however, that he could be emotional enough over the memory of yesterday's catastrophe. This Blood accounted reasonable until he came to perceive that the man's real concern was less with the sufferings of the people of Basseterre than with the possible consequences to himself when an account of his stewardship should come to be asked of him by the French Government.

Madame, her beauty sadly impaired by her pallor, her weariness and dishevelled condition, interrupted his lament to recall him to the demands of common courtesy.

"You have not yet thanked this gentleman for the heroic service he has rendered us."

Blood caught the sneer and perceived its double edge. At last he found it in his heart to pity her a little, to understand the despair which had driven her, reckless of what might betide others, so that she should escape from this boorish egotist.

Belatedly and clumsily M. de Coulevain expressed his thanks. When that was done, Madame took her leave of them. She confessed herself exhausted, and it was the old Negro, who had remained in attendance in the background, who came forward to proffer his arm and to assist her. On the threshold a Negro woman waited, all tenderness and solicitude, to put her weary mistress to bed.

Coulevain, heavy-eyed, watched her depart, and remained staring until Captain Blood's brisk voice aroused him.

"If you were to offer me some breakfast, sir, that would be a practical measure of repayment."

Coulevain swore. "Death on my life! How negligent I am! These troubles, sir . . . the ruin of the town . . . the abduction of my wife . . . it is too much, sir. You'll understand. It discomposes a man. You forgive me, Monsieur . . . I have not the honour to know your name."

"Vandermeer. Peter Vandermeer, at your service."

And then another voice cut in, a voice that spoke French with a rasping English accent. "Are you quite sure that that is your name?"

Blood spun round. On the threshold of the adjacent room from which Colonel de Coulevain had earlier issued stood now the stocky figure of a youngish man in a red coat that was laced with silver. In the plump, florid countenance Captain Blood recognized at a glance his old acquaintance Captain Macartney, who had been second in command at Antigua when some months before Captain Blood had slipped through the fingers of the British there. His momentary surprise at finding Macartney here was dispelled by remembrance of the English frigate which had passed him as they were approaching Basseterre.

The officer was smiling hatefully. "Good morning, Captain

Blood. This time you have no buccaneers at your heels, no ships, no demi-cannons with which to intimidate us."

So ominous was the tone, so clear its hint of the speaker's intention, that Blood's hand flew instinctively to his left side. The Englishman's smile became a laugh.

"Not even a sword, Captain Blood."

"Its absence will no doubt encourage your impertinences."

But now the Colonel was intervening. "Captain Blood, did you say? Captain Blood? Not the filibuster? Not . . .?"

"The filibuster indeed; the buccaneer, the transported rebel, the escaped convict on whose head the British Government has placed the price of a thousand pounds."

"A thousand pounds!" Coulevain sucked his breath. His dark, blood-injected eyes returned to the contemplation of his wife's preserver. "Sir, sir! Is this true, sir?"

Blood shrugged. "Of course it's true. Who else do you suppose could have done what I have told you that I did last night?"

Coulevain continued to stare at him with increasing wonder. "And you contrived to pass yourself off as a Dutchman on a Spanish ship?"

"Who else but Captain Blood could have done that?"

"My God!" said Coulevain.

"I hope, none the less, you'll give me some breakfast, my Colonel?"

"Aboard the *Royal Duchess*," said Macartney, evilly facetious, "you shall have all the breakfast you require."

"Much obliged. But I have a prior claim on the hospitality of Colonel de Coulevain, for services rendered to his wife."

Major Macartney – he had been promoted since Blood's last meeting with him – smiled. "My claim can wait, then, until your fast is broken."

"What claim is that?" quoth Coulevain.

"To do my duty by arresting this damned pirate, and delivering him to the hangman."

M. de Coulevain seemed shocked. "Arrest him? You want

to laugh, I think. This, sir, is France. Your warrant does not run on French soil."

"Perhaps not. But there is an agreement between France and England for the prompt exchange of any prisoners who may have escaped from a penal settlement. Under that agreement, sir, you dare not refuse to surrender Captain Blood to me."

"Surrender him to you? My guest? The man who has served me so nobly? Who is here as a direct consequence of that service? Sir, it . . . it is unthinkable." Thus he displayed to Captain Blood certain remains of decent feeling.

Macartney was gravely calm. "I perceive your scruples. I respect them. But duty is duty."

"I care nothing for your duty, sir."

The Major's manner became more stern. "Colonel de Coulevain, you will forgive me for pointing out to you that I have the means at hand to enforce my demand, and my duty will compel me to employ it."

"What!" Colonel de Coulevain was aghast. "You would land your men under arms on French soil?"

"If you are obstinate in your misplaced chivalry you will leave me no choice."

"But . . . God of my life! That would be an act of war. War between the nations would be the probable result."

Macartney shook his round head. "The certain result would be the cashiering of Colonel de Coulevain for having made the act necessary in defiance of the existing agreement." He smiled maliciously. "I think you will be sufficiently under a cloud already, my Colonel, for yesterday's events here."

Coulevain sat down heavily, dragged forth a handkerchief and mopped his brow. He was perspiring freely. He appealed in his distress to Captain Blood.

"Death of my life! What am I to do?"

"I am afraid," said Captain Blood, "that his reasoning is faultless." He stifled a yawn. "You'll forgive me. I was out in the open all night." And he, too, sat down. "Do not permit yourself to be distressed, my Colonel. This business of playing Providence is seldom requited by Fortune."

"But what am I to do, sir? What am I to do?"

Under his sleepy exterior, Captain Blood's wits were wide awake and busy. It was within his experience of these officers sent overseas that they belonged almost without exception to one of two classes: they were either men who, like Coulevain, had dissipated their fortunes, or else younger sons with no fortunes to dissipate. Now, as he afterwards expressed it, he heaved the lead so as to sound the depth of Macartney's disinterestedness and honesty of purpose.

"You will give me up, of course, my Colonel. And the British Government will pay you the reward of a thousand pounds – five thousand pieces of eight."

Each officer made a sharp movement at that, and from each came an almost inarticulate ejaculation of inquiry.

Captain Blood explained himself. "It is so provided by the agreement under which Major Macartney claims my surrender. Any reward for the apprehension of an escaped prisoner is payable to the person surrendering him to the authorities. Here, on French soil, it will be you, my Colonel, who will surrender me. Major Macartney is merely the representative of the authorities – the British Government – to whom I am surrendered."

The Englishman's face lost some of its high colour; it lengthened; his mouth drooped; his very breathing quickened. Blood had heaved the lead to some purpose. It had given him the exact depth of Macartney, who stood now tongue-tied and crestfallen, forbidden by decency from making the least protest against the suddenly vanished prospect of a thousand pounds which he had been reckoning as good as in his pocket.

But this was not the only phenomenon produced by Blood's disclosure of the exact situation. Colonel de Coulevain, too, was oddly stricken. The sudden prospect of so easily acquiring this magnificent sum seemed to have affected him as oddly as the contrary had affected Macartney. This was an unexpected complication to the observant Captain Blood. But it led him at once to remember that Madame de Coulevain had described her husband as a broken gamester harassed by creditors. He wondered what would be the ultimate clash of the evil forces he was releasing, and almost ventured to hope that in that, when it came, as once before in a similar situation, would lie his opportunity.

"There is no more to be said, my Colonel," he drawled. "Circumstances have been too much for me. I know when I've lost, and I must pay." He yawned again. "Meanwhile, if I might have a little food and rest, I should be grateful. Perhaps Major Macartney will give me leave until this evening, when he can come to fetch me with an escort."

Macartney swung aside, and paced towards the open windows. The elation, the masterfulness, had completely left him. He dragged his feet. His shoulders drooped. "Very well," he said sourly, and checked his aimless wandering to turn towards the door. "I'll return for you at six o'clock."

But on the threshold he paused. "You'll play me no tricks, Captain Blood?"

"Tricks? What tricks can I play?" The Captain smiled wistfully. "I have no buccaneers, no ship, no demi-cannon. Not even a sword, as you remarked, Major. For the only trick I might yet play you . . ." He broke off, and changed his tone to add more briskly: "Major Macartney, since there's no thousand pounds to be earned by you for taking me, should you not be a fool to refuse a thousand pounds for leaving me? For forgetting that you have seen me?"

Macartney flushed. "What the devil do you mean?"

"Now don't be getting hot, Major. Think it over until this evening. A thousand pounds is a mort of money. You don't earn it every day, or every year, in the service of King James; and you'll perceive quite clearly by now that you won't earn it by arresting me."

Macartney bit his lip, looking searchingly meanwhile at the Colonel. "It . . . it's unthinkable!" he exploded. "I am not to be bribed. Unthinkable! If it were known . . ."

Captain Blood chuckled. "Is that what's troubling you? But

who's to tell? Colonel de Coulevain owes me silence at least."

The brooding Colonel roused himself. "Oh, at least, at least. Have no doubt of that, sir."

Macartney looked from one to the other of them, a man plainly in the grip of temptation. He swore in his throat. "I'll return at six," he announced shortly.

"With an escort, Major, or alone?" was Blood's sly question.

"That's . . . that's as may be."

He strode out, and they heard his angrily-planted feet go clattering across the hall. Captain Blood winked at the Colonel, and rose. "I'll wager you a thousand pounds that there will be no escort."

"I cannot take the wager, since I am of the same opinion."

"Now, that's a pity, for I shall require the money, and I don't know how else to obtain it. It is possible he may consent to accept my note of hand."

"No need to distress yourself on that score."

Captain Blood searched the Colonel's heavy, bloodhound countenance. It wore a smile, a smile intended to be friendly. But somehow Captain Blood did not like the face any better on that account.

The smile broadened to an increasing friendliness. "You may break your fast and take your rest with an easy mind, sir. I will deal with Major Macartney when he returns."

"You will deal with him? Do you mean that you will advance the money?"

"I owe you no less, my dear Captain."

Again Captain Blood gave him a long, searching stare before he bowed and spoke his eloquent thanks. The proposal was amazing. So amazing coming from a broken gamester harassed by creditors, that it was not to be believed – at least not by a man of Captain Blood's experience.

When, having broken his fast, he repaired to the curtained bed which Abraham had prepared for him in a fair room above stairs, he lay, despite his weariness, for some time considering it all. He recalled the subtle sudden betraying change in Coulevain's manner when it was disclosed that the reward would go to him; he saw again the oily smile on the Colonel's face when he had announced that he would deal with Major Macartney. If he knew men at all, Coulevain was the last whom he would trust. Of himself he was aware that he was an extremely negotiable security. The British Government had set a definite price upon his head. But it was widely known that the Spaniards whom he had harassed and pillaged without mercy would pay three or four times that price for him alive, so that they might have the pleasure of roasting him in the fires of the Faith. Had this scoundrel Coulevain suddenly perceived that the advent in Mariegalante of this saviour of his wife's honour was something in the nature of a windfall with which to repair his battered fortunes? If the half of what Madame de Coulevain had said of her husband in the course of that night's sailing was true there was no reason to suppose that any nice scruples would restrain him.

The more he considered, the more the Captain's uneasiness increased. He began to perceive that he was in an extremely tight corner. He even went so far as to ask himself if the most prudent course might not be to rise, weary as he was, slip down to the mole, get aboard the pinnace which already had served him so well, and trust himself in her to the mercies of the ocean. But whither steer a course in that frail cockleshell? Only the neighbouring islands were possible, and they were all either French or British. On British soil he was certain of arrest with the gallows to follow, whilst on French soil he could hardly expect to fare better, considering his experience here where the commander was so deeply in his debt. If only he had money with which to purchase a passage on some ship that might pick him up at sea, money enough to induce a shipmaster to ask no questions whilst landing him on Tortuga. But he had none. The only thing of value in his possession was the great pearl in his left ear, worth perhaps five hundred pieces.

He was disposed to curse that raid in canoes upon the pearl fisheries of Cariaco which had resulted in disaster, had separated him from his ship, and had left him since adrift.

But since cursing past events was the least profitable method of averting future ones, he decided to take the sleep of which he stood in need, hoping for the counsel which sleep is said to bring.

He timed himself to awaken at six o'clock, the hour at which Major Macartney was to return, and, his well-trained senses responding to that command, he awakened punctually. The angle of the sun was his sufficient clock. He slipped from the bed, found his shoes, which Abraham had cleaned, his coat, which had been brushed, and his periwig, which had been combed by the good Negro. He had scarcely donned them when through the open window floated up to him the sound of a voice. It was the voice of Macartney, and it was answered instantly by the Colonel's with a hearty: "Come you in, sir. Come in."

In the nick of time, thought Blood; and he accepted the circumstances as a good omen. Cautiously he made his way below, meeting no one on the stairs or in the hall. Outside the door of the dining-room he stood listening. A hum of voices reached him. But they were distant. They came from the room beyond. Noiselessly he opened the door and slid across the threshold. The place was empty, as he had expected. The door of the adjacent room stood ajar. Through this came now the Major's laugh, and upon the heels of it the Colonel's voice.

"Depend upon it. He is under my hand. Spain, as you've said, will pay three times this sum, or even more, for him. Therefore he should be glad to ransom himself, for, say, five times the amount of this advance." He chuckled, adding: "I have the advantage of you, Major, in that I can hold him to ransom, which your position as a British officer makes impossible to you. All things considered, you are fortunate, yes, and wise, to earn a thousand pounds for yourself."

"My God!" said Macartney, rendered suddenly virtuous by envy. "And that's how you pay your debts and reward the man for preserving your wife's life and honour! Faith, I'm glad I'm not your creditor."

"Shall we abstain from comments?" the Colonel suggested sourly.

"Oh, by all means. Give me the money, and I'll go my ways."

There was a chinking squelch twice repeated, as of money-bags that are raised and set down again. "It is in rolls of twenty double moidores. Will you count them?"

There followed a mumbling pause, and at the end of it came the Colonel's voice again. "If you will sign this quittance, the matter is at an end."

"Quittance?"

"I'll read it to you." And the Colonel read: " 'I acknowledge, and give Colonel Jerome de Coulevain this quittance for the sum of five thousand pieces of eight, received from him in consideration of my forbearing from any action against Captain Blood, and of my undertaking no action whatever hereafter for as long as he may remain the guest of Colonel de Coulevain on the Island of Mariegalante or elsewhere. Given under my hand and seal this tenth day of July of 1688.' "

As the Colonel's voice trailed off there came an explosion from Macartney.

"God's death, Colonel! Are you mad, or do you think that I am?"

"What do you find amiss? Is it not a correct statement?"

Macartney banged the table in his vehemence. "It puts a rope round my neck."

"Only if you play me false. What other guarantee have I that when you've taken these five thousand pieces you will keep faith with me?"

"You have my word," said Macartney in a passion. "And my word must content you."

"Your word! Your word!" The Frenchman's sneer was unmistakable. "Ah, that, no. Your word is not enough."

"You want to insult me!"

"Pish! Let us be practical, Major. Ask yourself: would you accept the word of a man in a transaction in which his own part is dishonest?"

"Dishonest, sir? What the devil do you mean?"

"Are you not accepting a bribe to be false to your duty? Is not that dishonesty?"

"By God! This comes well from you, considering your intentions."

"You make it necessary. Besides, have I played the hypocrite as to my part? I have been unnecessarily frank, even to appearing a rogue. But, as in your own case, Major, necessity knows no law with me."

A pause followed upon those conciliatory words. Then: "Nevertheless," said Macartney, "I do not sign that paper."

"You'll sign and seal it, or I do not pay the money. What do you fear, Major? I give you my word—"

"You word! Hell and the Devil! In what is your word better than mine?"

"The circumstances make it better. On my side there can be no temptation to break faith, as on yours. It cannot profit me."

It was clear by now to Blood that since Macartney had not struck the Frenchman for his insults, he would end by signing. Only a desperate need of money could so have curbed the Englishman. He therefore heard without surprise Macartney's angry outburst.

"Give me the pen. Let us have done."

Another pause followed, then the Colonel's voice: "And now seal it here, where I have set the wax. The signet on your finger will serve."

Captain Blood waited for no more. The long windows stood open to the garden over which the dusk was rapidly descending. He stepped noiselessly out and vanished amid the shrubs. About the stem of a tall silk-cotton tree he found a tough slender liana swarming like a snake. He brought out his knife, slashed it near the root, and drew it down.

As Major Macartney, softly humming to himself, a heavy leathern bag in the crook of each arm, came presently down the avenue between the palms where the evening shadows were deepest, he tripped over what he conceived to be a rope stretched taut across the path, and spreadeagled forward with a crash.

Lying momentarily half stunned by the heavy fall, a weight descended on his back, and in his ear a pleasant voice was murmuring in English with a strong Irish accent: "I have no buccaneers, Major, no ship, no demi-cannon, and, as you remarked, not even a sword. But I still have my hands and my wits, and they should more than suffice to deal with a paltry rogue like you."

"By God!" swore Macartney, though half choked. "You shall hang for this, Captain Blood! By God, you shall!" Frenziedly he struggled to elude the grip of his assailant. His sword being useless in his present position, he sought to reach the pocket in which he carried a pistol, but, by the movement, merely betrayed its presence. Captain Blood possessed himself of it.

"Will you be quiet now?" he asked. "Or must I be blowing out your brains?"

"You dirty Judas! You thieving pirate! Is this how you keep faith?"

"I pledged you no faith, you nasty rogue. Your bargain was with the French colonel, not with me. It was he who bribed you to be false to your duty. I had no part in it."

"Had you not? You lying dog! You're a pretty pair of scoundrels, on my soul! Working in conjunction."

"Now that," said Blood, "is needlessly and foolishly offensive."

Macartney broke into fresh expletives.

"You talk too much," said Captain Blood, and tapped him twice over the head with the butt of the pistol, using great science. The Major sank forward gently, like a man asleep.

Captain Blood rose, and peered about him through the dusk. All was still. He went to pick up the leather bags which Macartney had dropped as he fell. He made a sling for them with his scarf, and so hung them from his neck. Then he raised the unconscious Major, swung him skilfully to his shoulder, and, thus burdened, went staggering down the avenue and out into the open.

The night was hot. Macartney was heavy. The sweat ran from Blood's pores. But he went steadily ahead until he reached the low wall of the churchyard, just as the moon was beginning to rise. On to the summit of this wall he eased himself of his burden, toppled it over into the churchyard, and then climbed after it. What he had to do there was quickly done by the light of the moon under the shelter of that wall. With the man's own sash he trussed him up at wrists and ankles. Then he stuffed some of the Major's periwig into his mouth, using the fellow's neckcloth to hold this unpleasant gag in position and taking care to leave his nostrils free.

As he was concluding the operation, Macartney opened his eyes and glared at him.

"Sure now it's only me: your old friend, Captain Blood. I'm just after making you comfortable for the night. When they find you in the morning, ye can tell them any convenient lie that will save you the trouble of explaining what can't be explained at all. It's a very good night I'll be wishing you, Major darling."

He went over the wall and briskly down the road that led to the sea.

On the mole lounged the British sailors who manned the longboat from the *Royal Duchess*, awaiting the Major's return. Further on, some men of Mariegalante were landing their haul from a fishing-boat that had just come in. None gave heed to Blood as he stepped along to the mole's end where that morning he had moored the pinnace. In the locker, where he stowed the heavy bags of gold, there was still some of the food that he had brought away last night from the *Estremadura*. He could not take the risk of adding to it. But he filled the two small water casks at the fountain.

Then he stepped aboard, cast off and got out the sweeps. Another night on the open sea lay ahead of him. The wind, however, was still in the same quarter as last night and would favour the run to Guadeloupe upon which he had determined.

Once out of the bay, he hoisted sail, and ran northward along the coast and the shallow cliffs which cast an inky shadow against the moon's white radiance. On he crawled through a sea of rippling quicksilver until he reached the island's end; then he headed straight across the ten miles of intervening water.

Off Grande Terre, the eastern of the two main islands of Guadeloupe, he lay awaiting sunrise. When it came, bringing a freshening of the wind, he ran close past Saint Anne, which was empty of shipping, and, hugging the coast, sailed on in a north-easterly direction until he came, some two hours later, to Port du Moule.

There were half a dozen ships in the harbour, and Blood scanned them with anxiety until his glance alighted on a black brigantine that was bellied like a Flemish alderman. Those lines were a sufficient advertisement of her Dutch origin, and Captain Blood, sweeping alongside, hailed her with confidence and climbed to her deck.

"I am in haste," he informed her sturdy captain, "to reach the northern coast of French Hispaniola, and I will pay you well for a passage thither."

The Dutchman eyed him without favour. "If you're in haste you had better seek what you need elsewhere. I am for Curaçao."

"I've said I'll pay you well. Five thousand pieces of eight should compensate you for delays."

"Five thousand pieces!" The Dutchman stared. The sum was as much as he could hope to earn by this present voyage. "Who are you, sir?"

"What's that to the matter? I am one who will pay five thousand pieces."

The skipper of the brigantine screwed up his little blue eyes. "Will you pay in advance?"

"The half of it. The other half I shall obtain when my destination is reached. But you may hold me aboard until you have the money." Thus he ensured that the Dutchman, ignorant of the fact that the entire sum was already under his hand, should keep faith.

"I could sail tonight," said the other slowly.

Blood at once produced one of the two bags. The other he had stowed in one of the water casks in the locker of the pinnace, and there it remained unsuspected until four days later, when they were in the narrow seas between Hispaniola and Tortuga.

Then Captain Blood, announcing that he would put himself ashore, paid over the balance of the money, and climbed down the side of the brig to re-enter the pinnace. When, presently, the Dutchman observed him to be steering not, indeed, towards Hispaniola, but a northerly course in the direction of Tortuga, that stronghold of the buccaneers, his growing suspicions may have been fully confirmed. He remained, however, untroubled, the only man who, in addition to Blood himself, had really profited by that transaction on the Island of Mariegalante.

Thus Captain Blood came back at last to Tortuga and to the fleet that was by now mourning him as dead. With that fleet of five tall ships he sailed into the harbour of Basseterre a month later with intent to settle a debt which he conceived to lie between Colonel de Coulevain and himself.

His appearance there in such force fluttered both the garrison and the inhabitants. But he came too late for his purposes. Colonel de Coulevain was no longer there to be fluttered. He had been sent back to France under arrest.

Captain Blood was informed of this by Colonel Sancerre, who had succeeded to the military command of Mariegalante, and who received him with the courtesy due to a filibuster who comes backed by the powerful fleet that Blood had anchored in the roadstead.

Captain Blood fetched a sigh when he heard the news. "A pity! I had a little word to say to him; a little debt to settle."

"A little debt of five thousand pieces of eight, I think," said the Frenchman.

"On my faith, you are well informed."

The Colonel explained. "When the General of the Armies of France in America came here to inquire into the matter of the Spanish raid on Mariegalante, he discovered that Colonel de Coulevain had robbed the French Colonial Treasury of that sum. There was proof of it in a quittance that was found among Monsieur de Coulevain's papers."

"So that's where he got the money!"

"I see that you understand." The Commandant looked grave. "Robbery is a serious, shameful matter, Captain Blood."

"I know it is. I've practised a good deal of it myself."

"And I've little doubt that they will hang Monsieur de Coulevain, poor devil."

Captain Blood nodded. "No doubt of that. But we'll save our tears to water some nobler grave, my Colonel."

10

GALLOWS' KEY

IT IS impossible now to determine whether Gallows' Key took its name from the events I am about to relate or bore it already previously among seafaring men. Jeremy Pitt in his log gives no hint, and the miniature island is not now to be identified with precision. All that we know positively, and this from Pitt's log of the *Arabella*, is that it forms part of the group known as the Albuquerque Keys, lying in 12° northern latitude and 85° western longitude, some sixty miles north-west of Porto Bello.

It is little more than a barren rock, frequented only by sea-birds and the turtles that come to deposit their eggs in the golden sand of the reef-enclosed lagoon on its eastern side. This strip of beach shelves rapidly to a depth of some sixty fathoms, and the entrance to the lagoon is by a gap of not more than twenty yards in the rocky amphitheatre which goes to form it.

Into this secure if desolate haven sailed Captain Easterling one April day of the year 1688 in his thirty-gun frigate the *Avenger*, followed by the two ships that made up his fleet: the *Hermes*, a frigate of twenty-six guns, commanded by Roger Galloway, and the *Valiant*, a brigantine carrying twenty, in charge of Crosby Pike, who once had sailed with Captain Blood and was realizing his mistake on making a change of admiral.

You will remember this scoundrel Easterling, how once he had tried a fall with Peter Blood, when Blood was on the very threshold of his career as a buccaneer, and how, as a consequence, Easterling's ship had been blown from under him and himself swept from the seas.

But laboriously, with the patience and tenacity found in bad men as in good, Easterling had won back to his old position and was afloat once more and in greater strength than ever before upon the Caribbean.

He was, in Peter Blood's own words, just a filthy pirate, a ruthless bloodthirsty robber, without a spark even of that honour which is said to prevail among thieves. His followers made up a lawless mob of mixed nationalities, subject to no discipline and obeying no rules save those which concerned the division of their spoils. They practised no discrimination in their piracy. They would attack an English or Dutch merchantman as readily as a Spanish galleon, and deal out the same ruthless brutality to the one as to the other.

Now, despite his ill-repute even among buccaneers, Easterling had succeeded in luring away from Blood's following the resolute Crosby Pike, with his twenty-gun ship and well-disciplined crew of a hundred and thirty men. The lure had been that old story of Morgan's treasure with which Easterling once had unsuccessfully attempted to beguile Blood.

Again he told that hoary tale of how he had sailed with Henry Morgan and had been with him at the sack of Panama; how – as was well known – on the return march across the isthmus there had been all but mutiny among Morgan's followers on a suspicion that the booty divided among them was very far from being all the booty taken; how it was murmured that Morgan had secretly abstracted a great portion for himself; how Morgan, becoming alarmed lest a mutinous search of his personal baggage should reveal the truth of the rumour, had taken Easterling into his confidence and sought his aid in what was to do. Between them they had buried that treasure – a treasure of pearls and precious stones to the fabulous value of at least a half million pieces of eight – at a spot on the banks of the Chagres River. They were to return to unearth it later, when opportunity should serve. Morgan, however, swept by destiny along other profitable pursuits, was still postponing his return when death overtook him. Easterling had never returned because never before had he commanded the necessary force for the penetration of Spanish territory, or the necessary strength of ship for the safe conveyance of the treasure once it was reclaimed.

Such had been the tale to which Blood had scorned to lend an ear but to which Pike succumbed, in spite of Blood's warning against joining forces with so unscrupulous a rogue and his freely expressed conviction that no such treasure existed.

Pitying Pike for his credulity, Blood bore him no resentment for his defection, and feared rather than hoped that the sequel would punish him sufficiently.

Blood himself at this time had been planning an expedition to Darien. But since Easterling's activities on the isthmus might put the Spaniards on the alert, he found it prudent to postpone the business. His fleet of five stout ships scattered and went a-roving without definite objective. This was at the beginning of April, and it was concerted that they should reassemble at Mosquito Keys, at the end of May, when the expedition to Darien could be considered anew.

The *Arabella*, going south by the Windward Passage, and then east along the southern coast of Hispaniola, came, some twenty miles beyond Cape Tiburon, upon an English merchantman in a foundering condition. She was kept precariously afloat so long as the sea was calm by the shifting of her guns and all other heavy gear to larboard, so as to keep above water the gaping wounds in her starboard quarter. Her broken spars and fractured mainmast told an eloquent tale, and Blood imagined that Spaniards had been at work. He discovered instead, when he went to her assistance, that she had yesterday been attacked and plundered by Easterling, who had put half her crew to the sword and brutally killed her captain for not having struck his colours when summoned to do so.

The *Arabella* towed her within ten miles of Port Royal, and daring to go no nearer lest she should draw down upon herself the Jamaica Squadron, left her there to complete alone what little remained of the voyage to safety.

That done, however, the *Arabella* did not sail east again, but headed south for the Main. To Pitt, his shipmaster, Blood explained his motives.

"We'll be keeping an eye on this blackguard Easterling, so we will, Jerry, and maybe more than an eye."

And south they sailed, since that was the way Easterling had gone. To the tale of his treasure, Blood, as we know, attached no faith. He regarded it as an invention to gull such credulous fellows as Pike into association. In this, however, he was presently to be proven wrong.

Creeping down the Mosquito Coast, he found a snug anchorage in a cove of one of the numerous islands in the Lagoon of Chiriqui. There for the moment he elected to lie concealed, and whence he watched the operations of Easterling, twenty miles away, through the eyes of friendly Mosquito Indians whom he employed as scouts. From these he learned that Easterling had cast anchor a little to westward of the mouth of the Chagres, that he had landed a force of three hundred and fifty men, and that he was penetrating with them into the isthmus. From his knowledge of Easterling's total strength, Blood computed that hardly more than a hundred men had been left behind to guard the waiting ships.

Whilst waiting in his turn, Blood took his ease. On a cane daybed set under an improvised awning on the poop (for the weather was growing hot) the buccaneer found sufficient adventure for his spirit in the verse of Horace and the prose of Suetonius. When physical activity was desired, he would swim in the clear, jade-green waters of the lagoon, or, landing on the palm-fringed shore of that uninhabited island, he would take a hand with his men in the capture of turtle, or in the hewing of wood to provide the fuel for the boucan fires in which their succulent flesh was being cured.

Meanwhile his Indians brought him news, first of a skirmish between Easterling's men and a party of Spaniards who evidently had got wind of the presence on Darien of the buccaneers. Then came word that Easterling was marching back to the coast; a couple of days later he was informed of another encounter between Easterling and a Spanish force, in which the buccaneers had suffered severely, although in the end they had beaten off the attack. Lastly came news of yet a third engagement, and this was brought, together with other precious details, by one who had taken part in it.

He was one of Pike's men, a hard-bitten old adventurer, who had given up logwood-cutting to take to the sea. His name was Cunley, and he had been rendered helpless by a gunshot wound in the thigh and left by Easterling's retreating force to die where he had fallen. Overlooked by the Spaniards, he had dragged himself into the scrub for shelter and thus into the hands of the watchful Indians. They had handled him tenderly, so that he should survive to tell his tale to Captain Blood, and they had quieted his alarms with assertions in their broken Spanish that it was to Don Pedro Sangre that he was being conveyed.

Tenderly they hoisted the crippled fellow aboard the *Arabella*, where Blood's first care was to employ his surgeon's skill to dress the hideous festering wound. Thereafter, in the wardroom, converted for the moment into a sickbay, Cunley told in bitterness the tale of the adventure.

Morgan's treasure was real enough. The buccaneers were bearing it back to the waiting ships, and in value it exceeded all that Easterling had represented. But it was being dearly bought – most dearly by Pike's contingent, whence the bitterness investing Cunley's tale. Going and coming they had been harassed by Spaniards and once by a party of hostile Indians. Further, they had been reduced by fever and sickness on that difficult march through a miasmic country where mosquitoes had almost eaten them alive. Of the three hundred and fifty men who had left the ships, Cunley computed that after the last engagement, in which he had been wounded, not more than two hundred remained alive. But the ugly fact was that not more than twenty of these were men of Pike's. Yet Pike had brought ashore by Easterling's orders the heaviest of the three contingents, landing a hundred and thirty men, and leaving a bare score to guard the *Valiant*, whilst fifty men at least had been left on each of the other ships.

Easterling had so contrived that Pike's contingent was ever in the van, so that it had borne the brunt of every attack the buccaneers had suffered. It was not to be supposed that Pike had submitted to this without remonstrances. Protests had grown increasingly bitter as the evil continued. But Easterling, backed by his earlier associate Roger Galloway, who commanded the *Hermes*, had browbeaten Pike into submission, whilst the ruffianly followers of these two captains, by preponderance of numbers which remained at comparatively full strength, had easily imposed their will upon the dwindling force of the *Valiant*. If all her present survivors got back to the ship, the *Valiant* could now muster a crew of barely forty hands, whilst the other two combined a strength of nearly three hundred men.

"Ye see, Captain," Cunley concluded grimly, "how this Easterling has used us. As the monkey used the cat. And now him and Galloway – them two black-hearted bastards – is in such strength that Crosby Pike dursn't say a word o' protest. It was a black day for all of us, Captain, when the *Valiant* left your fleet to join that blackguard Easterling's, treasure or no treasure."

"Treasure or no treasure," Captain Blood repeated. "And I'm thinking that for Captain Pike no treasure it will prove."

He rose from his chair by the sick man's bed, tall, graceful and vigorous in his black small clothes, silver-broidered waistcoat and full white cambric sleeves. His coat of black and silver he had discarded before commencing his surgical ministrations. He waved away the white-clad Negro who attended with bowl and lint and forceps, and, alone with Cunley, he paced to the wardroom ports and back. His long supple fingers toyed thoughtfully with the curls of his black periwig; his eyes, blue as sapphires, were now as hard.

"I thought that Pike would prove a minnow in the jaws of Easterling. It but remains for Easterling to swallow him, and, faith, it's what he'll be doing."

"Ye've said it, Captain. It's plaguey little o' that treasure me and my mates o' the *Valiant* or Captain Pike himself'll ever see. The thirty that's left of us'll be lucky if they gets away alive. That's my faith, Captain."

"And mine, bedad," said Captain Blood. But his mouth was grim.

"Can ye do nothing for the honour of the Brethren of the Coast and for the sake o' justice, Captain?"

"It's thinking of it I am. If the fleet were with me I'd sail in this minute and take a hand. But with just this one ship . . ." He broke off and shrugged. "The odds are a trifle heavy. But I'll watch, and I'll consider."

Cunley's opinion that it was a black day for the *Valiant* when she joined Easterling's fleet was now being shared by every survivor of her crew, and by none more fully than by Captain Pike himself. He had become apprehensive of the final issue of the adventure, and his apprehensions received the fullest confirmation on the morrow of their sailing from the Chagres, when they came to anchorage in that lagoon of Gallows' Key to which I have alluded.

Easterling's *Avenger* led the way into that diminutive circular harbour, and anchored nearest to the shore. Next came the *Hermes*. The *Valiant*, now bringing up the rear, was compelled, for lack of room within, to anchor in the narrow roadstead. Thus again Pike was given the most vulnerable station in the event of attack – a station in which his ship must act as a shield for the others.

Trenam, Pike's sturdy young Cornish lieutenant, who from the outset had been against association with Easterling, perceiving the object of this disposition, was not ashamed to urge Pike to take up anchor and be off in the night, abandoning Easterling and the treasure before worse befell them. But Pike, as obstinate as he was courageous, repudiated this for a coward counsel.

"By God!" he swore. "It's what Easterling desires! We've earned our share of that treasure, and we're not sailing without it."

But the practical Trenam shook his fair head. "That will be as Easterling chooses. He's got the strength to enforce his will, and the will to play the rogue, or I'm a fool else."

Pike silenced him by making oath that he was not afraid of twenty Easterlings.

And his air was as truculent when next morning, in response to a signal from the flagship, he went aboard the *Avenger*.

He was awaited in the cabin not only by Easterling, arrayed in tawdry splendour, but by Galloway, who favoured the loose leather breeches and cotton shirt that made up the habitual garb of a boucan-hunter. Easterling was massively built and swarthy – a man still young, with fine eyes and a full black beard, behind which, when he laughed, there was a flash of strong white teeth. Galloway, squat and broad, was not only apelike in build, with his long arms and short powerful legs, but oddly apelike in countenance, out of which two bright little wicked eyes sparkled under a shallow wrinkled brow.

They received Captain Pike with every show of friendliness, sat him down at the greasy table, poured rum for him and pledged him, whereafter Easterling came promptly to business.

"We've sent for ye, Captain Pike, because at present we're carrying, as it were, all our eggs in one basket. This treasure," and he waved a hand in the direction of the chests containing it, "is best divided without more ado, so that each of us can go about his business."

Pike took heart at this promising beginning. "Ye mean to break up the fleet, then?" said he indifferently.

"Why not, since the job's done? Roger here and me has decided to quit piracy. We're for home with the fortune we've made. I'll belike turn farmer somewhere in Devon." He laughed.

Pike smiled, but offered no comment. He was not at any time a man of many words, as his long, dour, weatherbeaten face announced.

Easterling cleared his throat and resumed. "Me and Roger's been considering that some change in the provisions o' the articles would be only fair. They do run that one-third of what's left over after I've taken my fifth goes to each of the three ships."

"Aye, that's how they run, and that's fair enough for me," said Pike.

"That's not our opinion, Roger's and mine, now that we come to think it over."

Pike opened his mouth to answer, but Easterling, giving him no time, ran on:

"Roger and me don't see as you should take a third to share among thirty men, while we share each of us the same among a hundred and fifty."

Captain Pike was swept by sudden passion. "Was that why ye saw to it that my men were always put where the Spaniards could kill them until we're reduced to less than a quarter of our strength at the outset?"

Easterling's black brows met above eyes that were suddenly malevolent.

"Now what the devil do you mean by that, Captain Pike, if you please?"

"It's an imputation," said Galloway dryly. "A nasty imputation."

"No imputation at all," said Pike. "It's a fact."

"A fact, eh?" Easterling was smiling, and the lean, tough resolute Pike grew uneasy under that smile. Galloway's bright little ape's eyes were considering him oddly. The very air of that untidy, evil-smelling cabin became charged with menace. Pike had a vision of brutalities witnessed in the course of his association with Easterling, wanton, unnecessary brutalities springing from the sheer lust of cruelty. He recalled words in which Captain Blood had warned him against associating with a man whom he described as treacherous and foul by nature. If he had hugged a doubt of the deliberate calculation by which his own men had been sacrificed on Darien, that doubt was now dispelled.

He was as a sleepwalker who awakens suddenly to find himself on the edge of a precipice into which another step must have projected him. The instinct of self-preservation made him recoil from an attitude of truculence which might lead to his being pistolled on the spot. He pushed back the hair from his moist brow and commanded himself to answer in level tones.

"What I mean is that if my men have been reduced, they've suffered this in the common cause. They will consider it unfair to break the articles on any such grounds."

He argued on. He reminded Easterling of the practice of matelotage among buccaneers, whereby every man enters into a partnership with another in which the two make common cause and under which each is the other's heir. In this alone lay reason why many of his men who were to inherit should feel defrauded by any change in the articles.

Easterling's evil grin gave way again to a scowl. "What's it to me what any of your mangy followers may feel? I'm admiral of this fleet, and my word is law."

"So it is," said Pike. "And your word is in the articles under which we sailed with you."

"To hell with the articles!" roared Captain Easterling.

He rose and stood over Pike, towering and menacing, his head almost touching the ceiling of the cabin. He spoke deliberately. "I'm telling you things is changed since we signed them articles. What I says is more nor any articles, and what I says is that the *Valiant* can have a tenth share of the plunder. Ye'ld be wise to take it, remembering the saying that who tries to grasp too much ends by holding nothing."

Pike stared up at him with fallen jaw. He had turned pale from the stress of the conflict within him between rage and prudence.

"By God, Easterling . . ." He broke off abruptly.

Easterling scowled down upon him. "Continue," he commanded. "Finish what ye has to say."

Pike shrugged despondently. "Ye know I dursn't accept your offer. Ye knew my men would tear me in pieces if I did so without consulting them."

"Then away with you to consult them. I've a mind to slit your pimpish ears so that they may see what happens to them as gets pert with Captain Easterling. You may tell your scum that if they has the impudence to refuse my offer they needn't trouble to send you here again. They can up anchor and be off to Hell. Remind 'em of what I says: that who tries to grasp too much ends by holding nothing. Away with you, Captain Pike, with that message."

Not until he was back aboard his own ship did Captain Pike release the rage from which he was all but bursting. And the sound of it, the tale he told in the ship's waist with the survivors of his crew about him, aroused in his violent followers a rage to match his own. Trenam added fuel to the flames by the views he expressed.

"If the swine means to break faith is it likely he'll stop half way? Depend on it, if we accept this tenth, he'll find a pretext to cheat us of all. Captain Blood was in the right. We should never ha' put our trust in that son of a dog."

One of the hands spoke up, voicing the feelings of all. "But since we've put it, we've got to see he keeps it."

Pike, who was leaning by now to Trenam's despondent view of their case, waited for the chorus of angry approval to subside.

"Will you tell me how we are to do it? We are some forty men against three hundred. A twenty-gun brig against two frigates with fifty guns of heavier weight between them."

This gave them pause until another bold one spoke. "He says a tenth or naught. Our answer is a third or naught. There's honour among buccaneers, and we hold him to his pledge, to the articles upon which the dirty thief enlisted us."

As one man the crew supported him. "Go you back with that answer, Captain."

"And if he refuses?"

It was Trenam who now thought he held the answer.

"There's ways of compelling him. Tell him we'll raise the whole Brotherhood of the Coast against him. Captain Blood will see that we have justice. Captain Blood's none so fond of him, as he well knows. Remind him of that, Captain. Go you back and tell him."

It was a powerful card to play. Pike realized this; yet he confessed that he did not relish the task of playing it. But his men turned upon him with upbraidings. It was he who had persuaded them to follow Easterling. It was he who had not known how to make a stand against Easterling's encroachments from the outset. They had done their part. It was for him to see to it that they were not cheated of their pay.

So back from the *Valiant* at her anchorage in the very neck of the harbour went Captain Pike in the cockboat to convey his men's answer to Captain Easterling, and to hoist the bogey of Captain Blood and the Brethren of the Coast, upon which he depended now for his own safety.

The interview took place in the waist of the *Avenger* before an audience of her crew and in the presence of Captain Galloway, who was still aboard her. It was short and violent.

When Captain Pike had stated that his men insisted upon the fulfilment of the terms of the articles, Easterling laughed. His crew laughed with him; some there were who cheered Pike ironically.

"If that's their last word, my man," said Easterling, "they can up anchor and away to the devil. I've no more to say to them."

"It'll be the worse for you, Captain, if they go," said Pike steadily.

"D'ye threaten me, by God!" The man's great bulk seemed to swell with rage.

"I warn you, Captain."

"You warn me? Warn me of what?"

"That the Brethren of the Coast, the whole buccaneering fraternity, will be raised against you for this breach of faith."

"Breach of faith!" Easterling's voice soared in pitch. "Breach of faith, ye bastard scum! D'ye dare stand before my face and say that to me?" He plucked a pistol from his belt. "Be off this ship at once, and tell your blackguards that if the *Valiant* is still there by noon I'll blow her out of the water. Away with you."

Pike, choking with indignation, and made bold by it, played his master card.

"Very well," said he. "You'll have Captain Blood to deal with for this."

Pike had reckoned upon intimidating, but neither upon the extent to which his words would achieve it nor the blind fury that follows panic in such natures as that of the man with whom he dealt.

"Captain Blood?" Easterling spoke through his teeth, his great face purple. "You'll go whining to Captain Blood, will you? Go whine in Hell, then." And on the word, at point-blank range, he shot Pike through the head.

The buccaneers standing about them recoiled in momentary horror as the man's body went backwards across the hatch coaming. Easterling jeered coarsely at their squeamishness. Galloway looked on, his little eyes glittering, his face inscrutable.

"Take up that carrion." Easterling pointed with his still smoking pistol. "Hang it from the yard-arm. Let it serve as a warning to those swine on the *Valiant* of what happens to them as gets pert with Captain Easterling."

A long-drawn cry, in which anger, fear and pity were all blended, went up from the deck of Pike's ship when the crew, crowding the larboard bulwarks, perceived through the rigging of the *Hermes* the limp body of their captain swinging from the yard-arm of the *Avenger*. So intent were these men that they paid no heed to the two long Indian canoes that came alongside to starboard, or even to the tall gentleman in black and silver who stepped from the accommodation ladder to the deck behind them. Not until his crisp dry voice rang out were they aware of him.

"I arrive a trifle late, it seems."

They turned and beheld him on the hatch-coaming, his left hand on the pummel of his rapier, his face in the shadow of his broad plumed hat, his eyes hard and cold with anger. Asking themselves how he came there, they stared at him as if he were an apparition, mystified, incredulous, doubting their vision.

At last young Trenam sprang towards him, his eyes blazing with excitement in his grey face. "Captain Blood! Is it indeed you! But how—?"

Captain Blood quieted him by a wave of the long supple hand emerging from the foam of lace at his wrist. "I've never been far from you ever since you landed on Darien. I know your case, and this is no more than I foresaw. But I had hoped to avert it."

"You'll call a reckoning from that treacherous dog?"

"To be sure I will, and at once. That hideous gesture demands an instant answer." His voice was as grim as his countenance. "You have men here to lay the guns. Get them below at once."

The *Valiant* had been swinging with the first of the gentle ebb when Blood stepped aboard; she stood now in the line of the channel, so that the operation of opening the gun ports could not be discerned from the other ships.

"The guns?" gasped Trenam. "But, Captain, we're in no case to fight. We've neither the men nor the metal."

"Enough for what's to do. Men and guns are not all that count in these affairs. Easterling gave you this station so that you should cover the other ships." Blood uttered a short, stern laugh. "He shall learn the strategic disadvantages of it, so he shall. Get your gun crew below." Then he gave other orders briskly. "Eight of you to man the longboat. There are two canoes astern well manned to assist you warp your ship broadside when the time comes. The ebbing tide will help you. Send aloft every man you can spare, to loose sail once we're out of the channel. Bestir, Trenam! Bestir!"

He dived below to the main deck, where the gun crew was already at work clearing the guns for action. He stimulated the men by his words and manner, and received unquestioning obedience from them; for, without understanding what might be afoot, they were stirred almost to enthusiasm by their confidence in him and their assurance that he would avenge upon Easterling their captain's murder and their own wrongs.

When all was ready and the matches glowing he went on deck again!

The two canoes manned by Mosquito Indians and the *Valiant*'s longboat were astern under her counter and invisible to those aboard the other two ships. Towing-ropes had been attached, and the men waited for the word of command.

At Blood's suggestion Trenam did not stay to take up

215

anchor, but slipped his cable, and the oarsmen bent to their task of warping the ship round. Labours which would not in themselves have sufficed were made easy by the ebb, and slowly the brigantine began to swing broadside across the channel. Already Blood was below again, directing the hands that manned the starboard guns. Five of these were to be concentrated on the rudder of the *Hermes*, the other five were to sweep her shrouds.

As the *Valiant* swung about and the warping operations became apparent to the men on the other ships it was assumed by them that, panic-stricken by the fate of their captain, the crew of the brigantine had resolved on flight. From the decks of the *Hermes* a derisive, valedictory cheer rang out. But scarcely had it died away, and hardly had it been taken up by the *Avenger*, when it was answered by the roar of ten guns at point-blank range.

The *Hermes* rocked and shuddered under the impact of that unexpected broadside, and the fierce outcries of her men were mingled with the hoarse voices of the startled sea-birds that rose to circle in alarm.

Blood was on deck again almost before the reverberations had rolled away. He peered through the rising cloud of smoke and smiled. The rudder of the *Hermes* had been shattered, her main-mast was broken and hung precariously suspended in her shrouds, whilst a rent showed in the bulwarks of her forecastle.

"And now?" quoth Trenam in uneasy excitement.

Blood looked round. They were moving steadily if slowly down the short channel, and were already almost in the open sea. A steady breeze was blowing from the north. "Crowd on sail, and let her run before the wind."

"They'll follow," said the young mariner.

"Why, so I trust. But not yet awhile. Take a look at their plight."

It was only then that Trenam understood precisely what Blood had done. With her broken rudder and shattered mainmast, the *Hermes*, whilst being herself unmanageable, was blocking the way and making it impossible for the raging Easterling to get past her and attack the *Valiant*.

Trenam perceived and admired, but was still far from easy. "If you've invited pursuit, it's true that you've certainly delayed it. But it will surely come, and we shall be as surely sunk when it does. It's just what that devil Easterling desires."

"Indeed, and I hope so; and, anyway, I've quickened those same desires of his."

They had picked up the crew of the longboat, whilst the Indian canoes could be seen making off to the north along the reef. The *Valiant* was now running before the wind and Gallows' Key was dropping swiftly astern. All hands were on deck. From the pooprail, where he leaned beside Trenam, Blood spoke to the man at the whipstaff below.

"Put up the helm. We go about." Perceiving Trenam's alarm, he smiled. "Quiet you. Have faith in me, and man the larboard guns. They'll not yet have disentangled themselves, and we'll give them a salute in passing. Faith, now, ye may trust me. It's by no means the first action I've fought, and I know the fool I'm engaging. It won't have occurred to him that we might have the impudence to return, and I'll wager your share of Morgan's treasure that he won't have so much as opened his ports as yet."

It fell out as he foretold. When they ran in, close-hauled, they saw that the *Hermes* had only just been warped aside to give passage to the *Avenger*, which with sprit-sail, sweeps, and the ebb to assist her, was crawling towards the channel.

Easterling must have rubbed his eyes at this reappearance of the *Valiant*, which he was imagining in full flight; he must have ground his strong white teeth when she hung there an instant with slatting sails and poured a broadside athwart his decks before going off again on a north-easterly tack. He replied in haste and ineffectively with his chasers, and whilst the mess made by the *Valiant*'s guns was being cleared up, he settled down vindictively to a pursuit which must end in the sinking of the audacious brigantine with every hand aboard.

The *Valiant* was perhaps a mile away to the north-east when

Trenam beheld the *Avenger* emerge from the narrow roadstead and take the open sea to come ploughing after them with
crowded yards. It was a dismaying vision. He turned to
Captain Blood.

"And now, Captain? What remains?"

"To go about again," was the surprising answer. "Bid the
helmsman steer for the northernmost point of the Key
yonder."

"That will bring us within range."

"No matter. We'll run the gauntlet of his fire. At need we
can round the point. But I've a notion the need will not present
itself."

They went about, and ran in once more, Blood scanning the
rocky coast of the island the while through the telescope.
Trenam stood fretful at his elbow.

"What do you look for, Captain?" he wondered with faint
hope.

"My Indian friends. They've made good speed. They've
gone. All should be well."

To Trenam it seemed that things would be anything but
well. The *Avenger* had veered a point nearer to the wind, so
as to shorten the work of intercepting them. From her forward
ports a gun boomed, and a round shot flung up the spray half
a cable's length astern of the *Valiant*.

"He's getting the range," said Blood indifferently.

"Aye," agreed Trenam with bitter dryness. "We've let you
have your way unquestioned, Captain. But what's to be the
end?"

"I fancy it's coming yonder under full sail," said Captain
Blood, and he pointed with the telescope.

Round the northern point of Gallows' Key surged a great
red-hulled ship under a mountain of canvas that gleamed like
snow in the noontide sunshine. Veering south as she appeared,
she swept majestically on before the wind, a thing of beauty
and of power, from gilded beakhead to lofty poop-lantern.
She was abeam of the *Valiant*, between the brigantine and
island, before the dumbfounded Trenam found his voice,

and before the voices of the crew were raised to cheer and cheer again.

Pale with excitement, his eyes sparkling, Trenam swung to Captain Blood. "The *Arabella*!"

Blood smiled upon him quizzically. "To be sure ye supposed I swam here, or crossed the ocean in a canoe; or maybe ye thought I wanted to be chased by Easterling just for the fun of running away and the joy of being drowned at the end of it. Ye hadn't thought about these things maybe. Neither had Easterling. But he's thinking about them now, so he is. Thinking hard, I dare swear."

But Easterling was doing nothing of the kind. His wits were paralysed. In the madness of despair, seeing himself beset by that formidable ship, which, moreover, had the weather gauge of him, he attempted to run for shelter back to the harbour from which he had been lured. Once there, with the guns of the *Hermes* to support his own, he might have held the narrow roadstead against all comers. But he should have known that he would never be allowed to reach it. When he ignored the shot athwart his bows, summoning him to strike his colours, a broadside of twenty heavy guns crashed into his exposed flank, and wrought such damage in it that he was bereft of even the satisfaction of replying. The *Arabella*, well handled by old Wolverstone, who was in command of her, went promptly about, and at still closer range poured in a second broadside to complete the business. Hard hit between wind and water, the *Avenger* was seen to be settling down by the head.

A sound like a wail arose from the deck of the *Valiant*. It startled Blood.

"What is it? What do they cry?"

" 'The treasure!' " Trenam answered him. " 'Morgan's treasure!' "

Blood frowned. "Faith, Wolverstone must ha' forgotten it in his fury." Then the frown cleared. He sighed and shrugged. "Ah well! It's gone now, so it has. Bad cess to it."

The *Arabella* hove to and lowered her boats to pick up the

survivors struggling in the water. Easterling, lacking the courage to drown, was amongst them, and by Blood's direction was brought aboard the *Valiant*. Thus was the iron driven deep into his soul. But deeper still was it to be driven when he stepped on to the deck of Pike's ship to find himself confronting Captain Blood. It had been no bogey, then, with which Pike's last words had threatened him. He recoiled as if at last, and for once in his life, afraid. The dark eyes smouldered in his grey face with the mingled fury and terror to be seen in those of a trapped animal.

"So it was you!" he ejaculated.

"If ye mean it was I who took Pike's place when ye murdered him, ye're right. Ye'ld have done better to have been honest with him. There's a maxim ye should have learnt at school, that honesty is the best policy. Though perhaps ye never were at school. But there's another maxim, of which I made you a present years ago, and which they tell me that ye're fond of quoting: Who seeks to grasp too much ends by holding nothing."

He waited for a reply, but none came. Easterling, his great bulk sagging, glowered at him silently with those dark feral eyes.

Blood sighed, and moved towards the head of the accommodation ladder.

"Ye're no affair of mine. I leave ye to these men you have wronged, and whose leader you have murdered. It is for them to judge you."

He went down to the boat that had brought Easterling aboard and so back to the *Arabella*, his task accomplished and his long duel with Easterling at last concluded.

An hour later the *Arabella* and the *Valiant* were running south together. Gallows' Key was falling rapidly astern, and Galloway and his crew aboard the crippled *Hermes* imprisoned in the lagoon were left to conjecture what had happened outside and to extricate themselves as best they could from their own difficulties.